LEGACY OF THE CLAW

ANIMAS

C. R. GREY

HOT
KEY
BOOKS

First published in Great Britain in 2014 by Hot Key Books
Northburgh House, 10 Northburgh Street, London EC1V 0AT

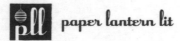

A CIP catalogue record for this book is available from the British Library.

ISBN: 978-1-4714-0129-9

1

This book is typeset in 11pt Sabon using Atomik ePublisher

Printed and bound by Clays Ltd, St Ives Plc

Hot Key Books supports the Forest Stewardship Council (FSC),
the leading international forest certification organisation, and is
committed to printing only on Greenpeace-approved FSC-certified paper.

www.hotkeybooks.com

Hot Key Books is part of the Bonnier Publishing Group
www.bonnierpublishing.com

for Aaron

Prologue

A LONELY CARAVAN TRUNDLED across the flat, brown terrain of the Dust Plains. In the back of one wagon, driven by two hunched men, a tarp covered a wealth of stolen goods: jewels looted from Gray City shops, two barrels of fine Parliament grog, and a girl with violet eyes.

The tarp stretched over her was backlit with sunlight and a shadow passed overhead. The girl heard a familiar squawk. A black carrion crow who followed the troupe was back from scouting. He was kin to the driver of the wagon, the man whom the girl understood to be the leader of this band of thieves.

The wagon soon came to a stop, and the girl could hear the sounds of a busy street. The wooden wheels creaked under her as the man and his companion stepped down from the wagon. Suddenly, everything was blinding light as the tarp was pulled back sharply. The girl shielded her eyes.

"Up. Up!" growled the man. He grabbed her arm and pulled her through a crowd, where he pushed her onto the center of a rickety wooden platform. There, he stood behind her with a huge hand on her shoulder. It wasn't a kind hand, or a comforting one. He was making sure that she didn't try to run.

The girl thought about the reassuring hands of her father. She remembered how his hands would move when he'd explain things to her or to his advisors in Parliament. Like the Animas bond. He'd placed one hand on his own chest, and with his other, he'd drawn a line from his heart to hers. *It's a vibration, a kind of knowing. It means that you're not just connected to an animal—you're connected to Nature, and to the world. The Animas bond is a force that connects every living creature. And a noble person, a noble ruler even, uses this force for good.*

"Who'll take her?" the man shouted into the gathered crowd. "Only twenty snailbacks!"

She wanted to cry out—she wanted to tell everyone who she was, but she was too afraid. Her father was the king of all Aldermere. But the king was dead.

She was alone.

"Eighteen snailbacks!" the man shouted into the silence. Finally, someone raised a hand in the crowd. Suddenly, everyone was shouting bids. The auction had begun.

She clenched her fists. She wouldn't cry. She saw the crow, perched at the edge of the wooden platform, blinking his cold, black eyes at her. It wasn't fair. The leader of the thieves had kin here, in this terrible place, and she had none. She had always been embarrassed to be Animas Pig, but she'd have given anything for the comfort of having her own kin close to her now. Even the thieves in the crowd had their doggish companions with them. Coyotes combed the mob, lifting snailbacks from unsuspecting pockets. But she was alone, alone. The crow cawed, laughing at her.

Her anger burned hot inside her until she thought she'd scream. Like an electric current, a terrible force moved through her whole body. She took her grief and terror and threw it, pushed it outward onto the kin of another.

The cawing of the crow became louder, sharper, as two coyotes from the gathered crowd lunged at him, brought him flapping and shrieking to the ground, and began to tear at his flesh and feathers. Her hands shook as she realized that she had caused it. She'd created violence like the violence she felt churning in her heart.

It was power like nothing she'd ever experienced. She could feel the bond that connected her not just to her own kin, but to *every* creature, just like her father had said. She could control it. She could *use* it.

As the crowd backed away, horrified—as the leader of the thieves bellowed for his comrades to help him pull the beasts off of his kin—the girl with the violet eyes remained still. Her mind turned toward her father and her little brother, now dead.

Why use our bond with Nature for good? she thought, as the teeth tore and the claws grabbed. It didn't save them. This new way of using the bond made her feel powerful, and in a world in which no one she loved still lived, she needed every ounce of strength she could muster.

One

TWENTY-SEVEN YEARS LATER

TWELVE-YEAR-OLD BAILEY WALKER ducked as a huge brown goose flew just past his head, coming to rest on the awning over the rigimotive station platform. The dark tortoiseshell cat, that only a moment before had startled the fowl into flight, wove between the legs of its human companions, meowing with satisfaction. Bailey patted down his messy, hay-colored hair, making sure no feathers had gotten caught in it.

"Are you ready, Bailey?" Emily, his mom, asked. She squeezed his shoulders with both hands before brushing a spot of dust off of his best shirt. "Just remember, no matter what anyone says about you—you are fine. You're more than fine. You're exceptional."

Yeah. Exceptionally weird, maybe, he thought. Bailey felt a sharp pang, but he nodded and smiled. He was leaving the Golden Lowlands and its pleasant farms, its rolling hills and sleepy, rambling towns—he was leaving his *parents*—for Fairmount Academy, the most prestigious school in Aldermere.

Where he would soon be labeled a complete freak.

"You listen to your mom, Bailey." Bailey's dad, a lanky man with dark, curly hair, had dressed in his nicest trousers and donned a crisp wool flatcap, just to see Bailey off. Herman Walker had been speaking for days about the chance to see the towering, four-story rigimotive (the biggest in the Lowlands!) that would take Bailey to Fairmount. The rigimotive was the only available means of long-distance travel, but since neither Bailey nor his parents had ever left the Lowlands, they'd never had the opportunity to see it.

Bailey couldn't wait to board. The two rigimotive cars were like giant red metal houses, with four rows of copper-rimmed windows looking out on the plains. Gold-painted spiral staircases inside each car reached all the way to the top. The yellow dirigible, a huge oval balloon, floated above the rigimotive.

Bailey's father had explained how the floating dirigible would help the crew navigate the rigimotive over any broken-down track, as well as propel the heavy cars forward. His father's enthusiasm for the technology of the Age of Invention was infectious. Growing up, Bailey's dad had told him all about the Royal Tinkerers—a group of professors and engineers that had invented the rigimotive before Bailey had been born. His father said they would've gone on to create a faster, more efficient train—but like so many plans that were made before the murder of King Melore, these had died along with him. Bailey often wondered if his dad hadn't taken up farming, like his parents before him, if he'd have become a tinkerer himself.

Today, even Bailey's mom had put on her best hat, a purple felt cloche with a bright yellow flower on the brim, and a pair of clicking brown heels to take him to the station. His dad's life-bonded hare, Longfoot, was excited too—Bailey watched as he swatted at the cat with mottled black and brown fur.

"You put the past behind you," his dad said, startling Bailey from his thoughts. "And don't worry about what other kids say. There's nothing wrong with you. Everyone moves at a different pace. You'll show them what you're made of."

Bailey had heard this speech, or some version of it, a thousand times before. But he nodded. "Thanks, Dad," he said, and meant it.

He would miss his mom and dad terribly. Emily and Herman Walker had adopted him when he was just a baby. Bailey had heard the story hundreds of times before: how he'd been found as a baby by his dad, crying naked underneath a raspberry bush, dangerously near the edge of the Dark Woods. He'd been underfed and very small. No one knew where he'd come from, or how he'd managed to survive on his own.

Bailey, of course, had no memory of being found. All he'd known growing up was that he was the adoptive son of an Animas Hare and an Animas Horse: both hardworking, kind, supportive . . . and, unlike Bailey, completely normal. They ran a wheat farm, and had raised him to work hard.

Work hard, and never turn down the opportunity to learn. He would forever be grateful to them. They'd always been so patient and encouraging—even when Bailey had started to show signs of being . . . well, *different*.

"Take care of yourself, my lovey!" His mom dabbed at her eyes. Oh, no. She was about to cry. Bailey hugged her quickly before she could make a scene—or call him "lovey" again.

"I will," he said. He disentangled himself from his mom's embrace and gave his dad a quick squeeze. His dad mussed Bailey's yellow hair, causing his mother to spring forward and comb it down again. Longfoot scurried over, and Bailey pulled away just before the hare could pee on his canvas shoe, which was the closest he came to expressing affection. "Bye, Mom. Bye, Dad. Bye, Longfoot."

"Don't forget to eat your grains!" his mom called after him, as Bailey threaded through the crowd. He heard laughter coming from a group of older students boarding the rigimotive ahead of him. His ears burned and he kept his head down. Maybe no one would know she was talking to him.

He could feel his mom's watchful and worried eyes on the back of his neck. He knew why she was worried—this was his first time away from home. He was anxious too.

But he was also excited. If there was ever a place that could give him, Bailey Walker, the hope of being normal— finally—it was Fairmount Academy, with the Animas trainer who might just have the answers Bailey needed: a man by the name of Tremelo Loren. His dad had scrounged some pamphlets on Fairmount's history from their local Lowlands library when Bailey had first been accepted. In one, which had been published quite a few years before, he saw mention of the young teacher, Mr. Loren, who had developed a reputation in the Gray City by training everyday people to develop stronger bonds with their animal kin. Bailey planned to seek him out as soon as he arrived.

There was a long line to board the rigimotive. The Lowlands was made up of small farming villages, and though it stretched over more than a third of Aldermere, this platform was one of the only rigimotive stops in the region. Some of the students in this line had traveled by cart and wagon for many miles already.

The stairs had once gleamed bright gold, but the rigimotive car showed signs of wear. The paint had flaked off significantly, showing dull, plain metal underneath. The stairs creaked under the weight of the students climbing up and down. Bailey reached the first floor of the second car, where his and the other travelers' trunks were being hoisted onto racks by two porters, and kept climbing. It was his first time traveling away from home, and he wasn't going to waste it by looking out the windows of the first floor.

Bailey wound his way up to the third floor. Stepping into the aisle, he scanned the wooden benches for a free spot. Bailey saw several older boys and girls sitting near the front, wearing telltale blue-and-gold ties loosely done under their collars. He suddenly felt very self-conscious, still in his linen shirt and his nicest pair of cotton work pants. A farm boy, at least until he got to Fairmount, where his trunk full of new school clothes and his official Fairmount blazer could finally be unpacked. He was about to slink quietly into a seat in the back of the car, out of sight, when he heard someone call his name.

"Bailey, right?"

The voice belonged to a familiar dark-haired, bespectacled boy, sitting alone on a bench with a thick book in his lap. He waved at Bailey.

"It's Hal, Hal Quindley."

Bailey had seen Hal around his old school, but they'd never been in class together. He wore a dark formal vest with the pattern of webbed wings on the shoulders. It looked new, and a little too big for him. Instead of a tie printed with the Fairmount colors, he wore a maroon silk cravat that looked as though someone had tied it for him.

"Hi," Bailey said. Relieved to see even a remotely familiar face, he slid onto the seat opposite, stowing his rucksack under the bench.

Hal stretched out his hand to shake.

"I'm glad you found me," he said. "I saw all the Year Ones listed in the *Fairmount Flyer,* and yours was the only name I recognized. Fairmount only accepts a hundred new kids a year, and so there's only room for a couple students from our town. Some pressure, huh?"

"Yeah," Bailey mumbled, impressed. "Wow."

He glanced out the window. His mom and dad were still waiting for the rigimotive to pull away. He felt a sudden, wrenching pang of homesickness.

"It's more than *wow*," Hal said, adjusting the thick,

copper-rimmed glasses on his nose. "They say you've got to be pretty exceptional to get in. Makes me wonder how I managed to sneak by!"

Bailey smiled. He heard his mom's voice in his mind— *You're more than fine. You're exceptional*—and the momentary homesickness melted away into anticipation once more.

But before he could respond, a heavyset man in a bulging overcoat plopped down on the seat next to Hal, panting loudly. The man's coat had several cargo pockets lining the front and sides, all of them overflowing with cuttings of various plants. A portly badger sauntered into the row after him and curled up underneath the bench, his wet nose poking out through the folds of the man's coat.

"Third floor, Hal?" asked the man, out of breath. "Couldn't have given Dillweed here a little rest this morning?"

Instantly, Hal's face turned red. "This is my Uncle Roger, an apothecary. And that's Dillweed," he explained, pointing at the snout on the floor. "They've got some business in the Gray City, and Fairmount's on the way. Uncle Roger, this is Bailey. He goes to my school—I mean, he *went* to my school. I mean . . . He'll be in Fairmount with me."

Roger turned to Bailey with wide, interested eyes—eyes that peered through the frames of glasses as thick as Hal's.

"Well, well! Making fast friends already, are we!" he exclaimed. Dillweed's protruding nose huffed under the coat. "Doesn't get better than that. You'll have plenty of time to chitchat before we get to Fairmount. Two whole days on a

11

rigimotive! When I think that it would take only half a day if we were allowed through the Woods to the mountains, I tell you . . ." Roger threw up his hands. "Well, well. We'll just have to get cozy." He turned his attention back to Hal. "I don't suppose you've seen your brother yet, have you?"

Hal made a face and pointed over his shoulder to the group of older students Bailey had noticed earlier. They were clapping and laughing loudly as one boy, with dark hair like Hal's, played keep-away with another boy's rucksack. The same tortoiseshell cat from the station platform sat nestled in the compartment overhead, batting at the rucksack as it passed. Roger rose from his seat with an exasperated sigh, and waddled over to put a stop to the game.

"That's your brother?" Bailey asked. Hal nodded, obviously annoyed.

"Taylor. He's Year Three, thank Nature, so I'll only have to put up with him for two years at Fairmount. He's a Scavage player," Hal said matter-of-factly. Scavage, a game in which members of two opposing teams had to find and capture the other team's flag with the help of their kin, was the most popular sport in the kingdom. Bailey had watched some Scavage games at his school, and his dad liked to listen to the big tournaments on the radio.

"Scavage is the *only* reason he got into Fairmount," Hal continued. "Taylor has one other talent and that's being a jerk." Hal removed his glasses and scrubbed at the lenses vigorously. Without them, his eyes looked almost crossed. "I'm Animas Bat, like my grandfather. And Taylor's Cat, so we don't exactly get along. They're *all* Animas Cat"—Bailey assumed Hal meant his family—"and that's why I live with Roger."

Bailey nodded. It wasn't uncommon for families with different types of kin to have problems, especially when one type of Animas was more aggressive than the other. Bailey remembered now why he'd seen so little of Hal at school. His wealthy uncle Roger lived near the periphery of the Dark Woods, and Hal was always whisked away right at the end of the last class, so they would get home before nightfall.

Looking at Hal now—his skinny arms, his outdated haircut and formal attire, and the thick glasses that made him look constantly surprised—Bailey found it hard to believe that he lived so close to the edge of the Dark Woods. For most citizens of Aldermere, the Dark Woods were forbidden, and the only people brave enough to live within its shadow were Animas Bear or Wolf.

The dirigible suspended above the car caught a gust of wind and pulled the rigimotive forward with a start. Bailey waved to his parents. Roger huffed as he settled back into his seat. Behind him, Taylor and his friends returned almost immediately to their game.

"That must have been your folks I was speaking to outside," Roger said to Bailey, as he returned to his seat. "Nice people."

"Thanks," Bailey said.

"So which are you," Roger asked, "Horse or Hare?"

This was it: the one question Bailey had been dreading. His Animas. Most people inherited from one parent or another, though a few skipped a generation. Roger clearly

13

wasn't aware that Bailey was adopted, which meant that he didn't have *either* a Horse or Hare Animas.

And that wasn't the worst of it. He'd even considered lying about it, telling everyone who was sure to ask at Fairmount that he was a Bear or a Snake—even a Possum! Anything was better than the truth.

"I . . ." Bailey could feel his palms begin to sweat.

"You don't have to say, Bailey," Hal jumped in quickly.

"Say what?" Roger asked, looking confused. "I merely asked—"

"*Roger,* he's . . ." Hal began. Roger looked from Hal to Bailey, blinking with confusion. "He's the adopted one," Hal said, looking down at his shoes.

Bailey felt himself blushing. Something about the hushed way that Hal had said "the adopted one" made Bailey think that Hal knew something more than he'd said. That was only to be expected, really. There was no way Hal wouldn't have heard the rumors, the taunts on the school grounds. He just hoped that Hal, the only other kid he knew from his town, would be decent enough not to blab about it once they got to Fairmount—at least until Bailey had a chance to ask for help from Mr. Loren, the trainer he'd read about.

"Ah . . ." Roger's eyes grew even wider behind his thick glasses, and he fumbled in a pocket for a handkerchief. It was clear to Bailey that Roger had heard the same whispers. He reached out and patted Bailey's hand. Bailey resisted the urge to pull it away. "I'm sorry, son," Roger said. "Insensitive of me."

At that moment, the bag that Taylor and his friends had

been tossing sailed past Roger's head.

"Sorry!" one of Taylor's friends shouted.

"Ruffian!" Roger trumpeted, and grabbed the bag. He marched up to the front of the car and began shouting at Taylor, who was doing a very bad job of looking sorry. Dillweed curled into the shadows under Roger's empty seat, emitting a soft snore. The boys were quiet for a minute as Roger lectured the students up front on rigimotive etiquette.

Hal was the first to speak.

"Listen, if I wasn't supposed to say anything . . ." He faltered. "It's just that I thought *everyone* knew."

"Not *everyone*," Bailey said. Bailey turned to watch the fields and pastures of the Golden Lowlands slide by, hoping Hal would take the hint: he didn't want to talk about it.

Riding the rigimotive turned out to be stranger than Bailey had imagined. Sometimes, when the wind was strong, the dirigible moved faster than the car's wheels on the tracks, and the rigimotive would sway and buck, causing Bailey to feel a little nauseous.

Roger had been right about the long journey too. The prospect of an overnight stay onboard wasn't pleasant, even though underneath the benches were narrow foldout cots for overnight journeys. Many of the overhead cubbies designated for traveling animals were being used for storage, so the raccoons accompanying one family on the second floor had come up to the third, and were blocking the aisles. The electro-current generated by the tracks was unreliable, and so, in addition to the electro-wired lights that occasionally flickered on and off, gas lamps had been hung every few feet along the central aisle of both the cars. Passengers had to duck as they walked to make sure they didn't get hit.

A dining area on the ground floor provided wrapped sandwiches—cucumber and onion, spinach and cheese, and city trout and tomato for those who ate fish. But Bailey could hardly stand the thought of food as the rigimotive rocked with each gust of wind.

By sunset, most of the passengers had given up on polite conversation, and were claiming benches and cots on which to doze. Bailey at last managed to keep down a city trout sandwich, and then he unfolded the cot opposite Hal. Roger, claiming not to be tired, was pacing the aisles. Dillweed had awakened from his nap, and he sat on the floor nearby, scratching various itches. Bailey rolled over and closed his eyes, trying to sleep under the flickering gas lamps and the hum of the huge dirigible above them.

He did sleep, at last. He dreamed of becoming a bird, and then a fox; then he was an ant, crawling under the shadow of a great mountain.

Bailey woke as something fluttered against the window. The gas lamps had been dimmed, and the sound of soft snoring filled the car.

"What's going on?" He sat up, balling his fists in his eyes. Roger was not in his seat. Hal was staring out of the window.

"It's just a bat," Hal said. "I couldn't sleep. Nothing new for me." He lowered his voice to a whisper, and leaned closer to Bailey. "We're coming up to the mountains. The Velyn Peaks."

Bailey shook off the haze of his dream. He squinted out the window. Beyond the glass, the trees of the Dark Woods towered above them. The moon hung high over the treetops. Through the tall branches, Bailey could see the tips of the legendary Velyn mountains, white and glimmering in the near distance. After another minute, there was a break in the tree line, and Bailey got a full view of the mountain range ahead, silhouetted against the pitch-black night sky. They looked empty and barren.

Bailey shivered. The Velyn Peaks stretched across the kingdom to the south of the Lowlands, and up toward the west, where the cliffs of Fairmount were. In the Lowlands, it was easy to think of the Velyn as very far away.

But as they drew closer to the academy, the looming, ominous presence of the mountains was undeniable. Boogeymen haunted the mountains. Ghosts and killers walked those white peaks—at least, that's what everyone said.

"Do you believe all the stories about the lost tribes of the Velyn?" he asked Hal. According to the stories, the Velyn were a mysterious group of men and women who'd been tough enough to live up there in the mountains, mostly because they shared the Animas bond with powerful beasts like grizzly bears, wolves, and giant mountain cats.

Hal shrugged. "You remember the History teacher, Mr. Elliot?" Hal asked. "He always told us that the Velyn were real people—escaped criminals mostly, people running from the law. But I don't know. My mom used to tell me that the Velyn men could turn into animals, and steal children who misbehaved. Only when I didn't eat my sprouts, though."

"My mom told me that one too," Bailey said, smiling. He turned back to the window. When he stared up at the mountains, he felt a flickering in the back of his mind, like the fluttering of wings.

Bailey tried to shut out the chugging of the rigimotive, and focus only on the silence in the trees, the faintest whisper of wind. He closed his eyes. His dad had tried to teach him so many times to connect with the animals around him, never with very good results. *You're not so different,* he'd said during those lessons. *You just need a little focus.*

He heard the branches of the trees scraping against each other in the breeze, and under that, a rustling, like the shuddering of dry leaves. It was a sound he was sure he hadn't heard earlier, through the window. It seemed to be buzzing in his very ears, as if he wasn't in the rigimotive car, but right out there in the trees, standing still, listening. He felt a leap of excitement.

"Something's out there," he said in a whisper, opening his eyes. The sound in his ears immediately died away. "I can feel it."

"What do you mean?" asked Hal. "Has that ever happened to you before?"

Bailey stood up. He had to get closer. He moved down the aisle to the back of the rigimotive car. Hal followed him.

He *had* felt something different, a stirring that had never happened when he'd been training with his dad. If he could just get outside somehow, maybe that feeling would come back . . . He reached the back of the rigimotive car and grabbed ahold of the brass handle that opened the car door.

"Bailey!" Hal whispered fiercely. "We're not supposed to move outside the car!"

A couple of passengers stirred, and one bright-eyed raccoon popped up from a blanket to blink at him. Bailey ignored Hal and opened the door. The wind outside on the platform blew Bailey's hair back from his forehead, and the machinery chugging below echoed in his ears.

If only I could focus, Bailey thought. If only I could get closer. He stepped forward onto the platform. The tops of the trees were lit by silvery moonlight; shadows raced and skidded across the ground. Only yards away from the tracks, the trees began to come together and form a thick, leafy wall—the beginning of the Dark Woods. In the trees, Bailey saw a flash of something white. He blinked. Was it a trick of the moon?

No. It was an animal.

At least, Bailey *thought* it was an animal, but it wasn't like any animal he'd ever seen. It was huge, disappearing and reappearing in between the gaps of the trees, glowing in the moonlight. Like a ghost, he thought. It seemed to run along with the rigimotive as it passed the forest. Bailey felt his blood go cold in his veins. After a moment, the flash of white disappeared altogether.

"What in Nature do you think you're doing?" a man yelled.

Bailey felt a hand on his shoulder, pulling him back through the door into the dim light of the car. It was a conductor in a worn uniform, with sharp blue eyes. Behind him was Roger, with Hal's older brother, Taylor, close at hand. Dillweed the badger and Taylor's dark, sleek cat skittered up the aisle behind them.

"You could have gotten yourself killed, going out there while the rigi's in motion!" the conductor said as he closed the door behind Bailey with a loud *whump*. Bailey could hear the disgruntled murmuring of passengers who didn't appreciate being woken up.

"Already in trouble, and we're not even there yet," said Taylor, who looked down at Bailey with a mocking smile. "Got something to prove?"

"Bark off, Taylor," said Hal, appearing in the doorway behind his brother.

But Bailey was still reeling from what he'd seen. The animal he'd spotted seemed like something otherworldly, watching the train . . .

"You all right, boy?" asked Roger.

"I—I saw something *huge* out there," he blurted out.

Roger narrowed his eyes at Bailey. Taylor, who stood behind him, laughed with a snort.

"A wolf?" he asked. "There are plenty of wolves in the Dark Woods."

"No, it wasn't that," said Bailey. "It was all white . . ."

"That doesn't sound like anything in these parts," said the conductor dryly. "Sometimes a bear will wander close to the tracks, but they're your average brown or black variety."

"Too true," said Roger loudly, clapping a heavy hand on Bailey's shoulder. "Must have been a trick of the light."

"It was there," said Bailey. "It was much bigger than a

bear—and it was so bright. It almost glowed . . ."

"Was it a gh-gh-ghost?" asked Taylor, wiggling his fingers in a mocking gesture.

"Go back to the front, Taylor, before you get on my last nerve," snapped Roger. "And, Bailey, come sit down and calm yourself. You just saw a wolf or coyote, that's all. Enough of these stories."

Bailey hung back, angry and embarrassed, while Roger and Taylor returned to their seats. Other passengers in the car were looking at him. His ears were hot. He knew that he had seen something—hadn't he? For a second, he wondered if Roger were right and he had mistaken a wolf for something else. But no. The creature he'd seen had been large enough to spot from several yards away, and had been a pure, snowy white.

"I know what I saw," said Bailey quietly to Hal.

"Sure, I believe you." Hal sat down on his cot, but didn't climb in just yet. He was still fidgeting; Bailey could tell he wanted to say something more.

Around them, the excitement of Bailey's scolding had died away, and the murmurs of their fellow passengers had been replaced with low breathing, snores, and the occasional rustle of feather and fur.

"Look," said Hal. "I just want you to know . . . I'm not going to tell anyone about . . . *you* know. If you want to keep it a secret when we get to Fairmount, you can count on me."

"Keep what secret?" Bailey asked, even though he already knew what Hal was talking about. But he wanted to know for certain just how much Hal knew about him. "What have you heard?"

Hal breathed in deeply, as if to steel himself against the words. He leaned in close to Bailey's ear.

Then he said them, the words that hurt Bailey like a physical blow, like nothing but the truth could do:

"You have no Animas."

Two

FAR FROM THE LOWLANDS and the dim gas lamps of the rigimotive, a small, dark shape circled the sooty factories of the Gray City, sweeping high over a stream of acrid smoke. It dipped past the far edges of the skyline, pulling its wings closer to its body as it careered over the rooftops, then spread them wide as it finally came within sight of the copper roofs of the palace, the home of Parliament. It let the air currents carry it straight to a window ledge halfway up the wall of a rickety tower on the palace's western side. A scar of smoke damage from the fire that had burned down half the building almost thirty years ago still showed on the tower's outer wall.

The owl settled on the sill of an open window, which overlooked a narrow, twisting staircase. At the bottom of the stairs was an archway that let in a shaft of light from the hall. Around the corner, a group of officials talked loudly about Parliament business. In a moment so quick that only the owl saw, a foot in a canvas shoe appeared in the shaft of light from the door, then was quickly pulled back into the shadows.

The owner of that foot, a thirteen-year-old girl named Gwen, stood very still in the dark corner by the archway and waited breathlessly for the Parliament members in the hall to move on. The owl on the windowsill cocked its head, but made no noise. The officials in the hall at last ambled away.

Gwen exhaled for the first time in what seemed like entire minutes. The members of Parliament were used to Gwen—she was apprenticed to the Elder, who had been in Parliament since the time of King Melore. But tonight, she needed to remain unseen. The Elder was leaving on a secret mission, and she was determined to go with him. She hoisted her rucksack onto her shoulder and ran her pale fingers through her short, flame-red hair. She'd tried to give up the habit a thousand times, but she couldn't help it. She felt jittery, as though feathers were rustling in her belly.

The owl hopped once on the windowsill as she passed it on her way up the stairs, and then took off again into the night. She could feel, however, that it had not gone far. She was learning (slowly) to distinguish individual members of her kin when there were several of them around, even getting so close as to intuit their names. She felt a warmth, a kind of buzzing in her chest as she sensed the group of owls in the tower room above her, and one flying, buoyed by the wind, just outside.

At the top of the steps, Gwen lingered in the darkness by the open door to the tower room. Sure enough, a cluster of owls sat together in the rafters, looking down at the shelves and shelves of dusty old books, and at the room's only human occupant: Elder, an old man with wild gray hair and shrewd eyes. He was busy stuffing objects into a canvas sack. His worn jacket and waistcoat had once been carefully embroidered with the patterns of wings, but those patterns were now an almost illegible tangle of loose brown and silver threads.

The Elder had known her since she was just another ratty orphan of the Gray City. He was Animas Owl, like her, and when he'd caught her trying to pick his pocket one day in the Gudgeons, a grimy, crime-riddled slum in the Gray City, he hadn't gotten angry. Instead, he'd taken pity on her, and brought her back to the palace to be his apprentice. Apprentices slept in clean, warm rooms downstairs near the kitchens, and attended morning classes until the age of twelve, after which their only charge was to serve a member of Parliament. But apprentices had fallen out of fashion since the days of Melore, and her classmates had been few and far between. Most of her learning came from the Elder himself. Before he took her in, she had been dirty, alone, and half-starving, with no companions except a small band of other child thieves. She'd known then that she was Animas Owl, but had never known how to connect to her kin, how to slow her breath and clear her mind so she could sense them and learn from them. The Elder had taught her that. He was the closest thing to a father she had. If he was leaving, then she would go too, even if it meant following him out of the palace in secret.

The Elder sighed. "Gwendolyn," he said softly, without turning around, "if I were a pair of hardy boots, where in this study would I be hiding?"

25

Gwen exhaled. How could she have thought she would remain undetected? The Elder must have known she was coming as soon as the owls perceived her.

She stepped out from the shadow into a cramped, cluttered room. There was barely enough space for the two of them to stand next to the Elder's claw-footed desk and the many shelves of books that lined the hexagonal walls.

"Did you try the closet?" she asked.

The Elder shook his head. "Would you believe, it's only full of more books?"

Normally, Gwen would have laughed. But instead she gripped the strap of her rucksack tightly and steeled herself.

"I'm coming with you to the Seers' land."

The Elder didn't stop packing. He didn't even look at her.

"My rain cape has also gone missing, it seems . . ." he murmured.

Gwen peeled away from the doorway and located his rain cape, which was inexplicably balled up under his bed. She stuffed it into the traveling bag on the desk for him.

"I worry about you," Gwen couldn't stop from blurting out, even though she knew she could say nothing to stop him from leaving the palace. "You need me with you."

The Elder rested his eyes on her momentarily. "You're right, child. I do need you. But I need you *here*. I need your eyes on Parliament while I'm gone. There's no longer any doubt in my mind that Viviana is taking steps to overthrow them." He lowered his voice. "Her Dominae party becomes larger every day."

The Elder sorted through the random pile of objects

he'd recovered from a cupboard under the bookshelves: a shoehorn, a bundle of maps tied with string, and finally—

"Aha!" he crowed, tossing the boots toward Gwen, who caught them and set them beside his bag.

"Since her reappearance here in the city, Viviana has let her anger and stubbornness guide her. As Melore's daughter, I had some hope that her emergence might mean a return of prosperity for Aldermere, after so many years of the Jackal's rule. Parliament was right to chase the Jackal from power—but they've lost their way. When Melore presided over them, Parliament was efficient and fair. Now there's so much corruption. We take from the people, and yet nothing is accomplished, no progress at all . . . We need a real leader." He straightened up and moved over to the shelves. On one of them stood a silk toy piglet, which looked as if it had once been loved dearly. The Elder picked it up and ran a finger along its stitched back.

"Those were better days," he said quietly, and Gwen knew that he was remembering Viviana as a child. He'd told her about Viviana—beautiful and stubborn, with untamable black hair and curious, violet eyes. She could imagine the young princess, before her father's murder, clutching the silk toy as she ran about the halls of the palace.

He sighed. "For so long the people have believed in a half-cooked prophecy about the return of a true leader—and I admit, when Viviana first announced her return to the city, I myself almost believed those rumors. But her behavior, her cruel ideas about Dominance—she's not the child I knew. She has nothing in common with her father. I'm convinced that she is beyond my help, or my friendship." He shook his head, regret written plainly on his thin, weathered face. "If only her brother had lived—" The Elder's voice broke. It obviously still pained him to think of Trent, the child he could not save, who had burned along with half of the palace.

Gwen shivered, and placed her hand on his arm.

"If so much troubles you here in the city, why leave? The Seers haven't spoken to anyone in years. Some say—some say there are no Seers left." She swallowed.

The Elder patted her hand warmly, cleared his voice, and continued. "I must go to the Statue of the Twins, where the Seers once resided. Clears my mind. There are rumors of unrest in the forests and the Lowlands as well. I must seek out what allies we may have left."

"All the more reason I should go with you! You'll need someone to protect you," she said, even though she knew what his answer would be.

He shook his head. His gray hair was tufted like the feathers of one of their owls. "You must stay here and make sure that no one tries to take over my study again, eh?"

Gwen nodded stiffly. The Elder's joke did not seem funny to her. For too long the Parliament had been divided. Some senators wanted to bleed out the corruption and elect a new monarch; others wanted absolute power for themselves, and often bought and received favors in order to get it. Chambers in the palace seemed to shift as often as allegiances. After many years of occupying a study near the royal apartment, the Elder had been shuffled out and up, into a cramped tower that looked out over the ports and the harbor market of the

Fluvian river. Every time the wind blew from the south, it caused the tower to sway slightly, and carried with it the pungent smell of fish.

The Elder moved to the desk and opened the smallest drawer.

"Here," he said. Gwen watched, surprised, as the Elder pulled the drawer completely out from the desk, revealing a hidden compartment. The Elder set the drawer on the desk and removed a thin leather box, only as long as the palm of his hand.

"I want you to keep this safe while I am gone. It is an instrument of great power."

Gwen marveled at the box before opening it. The real leather, very rare, used only for special objects, was smooth and almost red. The use of an animal's skin meant that the object had great value, and was made to honor the animal who died, most likely of old age. The box had been lovingly embossed with the emblem of a boy and a fox—the Twins of legend. She opened the box, her hands shaking slightly. But almost immediately, she felt disappointed. Inside was nothing more than a rusty old harmonica.

"I . . . I don't know how to play," Gwen said, trying to conceal her confusion.

"That doesn't matter," said the Elder. "It's a relic of the last True King. The leather is pigskin, made as a gift to the king in honor of his daughter's eighth birthday, when she Awakened to her Animas, the pig, like her mother. But the instrument—that is much older. Melore believed that its music could strengthen the Animas bond."

29

"How can that be?" Gwen asked, baffled.

The Elder lowered his voice. "Melore was a good king," he whispered, "and very intelligent. He believed that the Animas bond did not only exist *here*"—the Elder pointed to his head—"but all around us. He believed it was a frequency, a vibration. It was everywhere."

Gwen looked up at the owls clustered on top of the high bookshelves. One among them was a dark brown barn owl named Grimsen, with whom the Elder had bonded for life. Once life-bonded with a member of their kin, a human could see through their eyes, like looking at a photograph, almost at will. Life-bonded humans and their kin were like two halves of the same soul, and one's well-being was intimately tied with the other's. Gwen had not experienced this with one particular animal, an owl like Grimsen that she could consider part of her own self. She looked at the small instrument in her hands. How wonderful it would be if just learning to play a few notes—the right notes—would strengthen her Animas connection, making her strong enough to bond with one particular owl, to see clearly what it saw. Maybe then she could be of more use to the Elder.

"Keep it safe," the Elder said, and his voice turned stern. "You never know when a tune might come in handy."

Gwen forced a smile.

Above them, Grimsen screeched, and a large brown feather fell to the floor. The Elder closed his eyes as though listening. And he *was* listening, Gwen knew. He was listening and seeing as the owls saw.

"Stirrings," the Elder said, after a minute. He opened

his eyes again. "An old presence in the Dark Woods has emerged anew . . ." The Elder turned to Gwen and smiled, with a hint of mischief flashing in his eyes. "Dangerous times ahead. Oh, yes. Dangerous and exciting times."

Three

AFTER THREE MINOR DERAILINGS, a variety of prepackaged sandwiches from the dining area, and another restless night listening to Roger's snoring, Bailey was so glad to hear the loudspeaker's tinny *"FairMOUNT"* call that he cheered. He wasn't alone—Hal and his brother, Taylor, and Taylor's gang of rowdy friends all sent up a celebratory whoop, and Roger audibly thanked Nature they had arrived.

The rigimotive turned a corner around the base of a steep mountainside, and the boys could see the towering cliff on top of which the academy was perched, overlooking the wide Fluvian river. At the base of the cliff was a giant wooden waterwheel that created electro-current for the whole school. Here, where the river grew narrower, the water was forced through the wheel, which churned and sputtered and sent sprays of mist up the side of the cliff.

"How do we get up there?" Hal asked his uncle.

Roger groaned. "You can see the tracks, can't you?"

Bailey squinted. The late afternoon sun glared off the wet cliff face, but Bailey could see a thin set of tracks snaking their way straight up the side of the cliff—directly to the Fairmount buildings.

"Whoa" was all he could muster.

"*Seat belts on. Secure packages please,*" came the voice from the loudspeaker.

"Here we go," said Roger with the enthusiasm of a slug about to encounter a trail of salt. Dillweed burrowed under the seat once more, bracing himself against Roger's legs. "No matter how many times I make this trip, it never gets any easier. . . ."

As the rigimotive passed the waterwheel, a spray of river water splattered the windows. Then, a resounding creak, a screech of the wheels, a *whoosh* of the dirigible above, and suddenly the rigimotive and all its passengers were jolted back into their seats as the car came to a halt just inches in front of the face of the cliff.

"What's happening?" Bailey asked Roger, who looked a little ill.

"They're harnessing the front wheels to the tracks," he said matter-of-factly. "And they'd better do it right, by Nature . . ."

Bailey and Hal exchanged a worried look. Clanks and thuds echoed through the windows from the rock wall in front of them. The yells of the conductors were muffled, but soon Bailey heard what sounded like an order to go. With a jolt, the rigimotive car was shaken—not forward, but *up*. Bailey jumped in his seat. Roger held his handkerchief in front of his face and closed his eyes.

The rigimotive clanked its way straight up the side of the

cliff. Every two or three jolts, the second car—where Bailey, Hal, and Roger were sitting—would seem to lean back, as if the weight were too much, and Bailey's heart would pound until the dirigible's steady ascent pulled the car right. Bailey could see at once why Roger was so nervous—and many of the other passengers too. Everyone on two legs in the rigimotive car had their hands clenched around their seat bottoms, and the family of raccoons that had spent a sleepless two nights in the aisle were skittering up and down between the seats anxiously. Someone's hawk was flying wildly, attacking the windows as if it could get out.

Roger had turned from ghostly pale to a sort of yellowish-green. Thankfully, after only a few minutes, the rigimotive made another grand creaking sound and righted itself, sliding back onto horizontal tracks at the top of the cliff.

They had made it.

Bailey's stomach made another leap, this time into his throat. Fairmount Academy's gleaming ivy-covered marble buildings were pink and orange in the early evening sun, and already a small crowd of students and teachers were gathered near the rigimotive platform to meet them. Bailey had never seen so many different kinds of animals in his life. Most of his schoolmates in the Lowlands were kin to farm or house animals. But here, the platform was packed with lizards and monkeys and large birds as well as sheep and guinea pigs. A pelican perched on the roof of the station, looking protectively at a man with a long nose standing below on the platform, checking off a list as trunks were unloaded onto the platform. Some men hoisted the larger luggage and suitcases from the first floor of the rigimotive onto a cart, where a pair of donkeys waited patiently to take them to the dorms.

Bailey and Hal hurried down the stairs with Roger trailing behind them. Once outside, they followed the crowd of arriving students off of the platform and through the small station, where bags were being organized and returning students were shouting, hugging, and exchanging high fives. Rabbits, deer, and even one or two bears circled the station yard and scampered up the path to the main campus. The path itself was lined with impressive hedges trimmed to look like a menagerie of forest creatures.

"Looks like everything's well in hand, boys, so if you don't mind, I have a parcel to drop off before the rigi moves on without me!" said Roger, clapping them both on the back. From the looks of the chaos in the station, Bailey wasn't sure *anything* was in hand at all.

"Ah, to be young," Roger bellowed, mopping his face with his ever-present handkerchief. "Don't get yourselves into too much trouble, boys. If I hear of any misbehavior"—he pointed a meaty finger at Hal, who, wide-eyed, looked like the last boy in the kingdom who'd ever dream of breaking a rule—"I'll send you home to your mother in the blink of a badger's eye." With that, Roger ruffled Hal's hair and was off, back into the crowd. Hal waved halfheartedly, then turned to Bailey.

"He says it all the time," he said, smiling, "but I don't *think* he means it."

"What did he mean, a parcel?" asked Bailey.

Hal shrugged. "He's always got orders coming in for his herbs and plants and things. Probably an order from a Botany professor."

Outside the station, the crowd was even thicker and the chaos even less contained. Several sheepdogs ran circles around groups of confused students as the teachers tried unsuccessfully to corral students and their animal counterparts into lines according to year.

"Year Ones over here!" Bailey heard someone shout, but he couldn't see where the shout had come from, since as soon as he turned, a deer ran through the crowd, and a group of older girls went chasing after it, *ooh*ing and *ahh*ing.

Bailey turned and saw Taylor approaching with his friends from the rigimotive and some other tall, broad-shouldered boys. They were followed by their kin, a mixed group of cats, dogs, and even a long-eared jackrabbit that made Bailey suddenly a little homesick.

"Hey, little brother!" Taylor said, too loudly, as he clapped Hal—too hard—on the shoulder. Hal stumbled forward, nearly losing his glasses. "We were just talking about you."

"I bet," mumbled Hal.

"I was trying to tell my friends about Bailey's adventure on the way here, but I just can't get the details right." Taylor grinned at Bailey. "Please tell the story for us, Bailey."

Bailey remembered the reaction from those around him on the rigimotive: the laughter, the whispers.

"I don't want to talk about it," he said. He tried to push through the group, but Taylor held out a hand to stop him.

"Come on," said Taylor, his voice changing into something

almost resembling sincerity. "It's such a great story. Just tell us what it was like out there, on the platform. That was pretty crazy of you, little man."

Bailey shrugged. "I was curious."

"You weren't scared?" asked Taylor. Bailey looked around the assembled group of students. They were all watching him carefully.

"Not really," he said, and he realized it was true. He really hadn't been scared. He'd felt excited.

The other boys began to whisper.

"Not even when you saw the ghost?" asked Taylor loudly. There was a snort from the crowd, then several bursts of laughter.

Bailey frowned.

"I didn't say it was a ghost."

"You said it was white and it glowed—what else, Walker? Did it float and say *Boo*?"

"You don't know what I saw," Bailey said. "You weren't there."

"What did I tell you?" Taylor began to laugh too, and he and one of his friends slapped hands.

"I'm guessing you're Animas Weasel," said a broad-shouldered boy with a flat, wide forehead, as though he'd fallen on his face once too many times running in Scavage matches. "You can always tell a liar by the smell of Weasel!"

"Who knows *what* your Animas is, though?" Taylor added. "I don't see any of your kin around. Not on the rigi, not here. I guess not even your own kin want to be around you . . ."

37

Bailey felt his face heat up.

"Leave him alone, Taylor," said Hal.

"*Leave him alone!*" Taylor mimicked Hal's voice. "*I'll protect you, Bailey!*"

"Bark off, I mean it!" said Hal.

Taylor was still smiling, but there was a flash of anger in his eyes when he looked at Bailey. "You're just lucky we came along to pull you in from the platform, or who knows? The *bats* might have nibbled on your fingers. And you know what they say about bats—they carry all kinds of diseases."

Hal lunged for his brother, but Taylor sent him tumbling backward onto the lawn with a single push.

"Hal!" Bailey went to help Hal to his feet.

Suddenly, there was the loud clinking of machinery. A puff of foul-smelling smoke split the group apart, and a rickety motorbuggy came to a crashing halt in front of Taylor and his friends.

The contraption looked as if a stiff wind could blow it apart. Gears and bolts and other mismatched pieces were hammered against one another as the motorbuggy's steam engine kept puffing away. The man inside—at least, Bailey *thought* it was a man—reached up with his ridiculously oversized gloves and removed a pair of bug-eyed driving goggles.

His face, except for the part where the goggles had been, was coated with coal dust. Even his thin black mustache was dusty. He had a young face, but Bailey saw tired lines under the man's eyes. A red fox sat perched next to him on the seat of a sidecar, wearing a homemade pair of miniature goggles of her own, her red fur tinged in places with grease and black coal. The clutch and steering wheel were ornate and shiny—as if they were polished often. Whoever this man was, he truly loved his sputtering, handwrought motorbuggy.

"Taylor Quindley!" the coal-dusted person barked. "What are you and your teammates doing here, harassing young persons?"

Instantly, Taylor's attitude shifted. He shoved his hands in his pockets and muttered an apology, and the group quickly dispersed.

Bailey pulled Hal to his feet. The person in the motorbuggy was wrestling with a set of assorted knobs, trying to get the unsteady thing started again.

"I, um . . . you . . . thanks," Hal managed to say. Bailey noticed the top of a metal flask sticking out of the man's vest pocket.

"Don't thank me," the man said, without looking up. "I have three pastimes in life: machines, music, and making people squirm. You might be next."

"Are you Mr. Loren?" Hal asked, stepping forward with a hand outstretched. "I'm—"

"I don't use that name, and so I can only conclude that you're new around here." The teacher scowled. "It's Tremelo, but don't go thinking that a first-name basis makes us 'pals.' That goes for both of you."

With that, the motorbuggy roared into clinking, clanging action, and several students scrambled to get out of its way. The fox in the sidecar yipped at Bailey as it passed. Bailey gaped. His heart started beating loudly—he'd just encountered the very professor he'd meant to find.

"*That's* Tremelo Loren?" Bailey asked Hal. "I didn't think he'd be so"—he struggled to find the right word—"dusty."

Hal cleaned his glasses on his shirt; they had been knocked in the dirt when he'd fallen.

"You've heard of Tremelo?" Hal asked.

Bailey nodded. "I read something about him, that he's a trainer—he can make people's bond with their kin stronger."

Hal squinted through his glasses, confused. "Really? I thought he just teaches Basic Tinkering—mechanics and stuff. Taylor says he's a useless teacher. Then again, my brother isn't exactly the most reliable source. I mean, just look at that motorbuggy; it's impressive for having built it himself."

In the distance, the motorbuggy let out a rich belch of smoke as it backfired, scattering a group of girls and their goat kin. The goats took off toward some shrubbery at the edge of the grounds.

"Don't let those creatures near my berries!" called a red-faced woman with two buck-toothed groundhogs riding on her shoulders. "I *just* pruned them!" She hurried after the fleeing goats as the girls laughed.

"So," Bailey said to Hal. "What now?"

Just then, a short, squat woman in a tweed suit hustled toward them.

"Are you new, boys?" she asked, as the wombat clinging to her head removed a hairpin from her messy bun.

"Um . . . yes?" Bailey answered, watching the wombat chew on a piece of the woman's hair.

"Excellent. Welcome to Fairmount. Here you go."

She shoved a map into Bailey's hands. "You've just come from . . . ?" the harried woman asked them.

"The Golden Lowlands," Bailey answered.

"Excellent—I don't suppose either of you know a"—she stopped to scan a clipboard held in her tightly clenched hand—"Bailey Walker, would you?"

Bailey gulped.

"That's me," he said, through a mouth as dry as sand.

The woman looked relieved enough to hug him.

"Thank Nature. We've been looking for you—you're to come with me. And your friend?"

"Hal Quindley," Hal offered.

The woman checked her list again. Her wombat eyed Bailey as if he were a piece of especially ripe fruit.

"Quindley, you're in the Towers, dear. Walker, with me!" She turned and walked quickly through the throng of bustling students toward the central campus. Bailey looked at Hal, stricken.

"I'm sure it's nothing," said Hal, sounding very much like his uncle.

"Yeah. I bet you're right," Bailey answered, though his mind was racing. His hands shook as he followed the woman, her wombat bobbing above the crowd. He turned back and saw that Hal was watching him anxiously.

"I'll see you soon," Hal called, waving. Bailey hoped he was right.

The woman introduced herself as the dean of students, Ms. Shonfield. She led Bailey to the administration building, which housed the staff offices and the library. Bailey caught a glimpse of the meeting hall being decorated with garlands and banners for the welcoming ceremony scheduled for the next morning. Ms. Shonfield's office walls were packed with yellowed photographs of Fairmount headmasters of old, posing with members of Parliament and once-famous tinkerers. Bailey was especially impressed by a very grainy photo that showed men and women in formal dress during the Age of Invention, cutting a ribbon in front of a new, shiny rigimotive car. Ms. Shonfield caught him looking.

"The maiden voyage," she said proudly. "A few of our own professors were on the team that developed the rigimotive, back when our engineering program was a tad larger. We used to be much more of a research academy, but when Melore was killed . . . well, things got a little leaner."

Bailey noticed the tall, dark-bearded man holding the scissors. His striped suit was covered by a long greatcoat, intricately woven to look like soft, wild fur. His smile was wide under his top hat, his eyes sparkling.

"Who is that?" he asked.

Ms. Shonfield shook her head.

"It's a miracle that picture has survived," she said, a note of wistfulness in her voice. "So many photographs from that era were destroyed when the Jackal took power. That's Melore, the fallen king. This photo was taken only *one week* before his assassination at the Aldermere Progress Fair, and his palace invaded and burned . . ." She trailed off, lost in the pull of history. The wombat sat on her desk, chewing on a piece of paper and looking wistfully into the distance.

"Wow," said Bailey. He'd heard about King Melore, of course. Though twenty-seven years had passed since Melore had died, most people Bailey knew remembered the king fondly.

"Yes, well, what's done is done," she said, rousing herself. "I didn't bring you here to speak of dead kings. Go on. Take a seat." She gestured to a chair across from her desk. "I'll be frank with you, Mr. Walker. We don't know where to put you."

Bailey shifted in his seat, dreading the questions to come.

"I thought it was clear on the registration forms," she said, shuffling several papers on her desk. "We absolutely must know what Animas you are, so we know where to house you and get you registered for the most appropriate courses."

"Oh," said Bailey. He took a deep breath. "I haven't really got a . . . I mean, I haven't . . ."

Ms. Shonfield leaned in, listening intently.

"No matter what your Animas is, Bailey, there's no need to be ashamed! We take all kinds here at Fairmount. Not like the old days! Had an Animas Sloth graduate last year and you know, when he wasn't sleeping in class, he was absolutely lovely."

Bailey looked down at his hands, resting on his now dirty work pants, wrinkled and worn after a two-day ride on the cramped rigimotive. He just wanted to get to his trunk, and crawl into a real bed.

"I haven't Awakened to my Animas yet," he said. "I don't know what it is." Or if I have one at all, he thought.

Ms. Shonfield sat back in her chair and snatched her glasses off of her face. She squinted at him.

"An Absence," she said breathlessly. "That's quite . . . unique."

"I guess so," said Bailey, as the word *Absence*—so final, so bleak—echoed in his ears. His mom and dad had made a point never to use it. People with a lifelong Absence were rare to the point of myth. In the stories Bailey had heard, they always ended up insane, or worse.

"It's not *permanent,* I'm just developing slowly, that's all," he added quickly, just in case she was about to tell him he couldn't stay. "I'm adopted, so it's taking me longer to figure out what kind of animal I bond with. I . . . I'm always looking, though." He tried to sound cheerful. He tried to think of his father, encouraging him to be patient, telling him that his Animas could be anywhere—just someplace he hadn't looked yet.

Ms. Shonfield pinched her lips together and appeared to be working out a puzzle in her head. Bailey's stomach felt like it was made of lead.

"I just need a little time, and training," he said, feeling increasingly desperate. "You—you won't send me home, will you?"

"Of course not," Ms. Schonfield said. Bailey relaxed. "But you'll have to miss out on a couple of core courses, I'm afraid. Biology and the Bond, for one. The class will be of no use to you without an Animas. It's fairly hands-on, you see. Unfortunately, we haven't offered one-on-one Animas training in many years."

Ms. Shonfield leaned forward on her staunch elbows and looked closely at Bailey.

"My boy, you have a hard road to go here, I won't lie to you. I'm sure you know most children Awaken to their Animas at approximately age nine. The latest I've ever met is eleven. This isn't to discourage you, dear—but to let you know what you're in for."

Bailey looked up from his hands as she continued.

"We will find appropriate courses for you, don't worry about that, and we will wait and see how you take to school life. But there will be plenty of students—and yes, though I'm sorry to say it, adults—who won't understand your Absence. Who may try to treat you differently as a late waker. But you won't let them, will you? You belong here, Mr. Walker. We chose you, based on your aptitude, your intelligence, and the word of those who love you, not which corner of Nature's kingdom you may hail from. You're late to Awaken, and I'm sure this has brought you some pain, but I assure you, when you *do* Awaken to your Animas—and I have no doubt that you will—we here at Fairmount will be at the ready to help you as you grow into it. Don't ever doubt that you belong here."

Bailey nodded, solemn and grateful.

"That said, Mr. Walker, I think it's best to put you in the Towers as well for now. I'll arrange for your trunks to be directed there."

Four

AS A CLOUD-FILLED MORNING dawned over the foul-smelling docks of the Gray City, a striking young woman with violet eyes stood overseeing a busy factory.

From a distance, Viviana Melore was quite beautiful. Up close, it was possible that the cheekbones were angled a little too neatly; that the mouth, painted with maroon lipstick, was a little too cruel; and the forehead, which closely resembled her dead father's, the former king, was a little *too* high.

Viviana clutched a rusted rail, surveying a large, open workroom that reeked of hot ink and oil, and the pulp of freshly made paper. Below her, workers were busily attending to printing presses and assembly stations, tinkering with gears and folded paper with fresh ink.

Through the room's wide, grime-coated upper windows, she could see what the many workers at their stations below her could not: across the river, the towering dome of the Parliament, its grand copper roof tarnished to green. From here, she could not see the palace wing she'd escaped—but simply knowing it was there made her fingers twitch. She would tear that building down the moment she had the chance.

The taking of Parliament would not be difficult, of that she was sure—it was made up of weak, corrupt men and women. Since deposing the Jackal, they'd all but ignored the people, and the people were poor, desperate, and angry. The city was like a stone wall with too many cracks, and rather than working to fix them, Viviana was determined to blast them into rubble.

She breathed deeply, inhaling a wisp of thick smoke that rose up from the machine on the floor. It filled her nostrils and triggered a memory from long ago. *Smoke, flames rising, the desperate pounding on the other side of the door . . .* She straightened her shoulders and banished the memory from her mind. Just another piece of unpleasantness from the past.

She took a moment to adjust her suit. While many wealthier citizens in the Gray City chose ensembles embroidered with the image of their Animas, Viviana's decoration of choice was black silk thread, depicting not only her Animas, the pig, but many others, their claws outstretched, teeth bared.

Joan, her assistant, gave her weekly report. "Everything is going smoothly so far," she chirped over the whirring of the presses. "We've completed production of the Orsas that will fly to Red Street. Those for the fish market are preparing for takeoff any moment now."

Joan handed a small paper object to Viviana for her approval. A windup paper bird, no more than three inches high, with Viviana's crest printed on it wings. Joan delicately pulled a loose bit of paper sticking out from behind one of the bird's wings, and those wings began to whir into action. Viviana held on to one of its delicate paper feet to keep it from flying away.

"It's an On-the-Spot Orsa," Joan explained. "Designed to drop instantly."

As she spoke, the paper bird began to unfurl. The tiny rolls of paper that made its wings and back burst open, forming a small poster in Viviana's hands that read, WE WILL BE FREE, OR WE WILL BE NOTHING. By the time NOTHING had been revealed by the unfolding paper, all that remained of the shape of the bird was a tiny chirping beak that made a sound like a gasp for air. As the beak finally unfolded and gave way, the word DOMINAE joined the rest in a perfectly square billet, the size of Viviana's hand. All that remained in Viviana's palm was a tiny spring motor, its spinning barrel slowing to a stop.

Viviana smiled.

"*Very* well done," she said, which was, for her, an enormous compliment. "But you said the market? What about the Opera Square? Can we reach as far as the Gudgeons?"

"Some of the larger Orsas have been engineered to fly longer distances," Joan said. "But we will not rely on the Orsas alone."

Joan took Viviana's arm, leading her along the walkway to a spot overlooking a stretch of long worktables, where a group of men and women were busy cleaning a mess of discarded copper gears and wire. Something large—or many somethings—had been assembled here.

Joan whistled, and a tall, thin man in a three-piece navy suit—which Viviana could see was coated with a layer of dust—looked up, and began hurrying up a clanking metal staircase, beckoning to several of the workers to follow him.

"You've met Mr. Clarke, the tinkerer," Joan said as the man strode toward them on the walkway. The workers behind him, almost tripping over their long, heavy aprons, carried several enormous wooden crates in their arms. Viviana could see how shabby Clarke's suit was up close, how pale and sallow his skin—but there glinted in his eyes something proud and intelligent.

Clarke bowed low, smiling broadly, displaying a mouth of long, yellow teeth under his beak-like nose. He gestured to one of the workers behind him to open the box in his arms.

Out of the box fluttered—no, clanked—a metal raven, easily three times the size of a natural raven, made entirely of gears and bolts and expertly manipulated copper. Under a translucent layer of black paint, its metal workings gleamed, reflecting the gas lamps hanging above the workroom. A perfectly round mechanical eye whizzed and whirred in its socket as it looked first at Viviana, then Joan, then at Clarke, who nodded to it as if to an obedient child. The raven unfolded its wide copper wings, which clicked as its many gears turned, and flew to the railing of the walkway. It fixed its eyes on Viviana and opened its metal beak menacingly.

Viviana's own voice boomed forth from the inner whirrings of the bird's mechanical ribs and out of its throat, the beak serving as a perfect gramophone trumpet. "*My human brothers and sisters,"* it echoed, *"we will be free, or we will be nothing!"*

As the sound of Viviana's amplified voice died away, the bird closed its beak.

"It's brilliant," Viviana said, and she meant it. "What do you call them?"

"I have been calling them the Clamoribus, but of course you are free to—"

"Perfect," Viviana said, cutting him off. "'The Screams.' I like it."

"Their timing couldn't be more perfect. Parliament has taxed the people to exhaustion and the city has nearly crumbled with disrepair. People see how Parliament stuffs its pockets," said Clarke, as the raven restlessly—just like a real bird—shuffled its feet on the railing. The light from the window shone on its black-painted talons. "The Gray City needs someone with vision."

Viviana looked over at her beaming assistant. She had known Joan since they were girls in the Dust Plains. Joan's cute blond bob and sparkling blue eyes had always been misleading—she had the look of a cheerful simpleton, but Viviana had known for years that Joan was capable of anything.

"My clever Joan, you've found us such an ingenious tinkerer," Viviana said sweetly. "If only every part of this campaign could be left in your hands, I would have no worries in the world."

"Nor should you," Joan said, smiling gratefully. "It is as you have always said—"

She didn't get to finish. Below them, a female worker shrieked. The sound cut over the noise of the machinery.

"What's happened?" demanded Viviana sharply.

"I saw one! A rat! A filthy spy!" The worker's shrill voice echoed over the din of the presses.

In an instant Viviana lifted a silver whistle to her lips. The shrieking noise overpowered the clanking machines. At once, several of the starving alley cats along the wall sprang toward the poor worker who'd sounded the alarm. They found the squealing rat underneath the press and dragged it out into the open, tearing at it without mercy. The worker covered her eyes with her ink-stained apron as the cats clawed the helpless rodent to bits. When Viviana could see from her perch that the rat had been sufficiently decimated, she gave the whistle a second blow. The cats returned to their places against the wall, silently licking the blood from their paws.

"That's a very impressive trick," murmured Clarke.

Viviana accepted the compliment wordlessly. It was more than a trick—this was years of practice and focus, all her bitterness and rage channeled into usefulness. No one but the most gifted humans had the power to assert full control over the minds of their kin, and no one, not even those in the Parliament, would ever dare to attempt it.

This is how it should be, Viviana thought. The Animas bond meant having empathy for animals, which made a person weak, ignoring their own needs in favor of something lesser. Dominance, however, meant control. *We will be free, or we will be nothing.*

"Have someone nail what's left of the rat to the door."

Viviana raised her voice so that it echoed through the warehouse, just as it had out of the raven's mouth. "The resistance obviously needs to be told where they and their spies are not welcome." She waved a hand. "Now back to work, all of you."

From unwieldy wooden platforms, a team of men heaved on a set of ropes, and brought several more net sacks containing fluttering paper birds up from the workroom floor to the open windows. The men at the windows let go of the ropes, and the net bags burst open; the little mechanical paper birds poured out and briefly circled the ceiling of the factory, an enormous cloud of motion. Thousands of paper wings beat the air to shreds.

The mechanical giants in their boxes began flapping their heavy wings. They pushed off and out of their crates with sharply clawed feet, and rose steadily to meet their paper companions. As one, the birds flew through the open windows and over the river, casting dark shadows on the gray water, the huge winged gizmos leading the diminutive paper Orsas like soldiers in battle formation. Viviana's heart rose like those wings, and lifted off to join them.

She turned to Joan. Her capable assistant had another mission today besides overseeing the flight of a flock of paper birds.

"Only one more piece of business before you leave." Viviana spoke in a low voice, so no one else would hear. "One of my informants stationed on the King's Rigimotive Railway spoke to me this morning about some strange occurrences in the Dark Woods. One of the beasts may still be out there."

Joan smiled encouragingly. "Undoubtedly a rumor cooked up by your opposition. Don't give it another thought." Her eyes glittered as she rested a hand on Viviana's arm. "We'll soon know the full language of the Loon's prophecy—but no matter what it says, it will never keep you from regaining the throne. I'll make sure of it."

Five

HAL AND BAILEY'S ROOM was on the second floor of one of six wooden towers in the rambling dormitory. It had dark rafters and whitewashed walls, identical iron beds, and a large window that faced a sloping hillside. Because the Towers housed mostly students with nocturnal kin, the many common rooms were open at all hours, and stocked with board games, books, and plenty of candles for when the unreliable electro-current would flicker in and out at night.

The first day of classes began with an elaborate ceremony in the meeting hall of the administration building. Row upon row of gleaming wooden benches had been outfitted with blue and gold cushions for the students—and in some cases, their kin—to sit on. Many older students hugged and shouted greetings to their friends. The air echoed with voices, giggles, snorts, and barks. A large flag with the Fairmount crest, a golden lamb and crow on a bright blue background, hung above the stage.

Hal and Bailey found a spot near the front of the room as the Fairmount Academy choir began an upbeat rendition of an old melody, "Nature Is My Help and Joy." Afterward, the headmaster, a thin, prim-looking man named Finch, welcomed the new students with a long speech. Bailey dozed off and nearly fell forward onto a second-year's porcupine. Hal grabbed his shoulders just in time to avoid disaster, and Bailey smiled apologetically at two girls in the next row, who gave him a nasty look before whipping around toward the front of the room.

At last Finch concluded his speech and the students filed out to find their homerooms. Hal and Bailey had been placed together, in a room on the third floor of the Applied Sciences building. They passed the dining hall and emerged into a vast lawn known as the Circle, where Fairmount students lounged between classes, ate lunch outdoors, and picked up impromptu games of Scavage.

"That's Treetop dorm, where the reptile and bird Animae live," said Hal, pointing to the structures as they crossed the lawn. "And that's Garrett, with the tunnels. It's rodent and small farm Animae. And the barn and stables are up the hill a ways, as you get closer to the teachers' quarters."

"You memorized the whole map already?" Bailey joked.

Hal blushed.

"I wanted to be sure I was nowhere near Taylor. The Scavage pitch is farther into the forest, past the dorms. You can't see them from here, but they're huge! Which reminds me: tryouts are tomorrow afternoon . . ."

Hal trailed off as a group of chattering girls squealed loudly and pointed in his direction.

"Did I do something wrong?" Hal mumbled, tugging self-consciously on his blazer.

"Relax," Bailey said. "They're not pointing at you."

Bailey and Hal turned. Behind them, a girl was striding purposefully across the lawn toward the marble steps of the Applied Sciences building.

She was very tall and very pale, with long black hair and dark eyes lined with purple. Most of the girls Bailey had seen wore dresses and skirts with their blue Fairmount blazers. But this girl sported a pair of high-waisted tweed pants and a buttoned cotton shirt under her blazer. She carried a slouchy beaded bag over one shoulder.

"Isn't that the girl whose kin almost swallowed your mouse on the rigi?" said a blond girl, hugging a rabbit protectively to her chest.

The second girl, who was wearing a headband with a floppy flower sewn on it, nodded. "Freak," she said viciously. Bailey felt a twinge in his stomach. He hated that word, having heard it often enough.

As the black-haired girl came closer, seemingly indifferent to the reaction she was causing, Bailey saw a thin, black snake emerge from the top of the beaded bag and wind its way around her wrist.

"Wow," said Bailey. "I've never seen an Animas Snake before." He looked at Hal. "What about you?"

Hal didn't answer.

"Hal?" Bailey prompted.

"Snake," he murmured. "Wow."

Hal was so transfixed that he didn't notice the whizzing object headed straight for his head.

"Watch out!" Bailey yelled. He pushed Hal out of the way

just as the object was about to hit Hal square in the glasses.

Bailey looked down at the object as it skittered on the ground. It was long and wooden, like a fat paintbrush, with bristles at one end. He recognized it from pictures of professional Scavage games: a Flick. During Scavage games, camouflage and subterfuge were important, and the Flick was a tool used for marking the opposing players with brightly colored paint so they had no chance to hide.

Bailey turned around and saw Taylor and his friends laughing at Bailey and Hal. He'd thrown the Flick at them just like a dart.

"I think you *dropped* this," Bailey said casually, and lobbed the Flick back to Taylor. It flew straight and fast, forcing Taylor to dodge it. It stuck firmly a few feet behind where he originally stood, quivering in the ground. Taylor frowned. Bailey felt a rush of satisfaction—for once, Taylor had nothing stupid to say.

Hal and Bailey's homeroom looked more like a junk heap than a class. Shelves of papers lined the walls, in no apparent order: stacks of old student essays had been shoved next to a pile of yellowed documents that showed some kind of rigimotive design, with wings instead of a dirigible. Boxes of gears and screws were stacked on top of one another, their contents bursting from their tops. Glass cases over the shelves housed strange plants with spindly leaves that Bailey had never seen before. A dusty clock, missing both hands, hung above a door just behind the desk—Bailey figured it must lead to a private office. The desk itself was a catastrophe—an avalanche of papers and open books that spilled off of the surface and onto the floor. On a corner of the desk stood an empty bottle of red wine.

"Is this the right room?" Bailey asked Hal.

Hal squinted at his schedule as he tugged at his tightly starched collar, which was buttoned nearly to his chin. "'Homeroom. Applied Sciences Building. Room Thirty-eight. Miscellaneous Animae.' That's where we are, all right," Hal answered.

They chose two desks near the front of the room. There were a half dozen other students in the room, and they fidgeted in nervous silence. From his seat, Bailey could see that the writing utensils on the teacher's desk were covered with a layer of dust.

"Oh, no," breathed Hal softly.

"What?" Bailey said.

"*She's* here," whispered Hal, gesturing behind him. "No, don't look! Don't look!" Hal said, as Bailey tried to glance over his shoulder. But Bailey had already spotted her: the mysterious dark-haired girl they'd seen on the way to class. Her pet snake was dozing around her neck, its delicate head nestled against her collarbone.

"I can *hear* you, you know," she said loudly.

A group of girls sitting on the other side of the room giggled. A small parrot on the shoulder of a girl in the front row squawked. Bailey saw Hal blush bright red. He couldn't help but feel a little sorry for him.

Several minutes ticked by as they waited for their Homeroom teacher to appear. The other students began to whisper and fidget in their seats. One student, who had been followed to class by a pair of inquisitive newts, tried to engage the other kids into betting which of the creatures could climb the highest—but no one was in the mood. Instead, everyone sat in silence, wondering when—or if—their teacher would make an appearance.

The snake girl sighed. "In one minute, I'm out of here," she announced.

"We can't just go," Hal said, turning around in his chair to face her. "It's the very first class."

The girl's eyes narrowed. The snake lifted its head from its nap and flicked its tongue at them. "Nobody said you had to follow me," the girl said. "I wouldn't have pegged *you* for the type to cut class, anyway."

"What—what does that mean?" Hal sputtered, once again turning cherry-red.

Just then, a small red flash bolted in through the classroom doorway and leapt to the teacher's desk. A fox. She climbed to the top of the pile of papers and sat calmly, looking at the students as if she were about to call roll. Their Homeroom teacher sauntered in after her, picking his teeth with a fingernail and looking for all the world as though he were not a minute late.

"Uh-oh," Bailey and Hal whispered in unison.

It was Tremelo, the soot-covered man in the motorbuggy who'd made such an entrance in front of the station the afternoon before. Still wearing the same dirty driving coat, the professor surveyed the room.

"Is everyone here?" he asked.

The students looked at one another cautiously.

"Good," said Tremelo, before anyone had a chance to answer. With that, he opened the door behind his desk. Bailey caught a glimpse of more papers, more teetering stacks of junk, more chaos in the adjoining office. "I've got more important things to do today than spend half an hour going over the rules with a bunch of kids who are bound to break them anyway," he continued, "so listen carefully."

Bailey and the other students sat still as stones.

"Welcome to Fairmount. Steer clear of salmon pie Sundays if you value your intestinal health, and always, *always* be quiet while I think." Then he disappeared into his office, slamming the door and leaving the students alone again.

The snake girl snorted. Bailey and Hal exchanged a look.

"He must be kidding, right?" said Bailey.

"Taylor told me that last year, he set his own office on fire," Hal said. *"Twice."*

As if on cue, a small curlicue of smoke rose from the bottom of the office door. Bailey sniffed the air—nothing was burning, though he did smell a sweet, herblike scent that he couldn't place.

"What is that?" he asked Hal.

"It's myrgwood!" Hal said after one sniff, his eyes wide. "It's . . ." He lowered his voice to a whisper. "My uncle Roger says it makes you very . . . um . . . relaxed."

Low humming emerged from behind the door, followed by quiet, drowsy singing. *"I gave my love a darling stoat / Her badger ate it whole . . ."*

"Well, that does it," said the snake girl, standing up at

her desk. "I'm out of here. Who else has Sucrette's Intro to Latin?"

"We do!" Hal said quickly, and practically hauled Bailey out of his seat.

The girl rolled her eyes. "Great. All right, then. Let's go before we're smoked out."

Together, they stood up and made their way out in the hall. Bailey wasn't sure how he felt about leaving class early—then again, Tremelo hadn't exactly seemed eager for them to stick around.

"Hey, what's your name?" Hal asked as they made their way out of the building and into the early morning sun.

"Victoria Colubride," she said. "Tori." Then she sped ahead of them.

"I don't think she likes us very much," Bailey whispered to Hal.

"Tori's a pretty name, isn't it?" Hal said, and Bailey knew he hadn't heard.

They still had more than twenty minutes until their next class. Tori, Hal, and Bailey found their way to a pleasant set of stone benches in an L-shaped sunken garden by the building for Linguistics and Interspecies Communication. Tori pulled a bag of dried fruit out of her purse and began munching, seemingly uninterested in making conversation.

"Where are you from?" Hal asked her. "We're from the Lowlands, Bailey and I."

Tori sighed and looked toward the clock tower. Her snake wound its way around her neck again, settling its head underneath her left ear.

"The Gray," she said finally.

"That's fantastic," said Hal. "I mean really, wow, the *city*. So brilliant."

"It's *not*," Tori said. "Though at least everyone there dresses like they live in this century. Why do all the teachers here look like they've rolled straight out of the Age of Invention? I think my *grandfather* wore cravats." She rolled up the bag of fruit and went to put it back in her bag, as Hal tried to close his school blazer quickly over the paisley-patterned cravat that Roger had sent along with him. Bailey swallowed a laugh. As Tori moved her arm, he caught sight of a wide red scar on her wrist. Tori caught Bailey looking, and tugged her blazer's sleeve forcefully down.

Hal was blathering on about wanting to see the Parliament, and whether she had ever been to the fish market. Bailey stayed silent until Tori turned her purple-rimmed eyes to him.

"So, I heard you were playing jump-the-train-car on the way here," she said.

Bailey tried to judge whether she was making fun of him, and decided she wasn't. "I just needed some air," he said.

"*Hmmm.*" Tori narrowed her eyes at both of them. "You must either be really brave or a complete idiot."

Bailey laughed. "Let's go with brave, okay?"

"It was my idea," Hal blurted out, and Bailey didn't bother to correct him.

The bells in the clock tower rang after a while, and the three of them picked themselves up off the grass and made their way to the Latin classroom.

Ms. Sucrette was a brand-new teacher, and her classroom

was the exact opposite of Tremelo's mess. On all the brightly painted walls were long, crisp parchments that charted verb conjugations. Ms. Sucrette herself was right on time, dressed in a cheery blue drop-waist dress with a pink carnation pinned to the collar. She had short, wavy blond hair. Her Animas was clearly a bluebird: a small flight of them circled the room endlessly throughout the lesson, occasionally landing on a student's desk to stare blankly at them as roll was called.

"Welcome, welcome!" she chirped. "I'm sure you may have heard that this is my first year at Fairmount, so we'll all be learning together!" Bailey couldn't see Tori from where he sat, but he thought he could feel her rolling her eyes.

Ms. Sucrette began to call roll. Used to being called last on any list, Bailey let his mind wander. Clearly Tremelo, the great Animas trainer, would have to be won over—but Bailey *wouldn't* give up. He was making friends already, and Hal had promised not to tell anyone about his Absence. As long as he could keep it hidden, he had a chance to feel normal.

"Quindley, Harold," Sucrette called.

Hal cleared his throat.

"Present," he responded crisply. Sucrette smiled and made a mark on her list.

"Walker, Bailey."

"Here," Bailey answered, raising his hand. Ms. Sucrette smiled warmly at him.

"*Wel*come, dear," she said. Bailey felt his ears getting hot as the other students snickered.

Sucrette finished calling roll, then led the class in a lesson on conjugating verbs.

"*Amo, amas,* and . . ." Sucrette trailed off, surveying which student to call on. Though Bailey had taken a Latin class in his old school, he didn't dare raise his hand. He knew the answer was *"amat,"* but he couldn't take another of her strange, sympathetic smiles.

As the students dutifully repeated the conjugation, the door to the classroom opened and a small, pretty girl with dark skin and bright golden-brown eyes entered. Her pleated maroon dress looked new under her school jacket, but very plain and a little loose, as if her parents had bought a size up so she'd grow into it. Her right shoulder was covered by a scratched leather patch that buckled with thin straps under her arm. Ms. Sucrette looked at her roll call.

"Ms. Sophia Castling?" she asked.

"I prefer Phi," the girl said softly.

"All the way from the Dust Plains," Ms. Sucrette announced, accentuating every syllable so that it sounded like a very grand pronouncement. "*Do* choose a seat."

The only empty desk was right under Ms. Sucrette's nose, just a row in front of where Bailey and Hal were sitting. Phi walked quickly to the desk and sat down gracefully, staring straight ahead, ignoring the fact that everyone was watching her. Bailey had never met anyone from the Dust Plains before, a set of territories so remote that even by rigimotive, the journey to Fairmount took over a week. Student enrollment from the Dust Plains was incredibly rare. Bailey had heard all sorts of stories about life in those

64

territories, mostly about how tough everyone was, with tough kin as well.

When Phi reached into her bag to pull out her notebook, Bailey heard a rustling behind him. He turned to see a falcon, wings outstretched, perched on the windowsill. For a moment, it was still. Then it swooped into the classroom and shot straight to the highest bookshelf, where one of Sucrette's bluebirds was preening. Someone in the back row shrieked.

"Please quiet down, children," Ms. Sucrette chirped, seemingly oblivious to what was happening.

The falcon struck out with its sharp beak. The bluebird barely escaped, and the chase was on. Students ducked in their chairs as the birds swooped low over their heads. Chairs scraped against the floor, and more than one student tried to fan the falcon away with their notebooks and papers.

"Ms. Sucrette! The bluebird!" someone shouted, and finally Ms. Sucrette turned her attention away from the list of verbs on the board. The falcon captured the bluebird's foot in its beak. Ms. Sucrette, without even batting an eye, seized a heavy book from the front shelf and swiped at the falcon.

"Drop it! This instant!" she cried, chasing the falcon back to the windowsill. The bluebird fell to the classroom floor, where it thrashed its wings and hobbled, trying to right itself on its hurt leg.

Before Ms. Sucrette could shoo the falcon out the window, it glided over to Phi, settled onto the leather patch on her shoulder, and steadied itself with its sharp talons. Phi sunk visibly into her seat as the falcon affectionately nibbled on a bit of her brown hair.

Ms. Sucrette strode to the front of the room.

"Sophia," she said shrilly. "You must learn to control your impulses, or mishaps like this will happen far too often." She took a deep breath, clearly making an effort to calm down. "Boundaries are important! Your kin must learn respect."

Phi nodded. She was obviously mortified, but Bailey couldn't help but feel jealous. It was said that girls matured faster. Maybe that explained her close bonds with her kin. He couldn't even imagine what it must feel like to have such a fierce Animas—if only he could be Animas Falcon. Or Animas *anything*. At this point, he'd even take a bug.

"Now where were we?" Ms. Sucrette said, smoothing her hair. "Ah, yes. *Amo, amas, amat!* Repeat after me, children!"

"What a joke," Tori said, leaving the room with Bailey and Hal at the end of the lesson. Bailey looked about for the girl with the falcon as the class dispersed into the hallway, but she'd left quickly, slipping away before anyone could stop to chat with her.

"Who?" Hal asked Tori.

"*Ms. Suc-rette!*" Tori answered, mimicking the teacher's careful articulation.

"I don't know," said Bailey, surprised that Tori had fallen in beside them. "I thought she was . . . nice."

"Sucrette didn't even flinch when that falcon went after one of her kin," Hal said. "I think I'd have gotten sick or something."

"Please," Tori said, "she didn't even notice! If you ask me, that makes her even more of a joke! And so *boring*. I'd rather watch a snake shed its skin than hear her talk." She started to speed up, and then turned around abruptly. "See you two tomorrow."

"What's with her?" Bailey wondered out loud. "I can't tell if she wants to be our friend or if she wants to kill us."

"Girls." Hal sighed dramatically. "With them, that's always the question."

As Tori walked away, Bailey saw a small black snake raise its head from the back of her collar. It flicked its tongue, and the curve of its jaws made it look as if it were laughing at them.

"Oh, Mr. Walker!" called a cheery voice from the classroom door they'd just exited through.

Bailey and Hal turned to see Ms. Sucrette smiling at them, holding her hands primly at her front.

"Yes?" answered Bailey, retracing his steps to the classroom door.

Ms. Sucrette reached out and touched his shoulder delicately with the tips of her fingers.

"Mrs. Shonfield informed me about your condition," she said. "And I must admit, this is the first time I've ever met someone with . . . Well, I think you're very brave to be coming to school. Please just let me know if you need any extra help, or are having any trouble keeping up." Her awkward touch turned into a small pat, and with a smile, she retreated into the classroom.

Bailey stood stunned. He'd expected the taunts and

sidelong glances from other kids like Taylor if news of his Absence got out—but he hadn't expected a sting like that. At least, he thought, she had good intentions. But he still felt a little like a puppy that had been kicked.

"Whew." Hal whistled. "I think Tori might be right about that one. Not the brightest striped zebra in the pack." He clapped a hand on Bailey's back. "Come on; we've got Flora and Fauna next."

Bailey followed Hal away from the Latin classroom, and thought about his mom and dad, who had always done their best to make him feel normal. Fairmount, it seemed, would do anything but.

Six

THE NEXT AFTERNOON, Bailey and Hal met up after their final classes of the day, and together they cut across the common lawn and past the classroom buildings to the Scavage field.

"If I don't try out for the Scavage team," Hal reasoned for about the fourth time that day, "Taylor will just make fun of me for the rest of my life." Hal squinted as he took off his glasses to clean them. "But then again, if I do go, he'll still make fun of me, because I know I'll be terrible."

Hal had spent the last hour in Biology and the Bond. But since Bailey didn't have an Animas, he'd been placed in a low-level History course taught by a Professor Nillow. Bailey had borrowed a spare copy of the Biology and the Bond textbook from the library, however, and had spent most of Nillow's lecture on the birth of Parliament flipping carefully through its pages, and admiring the detailed diagrams of both human and animal energy systems.

"Do you really think it'll be that bad?" Bailey asked, glad to be out in the fresh air. "You never know, you might be"—he looked Hal up and down: his thick glasses, without which he couldn't see a brick wall in broad daylight; his skinny arms and legs—"um . . . good."

"Ha-ha," Hal said, pulling a face. "I'm just glad you're coming with me. You're going to try out too, right?"

"What?" Bailey had a sudden vision of Taylor running him down and pelting him with Flicks as sharp as arrows. "Are you insane?"

"Come on, I bet you'd actually be good at it!" Hal said. "What about that throw you made yesterday? You'd be wonderful! I mean"—he lowered his voice—"who cares if you don't have an Animas if you're on the Scavage team?"

"No, Hal," Bailey said firmly. "I don't need to draw any more attention to myself." He was too small to make the team, he was sure, and he knew that Scavage involved plenty of human–kin communication. Even *trying* to play might make his Absence obvious to the older students.

Hal stopped walking. They'd reached the top of a sloping hill. Behind them, the marble classroom buildings loomed, but in front of them was a cheery stadium with wooden stands built around a sprawl of forested terrain. Hal turned to Bailey.

"Listen," he said, his eyes wide behind his glasses, "maybe—just hear me out—maybe your Animas didn't exist in the Lowlands. But maybe it's here somewhere, and if you give yourself the chance, out on the Scavage field, it will *find* you. Who cares about the other students? You came here to push yourself, right? This is as good a chance as any."

Bailey still wasn't sure, but Hal's confidence moved him. Maybe he was right; Bailey, like Hal, was afraid of looking like an idiot out on the field, but he *had* come here to push himself.

"Okay," he said slowly. "But we get beaten to a pulp, it's on you."

Hal sighed deeply. "Thank you," he said. "I owe you one."

The Scavage field wasn't just a field. The playing ground was a solid quarter-mile of Fairmount land that contained everything from open grassy space to dense woods covered in undergrowth. The farthest edge of the playing field bordered a set of low rocky cliffs, nearly hidden by the trees. The stadium seating that extended around three sides of the field was high enough so most spectators could watch all the action. People seated in the lower rungs could hear a play-by-play called out during each game by three different announcers who perched in dangerously tall nest-like lookout points arranged on three sides of the field.

Bailey began to feel nervous as soon as he saw the crowd of students gathered by the gates to try out—and, even worse, people who had come to cheer on their friends and get a look at the new hopefuls. Scavage was a Fairmount invention, but had become so popular throughout the kingdom that a professional Scavage league had been created during the reign of King Melore—of course, it was populated mostly by Fairmount graduates. For this reason, the Fairmount team was intensely scrutinized; even their practices drew a crowd of eager spectators.

Bailey felt like he was about to go on stage in front of a packed auditorium without his trousers. His hands felt cold, and he couldn't feel his legs below the knee. Hal, meanwhile, looked like at any second he might throw up the three egg tartlets he'd eaten during lunch.

The first person to greet them as they entered the field was Coach Banter, a broad-shouldered man with a shaved head. He was Animas Bulldog, and he had two kin who followed him around.

"Welcome, boys," he said with a nod. He uncrossed his arms and pointed them toward the sign-in.

A large red-haired girl with gold shoulder padding and warm-ups watched as they wrote their names on the sign-in sheet.

"*You're* Taylor's little brother?" she said to Hal.

Hal squared his shoulders. "I am. So what?"

The red-haired girl smirked. "You don't look a thing like him, that's all."

It wasn't Hal's most impressive comeback, Bailey had to admit, but all the same he was glad to see Hal stand up for himself. He felt even better when he saw Phi, the Animas Falcon, sitting alone on the wooden benches where potential players were being asked to wait. She was looking longingly at the trees on the other side of the pitch.

The red-haired girl shoved two sets of kneepads and thin but durable fingerless gloves into their arms. "Put these on. Trust me, you'll need them."

"Great," Hal muttered, as he and Bailey headed toward the bench to suit up. "There's that boost of confidence I was hoping to get . . ."

"Don't worry," Bailey said. He was focused on the empty seat next to Phi. Her curly brown hair was pulled back into a tight bun, and she wore a faded pair of girls' athletic shoes that looked secondhand. Her leather patch had been buckled into place over her white athletic shirt, and she also wore similar leather gauntlets on both her forearms. Bailey thought she looked less like a schoolgirl Scavage player, and more like a warrior about to go into battle. He gathered his courage and sat down next to her. Hal followed, and stood by the bench fumbling with his kneepads.

"Do you always attract the same falcon?" Bailey blurted out. Phi barely glanced at him. "I mean . . . I saw . . . I'm in Sucrette's Latin class."

"I know," Phi said evenly. She paused, then said, "Yes, mostly. We're not life-bonded or anything. But she did travel with me from the Dust Plains. Her name is Carin. "

"That's really cool," said Bailey.

Phi shrugged, but one corner of her mouth crooked into a smile. "Thanks. My roommate doesn't think it's so cool. Carin's always terrorizing her snakes." She pointed to the stands behind them. There, among the rowdy group of students, sat Victoria, looking as sullen as if she'd been put there in time-out for bad behavior. A freckled boy sitting next to her asked her a question, and as Bailey watched, one of Tori's snakes reared its head out of her collar and hissed. The boy jumped. Tori pretended not to notice.

"Tori's your roommate?" Hal asked quickly, with feigned casualness.

"All right, newbies!" came a loud, harsh voice—the red-headed girl was demanding their attention from the field. Beside her stood Taylor, his mottled-brown cat winding

73

its way around his ankles. They both held clipboards for taking notes on the hopeful new students. "Let's get going. We're splitting you up into two squadrons and we'll get a scrimmage going. I'm Arabella, captain of Squadron Blue, and this is Taylor, captain of Squadron Gold. We're the co-captains, and if you're picked, you'll obey our every command as if your measly lives depended on it!"

"Which they do," Taylor said, grinning meanly.

Hal gulped.

Bailey, Phi, Hal, and the twenty or so other new hopefuls lined up so that Arabella and Taylor could have a closer look at them. Coach Banter, who seemed to be letting Taylor and Arabella run the show, was sitting with his feet up in the stands, pawing through a Gray City newspaper and making disapproving grunts.

"When we get to you, tell us your name and your Animas," Taylor barked. "As you know, the stronger your Animas bond, the more skills you'll bring to a team, so let us know up front what you think you can do. And then," he finished with a dark look, "we'll be the judge."

Bailey felt, all of a sudden, as though he'd been filled head to toe with wet sand. He wanted to run, but he couldn't. He couldn't even breathe.

Phi was first of his group to go.

"Sophia Castling . . . Phi," she said. "I'm Animas Falcon." As if she needed proof, there was a loud screech overhead. Everyone looked up beside Phi. Two falcons were circling the field.

Arabella raised an eyebrow. "So you are," she said. She

made a note on her clipboard.

It was Hal's turn.

"Um, I'm Taylor's brother," he said.

Taylor rolled his eyes and muttered, "Barely." Hal glared at him.

"*Name*, please," barked Arabella.

"Hal Quindley," said Hal. "Bat."

Taylor whispered something in Arabella's ear, and she laughed a little as she made a note.

Finally, they came to Bailey. His hands were freezing *and* sweaty.

"Bailey Walker," he said. Hal was staring at him. In fact, everyone was staring at him. "Well, I . . ." he stammered. He felt like the world had stopped, like the entire kingdom was staring him down. He wanted to disappear. "I . . ."

"Yes?" said Arabella impatiently.

Bailey looked at Hal. He gave Bailey an apologetic look.

"I don't want to say," Bailey said.

Taylor and Arabella narrowed their eyes at him.

"You *have* to say," said Taylor. He smirked at Bailey, and Bailey knew that he did have to say, even if he didn't want to. It was clear from Taylor's smirk that he'd heard the rumors in the Lowlands, and if Bailey didn't tell, *he* would.

"I . . ." Bailey trailed off.

Suddenly, a dark shape swooped toward Taylor and grabbed his clipboard from his hands.

"Hey!" yelled Taylor. It was Phi's falcon. It flew to the roof of the changing rooms and hopped back and forth there with the clipboard dangling from its talons.

"For Nature's sake," Arabella said. She and Taylor rushed to the bird to try and coax it down. Bailey breathed out loudly. Next to him, Hal laughed as Taylor jumped up and down, waving his arms at Phi's falcon. Bailey looked down the line at Phi. She looked straight ahead, as if nothing odd was happening.

Bailey felt a rush of gratitude ease the sting of humiliation.

Finally, the bird dropped the clipboard and flew off. In the chaos, Taylor forgot he hadn't noted down Bailey's Animas, and instead began helping Arabella divide everyone into positions for the two teams. Phi was chosen to try on Blue Squad as a Sneak.

"That's perfect for her," Hal whispered to Bailey. "Sneaks are the ones who have to infiltrate the other team's part of the terrain. She's so quiet, and her Animas connection is out of this world, don't you think?"

Bailey nodded, but he was still shaking with mortification. He couldn't even imagine what position Taylor and his comrades could come up with for him.

"Quindley, Gold Squat!" Arabella shouted. Hal had been chosen to play his brother's position, on his brother's squad.

"Great, just great," Hal said. He cast an almost forlorn look behind him at the stands. Bailey saw Tori watching them. "I can't believe *she's* here," Hal moaned. "I guess the only thing to do is fail gloriously."

"That's the right attitude," Bailey said, patting Hal on the back and sending him off with a wave.

Soon everyone had been called but Bailey and a few other smaller kids who looked like they'd never run a lap in their lives. There was only one tryout position left unfilled. Taylor and Arabella were arguing at the edge of the field. Arabella was gesturing wildly with her hands, and Bailey thought he saw her point in his direction. Taylor shook his head. Bailey was almost relieved at the thought that he might not have to play after all. At least he could get out of there, away from the whispers and the stares. But no.

"Walker! Slammer, Gold Squad! Come here. Everybody else, sorry. There's always next year!" Taylor strolled over to Bailey and put an arm around his shoulder, squeezing just a little too hard. "All right, Whatever-You-Are. Arabella wants to see what you can do," he said. "This should be *hilarious*."

The new players gathered in a clump in front of the field as Coach Banter, flanked by Taylor and Arabella, listed the rules. Even though the tryouts hadn't yet started, Bailey spotted several animals—a squirrel, two rabbits, and even Phi's falcon—creeping, crawling, and flying out onto the field, drawn from the woods by their human kin, and by the anticipation of competition.

"Listen up, everyone," he barked. "Each team has a flag. Each flag is hidden. Your job is to protect your team's flag using any means necessary—barring murder—and to locate and steal the opposing team's flag. Use of kin is encouraged. There are nine of you to a team, three to each position.

"Sneaks!" Coach Banter continued. "Your job is to scout out the flag and steal it. Simple. Then you've got your Squats—they're the home base. The main line of defense. Squats, you stay by your flag at all times! And Slammers,

77

you're in the middle. You find the Sneaks before they find your team flag. Get them off course, tackle or confuse them, and mark them so they can't grab your flag. That's what the Flick is for! But remember—even though marked players can't steal the flag, they *can* stay on the field until all three are out, and use any means to distract the rival team. Everyone got it? Good!" Coach didn't wait to hear an answer. He gestured for Taylor and Arabella to march the hopefuls out onto the field as the small group of student spectators cheered.

Taylor piloted Bailey toward a babbling creek in the densely wooded north corner of the terrain, just a few yards away from his team's gold flag. The flag was at half-mast, surrounded by a scaffold-like structure of wood and metal. Other students from Gold Squad were scattered around the flag at different points, anxiously awaiting the starting whistle. Once the signal came, these others—the Sneaks—would leave the home base to locate and infiltrate the opposing team's base. Their goal was to capture the Blue Squad's flag.

As a Slammer, Bailey got to have a Flick of his own. It was made of bristles and a handle that stored bits of paint. With the right movement of the wrist, he could send a blob of paint hurtling toward a target, making it impossible for them to capture the flag, or do exactly what their title said: sneak. Bailey had tested the Flick on the ground before the start of the scrimmage and was startled by the bright, sparkling gold paint that shot out of the end. Not even an Animas Chameleon could get away with hiding under that goo.

Hal's job as a Squat was to protect the flag at all costs. It was a high-risk position, as members of the opposing team would almost certainly try to ambush and restrain him so that the flag could be stolen. As he moved into position, he looked like he wanted to duck under the nearest bush and hide.

A shrill whistle echoed through the woods, followed by various shouts and whoops. The flags were hoisted by automatic pulleys to the tops of their scaffolded poles. The Sneaks immediately dispersed.

The game had begun.

As Bailey ducked through the trees, out of sight of the flag, he stopped to listen. All he could hear was the wind, the burbling of the small creek a few feet away, and distant shouts from the spectators in the stands.

Now what? He had no idea which direction to go, or when the other players might attempt to get close to the flag. He guessed he should just stay put until there was a sure sign that the flag was in danger. He brushed some dirt off of a carefully placed log and sat.

Bad idea.

Above him, a falcon circled low, and gave out an earsplitting screech. It could only mean one thing. Phi knew where he was, and probably where the flag was too. In an instant, Bailey was back on his feet, on the alert. He leapt over the creek and ran through the low branches of the trees, keeping his eyes on the sky. He found himself in a clearing. From here he could see the high spectator's seats of the stadium, and all the eyes watching him. He felt his

stomach flop. Everyone was waiting for him to do something
. . . but what?

As he stood there, too dumbstruck to know his next move,
he heard a roar from the students who'd come to observe
the tryouts. He looked behind him: Phi was running full-tilt
from one end of the clearing to the other, north, toward
his team's home base. Bailey tightened his grip on the Flick
and ran after her.

Bailey crashed into the bushes where he'd seen Phi
disappear and looked around wildly. Nothing. The falcon
had disappeared, and Phi might as well have been a ghost.
Bailey figured his best bet was to head back toward the
home base. But he felt so turned around it was hard to tell
from which direction he'd come in the first place.

Bailey wished he had an Animas like Phi's, an extra sense
that could help guide him. But he didn't. He would just
have to do his best.

Focus. Think. Breathe. He closed his eyes, trying to
visualize the terrain he'd already covered. He'd run both
to the south and the east when he started following the
falcon—that meant, he realized, that if he ran in a semicircle
north and west, he'd be sure to come across the base, or at
least get close to it.

Bailey took off running again. His heart pounded, his
legs ached.

The terrain was rockier here, with more hills and slopes,
and the fallen leaves made navigating these hills very slippery.
His Flick at the ready, Bailey snuck under what few bushes
were available, trying to remain as quiet as possible, hoping

that Phi would be careless enough to make a sound.

He didn't have to wait long. He'd been concealed beneath the bushes for less than a minute when he saw the flash of a blue canvas shoe just a few feet away. He crept slowly and silently out from under his cover, and watched as the quickly moving form disappeared over the next rise. Bailey ran at a crouch, thighs burning, in case Phi was waiting on the other side of the hill. At the top of the rise, he looked for footprints in the densely packed leaves on the ground. Yes—she'd gone in the wrong direction, heading down the creek away from where the flag waited at the top of the ladder. Bailey decided to head her off, and he ran straight ahead, to the ridge on the other side of the creek.

He'd thought right—almost as soon as he crested the ridge, he saw Phi heading west. *Wait*. No. Not Phi. The player he saw wasn't Phi at all, but a taller boy, another Sneak, he recognized from the lineup. He was sure he'd seen Phi earlier—where was she now?

There was no time to worry about it. Bailey careened down the hill to catch up with the new player and cut him off before he could double back to the other end of the creek, where the flag was hidden. The boy spotted him coming, and grinned as he started to run faster. Bailey sped up with all his might, dodging trees and bushes to keep up with the boy.

Suddenly, the boy veered sharply to the left, away from the flag again, and Bailey saw a flash in the tree branches above—Phi! He aimed his Flick at the branch where Phi had perched, but she dashed away and he missed her by a bare inch.

Bailey gritted his teeth.

She was scampering down the tree, still within range of his Flick. As Bailey rounded a trunk obstructing his sight line, she cut through a row of trees and ran beyond the clearing. Bailey followed, twisted his body to clear the tree, and shot the Flick. He hit Phi in her side, watching with satisfaction as, for just a second, gold exploded all over her back and shoulders, like newly sprouted wings—and then he crashed to the ground. His ankle gave out and, before he could stop himself, he was rolling down a short, steep incline toward the creek. He landed, sprawling, on a group of slick wet rocks. Lifting his head, he tasted blood. He'd bitten his lip.

Dazed, Bailey sat up, wincing.

It seemed quieter here, as though the game was something that was happening far away. Low-hanging branches surrounded the small curve in the creek where he'd landed. Though the short hills on either side of the creek bank made this spot cool and shady, the sun shone through the patches of leaves that hadn't yet fallen.

Bailey limped toward the creek and splashed some water—clear and cold—over his face and on his lip. As he straightened, the end of a branch brushed his shoulder. He turned.

These trees weren't like any he'd ever seen before. They didn't have leaves—instead they had strange pod-like appendages, hanging down like fingers, full of tiny yellow seeds.

Just then, the whistle blew from the stands, and he heard the Coach's gruff voice echo through a bullhorn.

82

"THANK YOU, ATHLETES! WE WILL BE POSTING OUR SELECTIONS IN THE DINING HALL AT THE END OF THE WEEK. YOU MAY LEAVE THE FIELD!"

Bailey looked back again at the strange tree before jogging back toward the stands.

"You think you impressed anyone?" a deep voice called out behind him. Bailey spun around to see Taylor stalking toward him. "Just wait. We'll see what you can do *off* the field."

Bailey looked around slowly; they were on an isolated part of the Scavage pitch and he had to admit he was scared. He straightened up to his full height and braced himself as Taylor approached—but Taylor only brushed past him roughly, throwing his shoulder into Bailey's side so he stumbled as Taylor continued to walk away, and Bailey remained in the clearing, shaking.

"Hey!"

Bailey turned. Phi had appeared to his right, smiling despite the paint drenching her. "You did a great job," she said.

"Thanks," Bailey said, trying to compose himself from the run-in with Taylor. "You too. You were hard to keep up with."

"I played some sports at home in the Plains," she said, shrugging. "Well, not sports, really. More just like . . . running." She bit her lip, then smiled again at Bailey.

Bailey wanted to thank her for what her falcon had done earlier to distract Taylor—and to ask her whether it had been deliberate. But he couldn't bring himself to say the words. Instead, they walked together in comfortable silence.

Seven

THAT EVENING, AS RAIN beat on the copper roofs of the grand Parliament building, the Elder at last returned to the Gray City after five days away. No one in the streets recognized the cloaked figure slipping into Parliament through the narrow door sunk into the cobblestone alley, and none of the guards took notice of him, either.

In the meeting hall, despite the late hour, the members of Parliament were clustered around a central table, illuminated by two gas lamps that flickered from the ceiling. The harsh wind had dismantled the main turbine, and the electro-current had sputtered and died only an hour into the meeting.

Gwen was sitting on a bench in the shadows, next to the other assistants and apprentices. She was trying to take notes, but was having trouble following the heated debate. Once again, talk in the Parliament meeting hall was of Viviana and the Dominae.

"Everyone knows we're loyal to the old king," one Parliament member, Animas Robin, was saying. "How can we reject Viviana, his daughter, and still remain loyal to the Melore bloodline?" This question was met with boos from the fifty or so men and women gathered in the hall. Three of the Parliament woman's kin fluttered above the meeting table anxiously, and the rustling sound of their wings echoed against the marble walls.

"The bloodline was broken when Melore was assassinated!" another senator said. "Viviana hasn't been raised to rule. She's a pretender, just like the Jackal was! She says she wants progress, but what has she offered besides this backward philosophy of hers? Dominance—"

"It's heinous!" someone yelled. "Encouraging humans to force their kin to work, or worse! It's almost as if she doesn't believe that animals have their own free wills!"

"But she's the rightful heir," said the Animas Robin. "The people might embrace her return. And once she's with us, we could encourage her to soften her philosophy."

"The people don't know what's good for them! We've ruled ever since the Jackal was deposed! What does this woman from the Dust Plains know about running a kingdom?"

"I beg your pardon!" someone shouted.

"The people think *we* don't know how to rule; what's to stop them from supporting her? They have no love for us!"

"And why should they? If you'd resolved to pass *my* laws, we wouldn't be in this mess!"

The grumbling rose in volume and pitch, and Gwen quickly lost track of individual voices. A throng of birds and rodents chattered on the marble doorframes that surrounded the main room.

Gwen closed her eyes and tried to focus on the image of an owl on a moonlit branch, alone, hearing nothing but the sound of its claws against the bark. Gwen could hear her own soft breathing, and the ruckus of the meeting room began to fade away . . . only to be replaced by another, urgent sensation. She felt the presence of a very familiar owl and the hurried, anxious approach of wings, pulling her attention toward the hallway outside . . .

She opened her eyes, shocked. Grimsen and the Elder were close.

The door to the meeting hall opened loudly, and immediately the noise in the meeting hall subsided as everyone squinted in the low light to see who had entered. The Elder stepped forward. Gwen's heart leapt.

"Forgive my tardiness," he said, addressing the now-silent room. He was holding an oddly shaped bundle, wrapped in a rag. "I hope to be quickly brought up to speed, but first, I must show you what I've found." He strode to the center of the room, and placed the bundle on the wooden table. Grimsen flew from the Elder's shoulder to join a hawk over the main arch. "You may tell me what you believe it means."

As the Elder unwrapped the bundle, Gwen made out a large piece of what seemed to be solid granite: the stone shape of a paw, weathered almost featureless by time and the elements.

"Some of you may recognize this stone," the Elder began. "For those of you who do not . . . this is part of the rubble that remains of the Statue of the Twins, the most important symbol of the ancient Animas bond." Gasps sounded sharply throughout the room.

"Several days ago I ventured to the Seers' Land, only to

find the statue destroyed. Do we interpret this as the action of the Dominae, at Viviana's request? The Dominae are for much more than the enforced servitude of animals—they seek to pervert the Animas bond, twisting it into something dark and terrible that will give humans all power over animals, without empathy. I have no doubt that this is their work, and a sign that more violence is to come. Some of you have been unwilling to declare Viviana a threat to Aldermere. But we must know what storms are brewing, and we must face them united." The Elder's speech met with an anxious silence from the fellows of Parliament.

Gwen held her breath.

Finally, one woman sitting several rows away from the central table stood. A baboon clung to her leg like a small child, and she shook it off impatiently.

"Can we take this—this . . . *demonstration* as a declaration of intent?" Mutters and whispers followed her question. "You would have us declare the only child of King Melore a traitor to the kingdom? You are treading on thin ice, Elder Finn."

Several people booed and banged the table forcefully. The Elder raised his hand.

"Friend," he said softly, "my time in this palace reaches its fingers far back into its past. I have learned that ignoring warnings can be a dangerous practice. I merely bring before you a sign. Choose to ignore it at your own risk." He wrapped the stone in its rag again, and walked toward the door. He stopped just before passing through the arch, and turned to face the assembly once more.

"And before you dismiss this omen as the mere ramblings of an old man, know this: the fallen statue is just the beginning. Viviana may appear to be merely a nuisance, but her followers are growing daily. A band of Animae Coyote and their kin from out of the Dust Plains are making their way along the Fluvian. I have learned through Grimsen that a pack of Weasels—humans and their kin—mean to join with them at the crossing of the Dark Woods. In fact, it is very likely that the horde is already met, and making its way north. To us."

Gwen looked around the hall at the faces of the assembled representatives. All were ashen and frightened.

"We banded together once, nine years ago, to depose the murderous Jackal and end his reign. We are not without strength— and we will need to use that strength again. The Dominae are powerful, and they are bending the Animas bond into something unrecognizable. I'm warning you, friends: we will soon be fighting for our lives."

Eight

THAT NIGHT, BAILEY LAY awake in the Tower bedroom. It had been a long, strange day, and Bailey wondered how much harder things would be if—he hated the thought, but couldn't shake it— he *didn't* Awaken to his Animas before leaving Fairmount. He'd been hoping Tremelo would help him. But Tremelo, it seemed, was completely crazy.

Bailey heard a tiny scraping sound from the door, and sprang up onto his elbows. There was a piece of paper stuck under the door. He got up, moved quickly across the room, and opened the door. No one. He strained to listen for the sound of footsteps, or even paws, but whoever had left the note had crept away quickly.

He unfolded it carefully and held it up to read in the moonlight.

The note was short. *Bailey: Flagpole. Midnight.*

Bailey sat down on his bed, his heart pounding. The clock on the washstand in the room read 11:40 p.m. He wondered if he should go down to the common room and show the note to Hal—maybe he would know who had delivered it.

Then again, reasonable, cautious Hal might try and convince him not to go.

Bailey pulled on his work pants and farming boots. He tiptoed out of the room and crept silently by the door to the common room, where he heard the soft shuffling sounds of a game of chess being played. He caught a quick glance of Hal engrossed in his Latin homework. Pete, another Year One, was showing a group of boys how his kin, a possum, could dangle from the room's rafters by its tail.

The Towers resident assistant, a Year Four named Benjamin, lived in a private room across the hall from the common area. Bailey thanked Nature that Benjamin's door was closed, and no light shone underneath. Still, he tried to stay as quiet as possible. Bailey held his breath as he slid silently past the doorway, down the rest of the hall, and out into the night.

To reach the flagpole in the center of campus, he'd have to pass the night guard's post—he remembered seeing that much on Hal's map—but he *thought* if he cut north to the dining hall, past the Garrett, he could circle back around by the administration building in the center of campus. The only question was whether or not a guard—or worse, a teacher—might also be out on the grounds. He would have to stay alert.

As Bailey cut through the herb garden behind the dining hall, a twig snapped behind him. He froze. The hairs on the back of his neck stood up. He was being followed. Could Taylor be planning to ambush him?

He spun around. "Who's there?" he called out.

He heard a footstep crunch in the gravel. Then whoever it was stopped in his or her tracks behind the corner of the greenhouse.

"I know you're following me," Bailey said. "You might as well show yourself."

"I heard you sneak out," said the voice behind the greenhouse, and Hal emerged from the shadows.

Bailey grinned. "I thought maybe you were your brother," he said, relieved.

Hal made a face, as though he'd just been forced to swallow turpentine. "Never say that again!"

"How did you see me sneak out? You were nose-deep in a book when I passed the common room," said Bailey.

Hal shook his head. "I didn't say I saw you. I said I *heard* you." He shoved his hands in his pockets as he approached. He was wearing his pajamas under his sweater, Bailey noticed, and had shoved on a pair of loafers. "What are you doing out here?"

Bailey took the note out of his pocket. "I wasn't going to tell you. I thought you might try to talk me out of going," he said.

"It sounds like a setup to me," Hal said, scanning the note.

"Maybe," Bailey said. "Only one way to find out."

Hal hesitated, then shrugged. "What's the worst that can happen? You get in trouble and get booted out of school."

"That's the spirit," Bailey said, grinning. He was actually relieved that Hal had followed him. It was nice to have company. "Let's go."

Together, the boys made their way to the lawn in front

of the classroom buildings, and peeked around the corner of the administration building.

The lawn seemed vastly different at night. It reminded him a little of the fields he was used to in the Lowlands, but the short, dark green grass made it seem more like a murky ocean (or at least pictures Bailey had seen of the ocean) and the ornate marble buildings looked like huge blocks of ice reflecting the moonlight. In the center of the circular common was the Fairmount clock tower, the oldest structure on Fairmount grounds. Each of the arms on the clock's enormous face was at least as tall as Bailey. And each of the numbers was represented by a different golden animal, surrounding the face of the clock like a mechanical parade. In front of the tower flew the Fairmount flag. It looked forbidding and impossibly tall, like a finger raised threateningly toward the clouds.

A small group of students were gathered around the flagpole just a few yards south of the clock tower. It was Taylor and his Scavage friends, along with a handful of Year Ones. Bailey wasn't a bit surprised.

"Come on," Bailey whispered to Hal. They moved closer, and hid behind a bush just across the yard from the clock tower, so they could see what was happening.

"Okay, Fresh Meat, watch this!" Taylor said, and pointed upward, to the face of the clock. Bailey felt his heart speed up.

The center of the clock opened inward, and a number of bats flew from their home behind the gold-painted face. Hal closed his eyes. Bailey knew that Hal was trying to feel his way into the bat's bodies, to hear and see what they did.

One of the older boys stepped through the opening onto a narrow stone ledge and Bailey's mouth went dry. The ledge had to be fifty feet above the ground.

He shot a nervous look over at Hal. "What's happening?" he asked.

Hal's forehead furrowed. "I don't know . . ." He shook his head. The bats resettled in a nearby tree, and Hal looked troubled. He rubbed his forehead. "I can't get anything clear."

The boy waved at his audience. Then, without hesitation, he jumped.

Bailey's heart stopped. The boy was plummeting toward the ground. Faster . . . closer . . .

Then he reached out toward the flagpole and grabbed the rope that dangled down from the top. In a split second, he went from falling to swinging.

Cheers and laughter erupted from the older boys. Bailey had unconsciously climbed to his feet. He felt exhilarated. The jumper landed safely among his friends, who clapped and patted him on the back.

"That was *crazy*," Hal exclaimed. "Who would *do* that?"

"I would," said Bailey.

"You wouldn't!"

"In a minute," said Bailey, and it was true. If jumping from a clock tower would prove that he wasn't some kind of weaselly freak, then Bailey would jump. "I've *got* to do it, Hal," he said.

"You don't have to prove anything to them," Hal said to Bailey. But Bailey knew he was wrong. Of course he did;

he had everything to prove.

The older boys were now herding the Year Ones into the tower, through a plain wooden door set at ground level. The younger boys all looked frightened, even panicked. As they began filing into the tower, three of them broke loose from the ranks and ran back in the direction of the dorms.

"Animae Chicken!" Taylor shouted after them. His friends began cawing and clucking.

"That's three down—how many to go?" one of the Scavage players boasted.

Bailey placed a hand on Hal's shoulder.

"Wait here," he said.

He jogged toward the clock tower. The laughter of the Scavage players died down. Taylor glared at him. Maybe he hadn't expected Bailey to show.

"I'm here to jump," Bailey said loudly.

Taylor smirked and narrowed his eyes. "You sure about that, Walker? It's a long way down."

"I'm sure," Bailey said. But even as he spoke, he felt as if he'd swallowed a bag of sand. He knew it was too late to turn back now, though.

The inside of the clock tower smelled like dust and old moisture. The spiraling stone stairs seemed to go on forever. Bailey steeled his nerves and began to climb. He could hear the laughter of the older boys outside, muffled through the stone, along with the ominous *ticktock* that echoed within the tower. As Bailey climbed higher, panting, he could hear too, the voices of the kids at the top, daring one another to make the jump.

"No way!" one boy said.

"They *can't* be serious?" said another.

"It's suicide!" another one whispered.

At last, Bailey reached the landing. There were three Year Ones standing at the top of the stairs. Bailey recognized one from his homeroom, and wondered what he'd done to Taylor to have been called here. The boys turned to him, white-faced and surprised. They huddled against the giant gears that powered the clock, as far away from the door that led to the open-air ledge as possible.

"Are you going to do it?" the boy from his homeroom asked, wide-eyed.

"Why not?" Bailey said with a shrug, trying to sound as nonchalant as possible. In reality, his heart was hammering. He ducked under a low-hanging gear and stepped through the clockface door out onto the ledge.

Immediately, everything around him seemed to fall silent. He couldn't hear the turning gears behind him or the murmuring students or even the ominous ticking of the clock itself. All he could see were the vast, dark grounds of Fairmount and the buildings with ribbons of mist curled around them. He could smell the river nearby, just vaguely, and for a moment, he felt a completely unexpected sensation: happiness.

He inched farther out on the ledge. A shot of adrenaline raced through his body and he realized he was shaking—no, more like *buzzing*. Below him, Taylor was standing with his arms crossed.

I'm not afraid; not of you, not of anything, Bailey thought.

But he couldn't help his hands shaking as he looked down. The ground looked impossibly far away. His legs began to wobble, and Bailey forced himself to breathe deeply. Just one little jump. Easy. Nothing to be afraid of.

Before he could change his mind, he crouched into a runner's stance, sucked in a breath, and leapt.

He fell for what seemed like whole minutes. Bailey could feel the wind whipping in his ears, and the strange heaviness of his body dropping through thin air. Time eased as the ground spiraled closer, as though he were dropping in slow motion.

And then he could see the rope just a few feet below him, and he reached out blindly. He felt the rope in his hands, and then the quick jolt of his body changing direction. Suddenly, instead of falling, he was swinging around the flagpole—suspended, flying! He'd never felt anything so wonderful before; he found himself laughing as the rope swung him around the pole.

He wondered if this is how it was for everyone else when, just by clearing their minds, they could see what an animal saw, or think the way an animal thought. For once, soaring above the grass, Bailey thought he knew what it must be like to feel *bigger*, to be something *other* than just Bailey Walker, freak.

As he hit the ground, he was a new person—a stronger person. Even the burning in his hands from clutching the rope felt good. The other Year Ones were peering out of the clockface, clapping and whooping at the sight of Taylor's shocked expression.

"Who's Animas Chicken now?" he said, grinning.

But Taylor didn't answer. He was wide-eyed and backing up slowly, as if Bailey had a contagious disease. "Ants!" he cursed. "Run!"

Bailey watched, confused, as the Scavage players began to scatter across the lawn, back toward the dorms. What had he done wrong?

"Young man!" a voice trumpeted out from behind him.

Bailey looked toward the assembly hall and felt his stomach dive to his toes. Tremelo, his Homeroom teacher, was walking swiftly toward him, his red fox trotting swiftly at his side.

Just my luck, he thought to himself. The only one to jump—the only one to get caught.

It was too late to make a dash for cover—Tremelo was already upon him. Besides, Bailey's legs were still so shaky from the leap that he really wasn't convinced he could walk just yet. Bailey scanned the lawn for Hal, but there was no sign of him. At least he had gotten away.

"A decent performance, but I hope you know that you could be expelled from this academy for less," Tremelo said, stopping in front of Bailey. He reached into his pocket and took out a small silver flask. He lifted it to his lips and indulged in a long sip. "Fairmount does not tolerate rule breakers, I'm afraid."

"Then how did *you* get in?" Bailey blurted out, and then immediately regretted it.

But, to Bailey's surprise, Tremelo threw his head back and laughed.

"Well done," he said, returning the flask to his pocket with a flourish. "You should thank Nature I'm not the headmaster, or you'd be kicked out before you could say 'Animas Platypus.'" Still chuckling, Tremelo clapped a hand on Bailey's back and began to steer him toward the main hall and the dormitories. "I'm unfortunately obligated to see you head back to your rightful place. Which is . . . ?"

"Towers," Bailey muttered.

Tremelo began humming an old Gray City tune. *I knew myself a lady, her Animas a snail!* The fox dashed in front of them as they walked, playing her own games with the dew-covered grass.

Bailey wondered what Tremelo was doing, wandering around the grounds by himself at night. But Tremelo was a teacher, and could wander where he pleased. As for Bailey, he'd only just arrived at Fairmount, and he'd been caught breaking about a hundred rules.

As they passed the small, copper-roofed shed that served as the night guard's post, Tremelo stopped.

"A moment, please," he said to Bailey, and he ducked inside. Bailey could see that Mr. Bindley, the night guard, and his two massive dogs were snoring. Bailey watched from the doorway as Tremelo sniffed the air inside the shed. He moved forward and picked up a small packet from Bindley's table, which lay next to a thick, gear-heavy object. Tremelo caught Bailey looking at the strange contraption.

"Night-vision monocle," he said proudly. "Special lenses refract moonlight, amplifying it. I made it for him years ago. Best watch yourself, when he's got this on . . . and he's awake."

Tremelo quickly placed the small package he'd picked up in his jacket pocket.

"Every year," he muttered, shaking his head. He looked at Bailey and winked. "The Scavage team makes a habit of stealing my myrgwood to put old Bindley to sleep, so they can run amok on the grounds."

They left Bindley's post and walked across the commons to the dorms. It was late—nearly one o'clock, and the entire campus was a chorus of crickets.

Then Tremelo suddenly said: "You're the boy with an Absence, aren't you?"

There was that word again. Bailey didn't even get to think of a lie or try to avoid the question. As Bailey had suspected, Tremelo already knew.

"Mrs. Shonfield told you?" Bailey asked.

"She did. You are, after all, my student. But she didn't have to. It's plain as day to me. We have much in common, Bailey."

Bailey wasn't sure what Tremelo was referring to. What could he possibly have in common with this man who, for all his strangeness, was supposed to be one of the most powerful Animas trainers in the kingdom?

"It's just coming to me slowly, that's all," Bailey said.

"You don't have to tell me about slow development," Tremelo said. "I was well into my eleventh year when Fennel found me, and before that I'd had myself convinced I was Animas Rat, like my father." From his jacket he removed the same pouch Bailey had seen him take from Mr. Bindley's table. He extracted a large pinch of a dark herb that Bailey had never seen before, and packed it into a pipe. "You don't mind, do you?" he asked. He didn't wait for Bailey to respond. Within seconds, the professor was surrounded by a sweet, slightly bitter-smelling smoke.

Bailey's mouth itched and his throat was dry. "Sir," he said, "I read something before I came to Fairmount. You've helped people Awaken, haven't you? You're supposed to be an expert in strengthening the bond."

Tremelo stared toward the distant trees beyond the dorms and shook his head.

"That part of me died some time ago, boy. I used to, in my first few years at Fairmount . . . but no more."

Bailey's heart sank.

As if he could read Bailey's mind, Tremelo clapped him on the back. "Don't think of it as hopeless, my boy. Think of it as a puzzle to be solved. After all, trees may bear seeds, but no fruit." Tremelo stared dreamily at Bailey through the thick cloud of smoke. His fingers moved in midair as though he were playing an invisible piano. "Kin rise from ashes, hand over paw / When Locusts turn Men from Treachery / The Sun calls to the Loon."

"What?" asked Bailey, confused.

"It's a riddle," said Tremelo, as though this should have been obvious. Bailey began to wonder what, exactly, was in that pipe. "Find the answer to the riddle, Bailey, and perhaps you'll find your Animas." He laughed. "That's what my father used to say, anyway . . . not that it helped. I still Awakened eventually, no thanks to his ramblings. . . ." Tremelo shook his head, chuckling at some memory that

Bailey couldn't know.

Bailey thought this over. Part of it sounded familiar to him, though he wasn't sure from what. His mom had sung many songs to him as a baby, and he wondered if the familiar line—"the Sun calls to the Loon"—was from one of those.

"I think I've heard something like that before," he said. "From a lullaby. Is that what it's from?"

Tremelo shrugged and made a dismissive *phh* noise as he exhaled a bit of smoke.

"My father *never* sang me lullabies," Tremelo said. "Unless his friends' pub songs count. I doubt you heard any of that in 'The Squirrel-Faced Girl from the Lowlands', but then, I'm a bit hazy on those lyrics as well. . . ."

They had reached the Towers. Tremelo released his grip on Bailey's shoulder.

"Chin up, Bailey," Tremelo said. "Now, back to Towers with you."

Nine

LONG AFTER HE SAW Bailey back into his dorm, and despite the two pipes of myrgwood he had smoked, Tremelo could not quiet his mind.

Meeting a boy with an Absence was about as likely as Nature herself emerging from a cave in the Velyn Peaks, materializing in a cloud of mist for a cup of tea and a cookie. Bailey seemed sharp too, and strong, whereas a typical Absence meant utter tragedy— poor health and insanity to boot.

Tremelo poured a glass of rootwort rum, lit his pipe once again, and sank into a groaning armchair, the only piece of furniture in his quarters not covered with books and papers. He reached over the arm to crank a gramophone next to the chair. The record began to circle, and Tremelo placed the needle and closed his eyes as the sounds of the Gray City Symphony poured out of the amplifying horn. Fennel the fox wound her way affectionately around his feet, and Tremelo could feel the soft pressure of the animal's mind, the wordless reassurances.

Though Fennel began to sleep, and this too Tremelo could

feel—the fog, the relaxation into the dark—he could not join her. He had never slept well. Too many dreams, always waking up feeling as though he were suffocating. But aside from the usual insomnia, he couldn't stop picturing the leap that Bailey had made through the air—the bravery that the boy must have summoned, the grace he'd shown. And no Animas? Was it even possible that a human without an Animas could have such determination, such power?

Perhaps it had been a bad idea to tell Bailey the riddle—to tease him with his father's old rantings. But then again, Tremelo reasoned, if it's only gibberish, can it really do the boy any harm? His own childhood had been a haze of tale-telling by people like his father—called the Loon—and the other men and women who took heart in the old myths, who were loyal to the fallen king Melore, who traded prophecies and tales like others traded idle gossip. Tremelo's hazy memories were clouded with riddles and stories, and had he really turned out so badly after all? Perhaps better not to answer, he thought to himself.

At his feet, Fennel stretched, and Tremelo had a brief image, as common to him as breathing, of a blurry flight through the woods, a rabbit's tail flashing in front of him.

I'm only thirty-two, Tremelo thought. But I feel so old. A puff of smoke left his lips and disappeared in the draft from the window. That must be why his father's stories and riddles were on his mind this night.

Tremelo reached under the chair and pulled out a small locked trunk. Resting the trunk on his knees, he reached into his pocket and produced the key. Inside the trunk was a book with a crumbling leather cover, which had been made of the hide of a mountain goat as a gift to his father many years ago. It had once been a prized possession of the Loon's, but had become worn and cracked with time and misuse. Tremelo caressed it the way he had seen the Loon do so many times. *Hello, old friend.* He started to open it, but stopped himself.

No. The book was nonsense, a series of scratches and dashes, as though each symbol were just a picture of a bunch of sticks. His father claimed it was taught to him by the Seers in the western mountains, and Tremelo had believed him, although he himself had never met the Seers, even in the many trips that he and his father took to those mountains when he was a boy. He had once been certain the scratchings were a code . . . but now he wondered whether his father had simply been mad. Trying to figure out what it meant now would only disappoint him, as it had so many times before.

Besides, the Loon was dead, along with his stories.

Tremelo shut the trunk quickly, and shoved it back under the chair. Fennel woke with a start.

"No more riddles," he said, answering the question in Fennel's eyes. "No more codes."

Best to pretend that the past had never existed at all.

Ten

TREMELO'S RIDDLE PLAYED IN Bailey's head for the rest of the week like a malfunctioning music box. It snuck its way into his recitations of Latin verbs, his memorizations of different shaped leaves for Flora and Fauna, and the names of famous members of Parliament for History. It danced through his mind just as he was about to fall asleep. *Trees may bear seeds, but no fruit . . . the Sun calls to the Loon . . .*

On Friday night, as he and Hal sat studying in the Towers common room, Hal led him to his first clue about what the riddle might mean.

"Are you nervous about tomorrow?" Hal asked him.

"Why would I be?" Bailey asked.

"It's Saturday. The Scavage results are supposed to be posted. You'll get to see if you made the team!"

Bailey hadn't even been thinking about the possibility of making the team. But he hadn't done that badly, all things considered. In fact, before he'd taken that tumble down the hill, he'd been doing pretty well.

That's when he remembered the tree he'd nearly collided with on the Scavage field—the leafless one, covered in seeds.

Trees may bear seeds, but no fruit. Was it possible that the tree was a clue?

He told Hal about the riddle, and about the strange tree. Hal listened skeptically, with one dark eyebrow raised behind his thick glasses.

"I'm not sure what the riddle is supposed to mean," Bailey said, "but if it can help me find . . . you know . . . then I have to try."

"If you think you can believe a word 'Mr. Myrgwood' has to say, then all right," Hal said skeptically. "If you want company, I'm always up for a stroll."

Bailey and Hal woke before sunrise the next morning. Bailey pulled his blue Fairmount blazer closely around him as they walked past the dorms and herb gardens and out to the Scavage field. The air was crisp with an early autumn chill, and a hazy fog covered the grounds.

Hal was wearing a pressed pair of trousers and a vest over his white shirt, and his customary cravat had been replaced by a bow tie. Bailey wondered if formal clothing was all Hal had brought to Fairmount.

"I just don't want you to get your hopes up too much about Tremelo," Hal said. "Remember, this is the same guy who spent the entire class time yesterday telling us that the best way to avoid getting eaten by a bear was to put syrup on its nose. I'm pretty sure that nonsense is his first language."

The entrance to the main gates of the Scavage field was locked, so together they headed toward the far end of the field, where it backed up to the forest. As the stands gave way to fences, and the fences gave way to dense patches of trees, Bailey felt his heart beginning to pound. He hadn't realized how close the Scavage field was to the Dark Woods, which beckoned just beyond the first half mile of harmless forest. Bailey knew that beyond those trees were the Velyn mountains, winding their way south to the Golden Lowlands. He shivered. The morning was chilly and the boys darted quickly into the trees, following the line where the Scavage fences ended, to the back of the field.

Finally, they located the steep hill where Bailey had fallen down a few days ago all the way at the end of the Scavage terrain that marked the edge of the playing grounds. The strange tree looked so much smaller in this gray light. The seedpods hung down like heavy weights, and the tree's branches bowed in sweeping curves.

Hal circled the tree, adjusting his glasses to look more closely.

Reaching up to touch the hanging seeds, Bailey found that the pods were dry and fragile as tissue. When he tried to press one between his fingers, the pod's skin flaked away, and the seeds contained in it fell to the ground and scattered around Bailey's feet. The riddle played over and over again in his mind. *Kin rise from ashes, hand over paw . . .* What did it mean?

"So what now?" Hal said.

Bailey shrugged. "I don't know." The thin morning light had been chased away, and bright shafts of sunlight shot through the branches around him.

Trees may bear seeds, but no fruit . . . Bailey sighed, picking up one of the seeds that had dropped on the ground.

It was soft and round. He squished it and saw that the insides were the somber purple color of cooked blueberries. Tossing the seed away, he straightened up. Something told him he wouldn't find any clues about his Animas here, unless his Animas was a jar of blueberry jam.

"I'm stumped," said Hal.

"It was a dumb idea." Bailey shoved his hands in his pockets. "Let's go."

As the two of them made their way back onto the main grounds, they saw that the herb gardens they'd passed earlier were not empty. A squat woman in rolled-up pants and a heavy, dirt-stained apron bent over the rows of pepper plants. Bailey remembered her from the first day, outside the rigimotive station: Mrs. Copse, the groundskeeper. Two roly-poly groundhogs chased each other down the row of tomato plants behind her back. Bailey felt a spark of hope again. Maybe Mrs. Copse could tell him more about the strange tree.

To his surprise, Mrs. Copse outright laughed at his description of the tree.

"Strange?" she repeated after him. "Those things grow like pests around here!"

Confused, Bailey felt his heart sink.

"It's just that I—we've never seen one before," Bailey said.

"You're from the Lowlands, is it?" Mrs. Copse asked.

"Yeah," Bailey admitted.

"No wonder. King's Finger Oaks grow thick as thistles on the backside of a badger up here."

King's Finger Oaks. The name sent a small shiver of

recognition through Bailey, though he was sure he'd never heard the name before.

"What about the seeds?" Hal asked. "Is there, I don't know, a certain kind of animal that eats them?" Copse's two groundhogs were busy rolling around together in the dusty garden, playing.

"Ha! *We* do!" Mrs. Copse said, tossing a withered vine into a compost basket and slapping the dirt from her hands against her apron. "Not the *most* delicious thing, a little tart, but mix them with something sweet, and they're fine. I remember when my own kids were young—those were the start of some dark days, you know, under the Jackal's rule, less to go around—we'd toast those seeds and eat 'em on our oatmeal. King's Children, they're called." Mrs. Copse grinned and gazed off into the distance.

Bailey and Hal said a quick thanks, and they walked swiftly back to the Circle, toward the dining hall.

The quiet Saturday morning that Bailey and Hal had encountered upon leaving their room was gone. It had been replaced with a bright, sunny madhouse of students crammed in front of one of the dining hall's windows. Some in blazers, some still in their pajamas; everyone craned their necks and shouted to one another. A playful pack of dogs ran circles around the crowd, and several birds perched on the trim above the windows, squawking. The whole campus seemed to be buzzing over a piece of paper on the outside wall.

"It's been posted!" Hal said.

"Hey, over here!" shouted a familiar voice. He saw Tori waving at them from the group, along with Phi. Phi's amber eyes sparkled as she waved too. Her falcon sat on her shoulder, and even *she* looked pleased. Hal and Bailey rushed to them, and together they pushed their way through the excited students to see the list of new Scavage players.

Bailey scanned the list of positions and names, written in blue and gold letters on the long sheet of paper. The first name he saw that he recognized was Sophia Castling, listed as Sneak.

"Congrats!" he said to Phi. She smiled, and pointed at the paper again.

"Keep looking," said Tori.

And then he saw it. *Slammer: Bailey Walker.*

Hal clapped him on the back. "Congratulations, Bailey!"

Bailey reeled forward a bit from the force—he seemed to have lost the feeling in his legs. Was this real? He'd made the team, without the aid of an Animas. He looked dizzily around him. Several students were waving and congratulating their friends, and though Bailey knew that was what he should have been doing too, he felt as shocked as he was excited. He looked at Hal in disbelief. For the first time it occurred to him that Hal's name was missing from the list.

"Hal . . ." His tongue felt swollen. "I'm really sorry."

"Don't be!" Hal looked genuinely happy. He leaned in and whispered, "To tell you the truth, I've never been so relieved in my life."

"Welcome to the team." Suddenly, a strong hand grabbed Bailey's shoulder and turned him around. It was Arabella, the co-captain from the day before. She shook his hand vigorously, and then did the same to Phi. "You're both going to be great!"

Finally, Bailey cracked a smile. "Thanks!" he said. The shock began to wear off, leaving room for nothing but gladness in its place. Across the group of students, though, he could see one person who did not seem to be pleased at all: Hal's brother, Taylor. His arms were crossed and his glare menacing. As Arabella rushed off to congratulate the other new members of the team, Taylor sauntered over to Bailey, Hal, Tori, and Phi.

"Congratulations, Walker," he said, though it sounded less like a compliment than it did a threat. "I hope your little *performance* on the field wasn't just beginner's luck."

"Buzz off, Taylor," said Phi, which surprised both Bailey and Taylor.

"It wasn't luck," Hal piped up. "Bailey's really good."

Bailey's heart was beating fast in his chest. He hoped Hal was right. What if it *was* beginner's luck? Bailey noticed Taylor's cat on the ground next to them, licking its lips.

"We'll see," said Taylor, with a narrow smile.

"Oh, Nature! My lands!" someone shouted outside. The hubbub around the Scavage results died down quickly as the students strained to see the commotion, gathering in the commons outside the dining hall.

It was Mrs. Copse, the groundskeeper with whom Bailey and Hal had only just been talking. She hurried toward the group with a look of despair on her face, pointing to the line of trees at the edge of the common lawn.

"Where's Finch? Where's Shonfield? Out of the way, students—*out* of the way!"

She stumbled past the onlooking students toward the

administration building. Headmaster Finch and Tremelo, who were walking from that direction, met her.

"Oh, Nature, Mr. Finch! It's terrible—I've never seen such a kill! And so close to the buildings!"

The students began to whisper among themselves, craning their necks in the direction Mrs. Copse had just come from. Bailey felt a tingle on the back of his neck. A kill meant one animal hunting and killing another. It happened all the time, but to see Mrs. Copse so upset . . . This must have been something out of the ordinary.

Finch tried to quiet Mrs. Copse, and shot the students a warning look.

"I'm sure there's no cause for a commotion," he said, gesturing with his thin hands for everyone to disperse. "Now, students, if you wouldn't mind—I hear the dining hall is serving leek-and-onion tarts for breakfast, so hustle along. I mean it," announced Finch after no one moved. "All students are ordered to go into the dining hall this minute!"

With groans and whispers, the students filed into the dining hall. Bailey and his friends were about to do the same, when Bailey heard Finch call his name.

"Mr. Walker and Mr. Quindley, if you'll please accompany us," said Finch.

Hal's eyes went buggy behind his glasses.

"Us?" asked Bailey. "Why us?"

"Come along," said Finch as he adjusted the collar of his plaid tweed jacket. He turned abruptly on his heel and began to walk toward the forest.

"I'm not missing this," said Tori quietly. She pulled Phi

along and followed the adults alongside Bailey and Hal. When Finch turned and gave the girls a questioning look, Tori's eyes grew wide in a look of concern.

"Quindley gets light-headed at the sight of blood, sir," she said, elbowing Hal in the ribs.

"They're here for moral support," Hal added.

Finch shook his head and continued walking. It seemed he would allow them to come along for now.

When they stopped at the edge of the lawn, Mrs. Copse put her hands to her mouth. Tremelo placed a comforting hand on her shoulder. Finch plucked a handkerchief from his jacket pocket and held it to his nose. As the students huddled in closer, Bailey could see what had caused Mrs. Copse so much distress.

A massive black bear lay dead in the grass between the trees. Its neck and side had been deeply wounded by enormous claw marks across its hide.

"Ants," said Tori. She gripped Phi's arm, and two girls watched solemnly as Tremelo circled the dead bear, observing what he could. Hal squinted at it through his glasses and made small humming noises, as if he was thinking very hard about something.

"*Very* interesting," Hal murmured.

"What could do something like that?" Phi asked. "The animal that did that must have been huge."

"Quindley, Walker," Finch addressed them, "Mrs. Copse said she saw you two near this spot earlier this morning. Did you happen to see anything?"

Bailey and Hal exchanged a worried glance.

113

"No," said Bailey. "We were just walking around."

"You're not in trouble," said Tremelo. "We're just trying to figure out what might have done this. It's odd to see a kill so close to campus, or so brutal."

Hal stepped forward. "It *is* odd, isn't it? Don't most large forest animals have the good sense to stay away from campus, even if their human kin are present? And look here," he said pointing to the claw marks. "Whatever made the kill didn't stay to enjoy it. It slashed and ran. Either it was scared off, or this was defensive."

"I'd say that's a fair assessment, Mr. Quindley," Tremelo said.

Finch looked Hal up and down, seeming to take in the lanky boy's formal clothing and professorly tone with no amount of amusement. "Answer the question, please," he said.

"Bailey and I were taking a walk around the edge of the Scavage pitch," Hal said. "We didn't see anything strange."

Finch nodded.

"Mr. Loren, can I prevail upon you to help Mrs. Copse arrange a funeral?" he asked Tremelo. "Best to handle this sensitively. We have at least two Animae Bear enrolled, I believe . . ." Finch kept his handkerchief firmly in place. "And you four—I'll thank you to join your cohorts in the dining hall now."

Tori and Phi turned to the two boys.

"Want to come back to the dining hall with us?" Tori asked. She and Phi linked arms, and Phi leaned a little on Tori, as though she needed comfort.

"Sure," said Hal. "Bailey?"

Bailey felt shaken. Everyone wondered what animal could have done this, and Bailey's mind returned to that ghostly, glowing white beast he had seen from the rigimotive. It was the only thing he'd ever seen that could be large enough to make this kind of kill, but he didn't dare say it out loud. It was too strange.

"I'll meet you there," he said.

Hal nodded, then he and the two girls walked back across the commons. Bailey caught Tremelo's eye.

"Don't encounter kills like this in the Lowlands, I imagine," Tremelo said.

Bailey studied the body of the bear. Its face was calm, as though it hadn't had time to be afraid when it was hunted down.

"I've seen a kill before," he said quietly. "My mom is Animas Horse, and we had a mare, Maple, that was attacked by coyotes one night. My mom felt terrible for weeks. She could barely get out of bed. But my dad said that it's just part of life . . ." He kicked nervously at the grassy dirt with his toe. "When another animal kills one of your kin, you can't blame Nature—not the way you can blame people for doing bad things. It's just part of life."

"Your father is very wise," said Tremelo. "We'll be sending the bear back to Nature in about an hour, if you'd like to watch," he added. "Normally teachers handle animal deaths without much of a fuss, but students *are* welcome to attend rites if they choose."

A few hours later, Bailey stood with Tremelo, Phi, Hal,

and Tori around the bear's body, which had been moved to a small patch of grass in the shadows of the woods. Mrs. Copse and Ms. Sucrette, along with two older students, a boy and girl, also attended. Mrs. Copse had changed out of her gardening apron into a smart floral dress and cardigan, which she wore above rubber gardening boots. The two tearful students who clung to each other must have been Animae Bear, and Bailey wondered if they had felt the pain of its death as sharply as the bear had itself.

The two Animae Bear had gathered long sticks from the surrounding undergrowth, and together they worked silently, weaving the sticks into a low rectangular fence around the bear's body. Bailey remembered his mother performing the same rite for the horse when it had been found dead at the far border of their wheat field. Like she had then, the two bereaved students scattered flowers and leaves inside the outline formed by the sticks until the bear's body was nearly covered. Tremelo stood by silently, waiting to light the makeshift pyre.

When they were finished, the girl wiped her nose with the end of her blue blazer sleeve and silently looked at the ground. For a few seconds, the clearing was completely silent. Finally, the girl looked up and glanced at the boy, who seemed too unnerved to move.

Mrs. Copse stood at the bear's head, and addressed the small gathering. "This animal was known—she had animal brothers and human sisters who felt her joys and sorrows. She lived, and we gathered here are connected to that life, and changed forevermore by it."

The words were similar to what his mother had said over the fallen horse—and just as he had then, Bailey felt a mixture of solemnity and a strange jealousy that made him feel guilty. This creature was "known" by more than just his friends or family, but by the entire kingdom of Nature. There was a sad, lonesome part of himself that desperately wanted to Awaken. He wondered if that loneliness would always be a part of him.

For the next week, the school was abuzz with talk of the killed bear—rumors flitted through the halls like fruit flies, landing on one ridiculous theory after the next.

"There's only one thing that could do that kind of damage to a black bear of that size," said one of Hal and Bailey's dormmates, Pete, sounding very serious. The rest of the boys gathered in the Towers common room waited for him to continue. "And that's a Liwolf. Part lion, part wolf." Laughter erupted, and another boy tossed a chess piece at Pete's head.

"Hey!" Pete said, ducking out of the way. "It's not impossible!"

Bailey's curiosity about Tremelo's riddle had been powerfully overshadowed by the mystery of the bear, but both these concerns soon faded in the wake of a full school schedule: Latin, Flora and Fauna, History, Introduction to Tinkering, and of course, daily Homeroom with Tremelo. And after a two-hour break each day, the Scavage team met at four for two hours of running, jumping, and Flicking. He'd never felt this busy in his life, even during the harvest seasons back in the Lowlands.

Scavage would have been a much pleasanter release for Bailey if it hadn't been for Taylor, who picked on Bailey at every turn. He'd unofficially made it his mission to prove that Bailey would fail as a Scavage player. When Taylor and his friends weren't trying to body check him on the field or Flick him in the face with paint, they were loudly talking about why Bailey's kin never followed him around.

"Maybe he's ashamed," Taylor taunted before warm-ups for Thursday's practice. His friends grinned and listened in, which made Bailey's blood boil. "Maybe he's Animas *Worm*."

"Or Animas Roach!" one of Taylor's friends interjected. Taylor cracked up and patted him on the back. Bailey sat on the bench putting on his kneepads and gloves, trying his best to ignore them.

"Or maybe there really is such a thing as Animas Ant," Taylor said. "Though I guess that's better than nothing, isn't it, Bailey? An anting *ant*."

Bailey bristled, and he wondered just how much Taylor had guessed about him. *Just don't say anything,* he heard his dad's voice tell him. *Don't let it on that it bothers you.*

"You know what happens to people who are Animas *nothing*?" Taylor crowed. "They go stark raving bonkers. Like their brains are just *wiped out*."

"There's no such thing," said one of the other Year Four players. He gawped, slack-jawed, at Taylor. "Is there?"

Taylor grinned.

"You've never heard of an Absence?" He spoke to his

friend, but his eyes were trained directly at Bailey, and there they stayed as he continued. "There's only been, what? Three known cases in the history of the kingdom? And all three went so insane they had to be locked up. Tried to rip their own hair out, tried to *kill* themselves, even. And wouldn't you? I mean really, if you were just . . . nothing. So dull Nature didn't even want anything to do with you? *I* would."

Bailey's face burned red. He'd have given anything to be able to punch Taylor in his obnoxious grin.

"It's a good thing Bailey here isn't one of those, huh?" Taylor said. "We'd have to lock him up for *everyone's* good."

Bailey clenched his fists and rose from his seat on the bench.

There was no telling what Taylor knew for sure—but it was clear that he'd heard the rumors in the Golden Lowlands and would make sure that those rumors followed Bailey all the way to Fairmount.

"Bailey!"

He turned and saw Phi walking toward him. She looked down at his fists and arched an eyebrow.

"I thought we could warm up together," she said, pointing her thumb to a spot on the other side of the benches. "Over *there*."

"Uh-oh, saved by the girlfriend," Taylor crowed, and the other boys made cooing noises. They stalked off toward the field then, where Bailey knew he'd have to prove himself even further if their taunting was ever going to stop.

"He's such a creep," said Phi. "It's amazing that he and Hal are even related."

The two finished putting on their gear and stretched by the edge of the field. It turned out Phi wasn't having the best week, either—the falcon Carin, the one who had caused so much havoc in Ms. Sucrette's classroom on the first day, had flown off after the bear's funeral and hadn't returned for several days.

"She does that all the time to hunt," said Phi as they lined up to take the field. "And I hate when she goes away. It makes everything even worse."

"What do you mean?" asked Bailey.

Phi lowered her head. Her dark eyes were hidden by her brown, curly hair.

"I don't know. Sometimes I don't really *like* having such a close bond with Carin. I mean, it's who I am. But no one told me how much the Animas bond changes you. It changed me, at least. I don't know if that's how everyone feels."

"What do you mean, it changed you?" Bailey asked. He was surprised by how open Phi was being was him. Normally, she hardly spoke at all. But now she couldn't seem to stop.

She gripped the sides of the bench so that her knuckles were little half-moons. "I want to fly the way Carin does," she blurted out. Then she looked away. "I know it must sound stupid. But when she flies away, I hate it. Wherever she is, I can't fly with her."

Bailey had never thought about the Animas bond that way, that it might actually pain Phi to be separated from her kin. He didn't know what to say except "It doesn't sound stupid."

Phi smiled at him.

"Thanks. I haven't told anyone that besides Tori. But I know I can trust you," she said. Bailey felt a rush of warmth through his whole body.

Phi looked up at the sky again, searching it for Carin.

"One nice thing about her flights, though," she continued, "is that when she comes back and we're near each other again, I feel like I've seen something new, even though I haven't. It's like when you go on a trip and come back and tell your friends about it, or when you write home to your parents. There's a crisp air that I can feel, or I remember seeing a flash of pine trees . . ."

Bailey listened, fascinated. He longed for a bond like the one Phi described. That she was unhappy made him feel a tightness in his chest.

"The woods are so different from the Dust Plains," she said. "When the bear was killed last week, I felt something from Carin, like she wasn't just scared for herself, but for me too. I couldn't see anything clearly. There are things in the woods that she fears, but I'm not sure what they are. I just feel an echo of what she felt when she saw them."

"That's incredible," said Bailey. "So you think Carin knows what might have killed that bear?"

Phi nodded.

"I didn't say anything that day because I wasn't sure what the feeling meant. But . . ." She hesitated.

"What?" asked Bailey.

"Whatever it is, it's still out there," she whispered. "It's waiting for something."

Eleven

THAT SAME EVENING, VIVIANA stood in front of a freestanding mirror in the center of her apartment as two tailors took her measurements. Her personal rooms were the former foreman's quarters in what had once, during the Melorian Age of Invention, been a factory. The space was plenty grand, with tall windows that faced the docks. The factory itself was filled with defunct bits of half-finished machinery, the bones of a more progressive time that she hoped to revive.

Outside her window the Gray City spread before her, and even from here, she could feel it broiling. Her Clamoribus birds were doing the trick—perched all over the city, they spewed her campaign slogans and incited shouting matches in the streets. Just the day before, a riot had broken out in one of the richer neighborhoods of the city, near Parliament—poor men and women from the Gudgeons, urged by the calculated wrath of the Clamoribus, had begun throwing rocks through shop windows.

Through her own open window, she saw a dark shape approaching the Gray City skyline.

"Leave," she said coldly.

"Only another moment, miss, and we'll be finished," the Animas Squirrel said. He was just fitting the sleeves of a new coat to her arms, while the other tailor made measurements around the cuffs.

Viviana whipped herself around to face him.

"I said *leave*. I will tell you when you may come back in."

The two tailors retreated quickly. The metal door slid shut behind them with a satisfying clang. Viviana turned back to the window, where one of Clarke's massive Clamoribus birds now stood. This one was a messenger.

She watched as it hopped down from the sill and settled in the center of the room. Even with its wings retracted, the raven was impressively large. Viviana pressed a shining golden button on the raven's temple and a red light in the bird's left eye blinked on.

The raven opened its beak, and somewhere in its gleaming innards, a recording spoke.

"I am here, Viviana, securely in place." Joan's voice flowed from the beak of the raven, and calmed Viviana's nerves, as it so often had over the years. Her reliable assistant. They'd both cleaned up well since their days as Dust Plains chattel. *"No one suspects me,"* Joan's voice echoed. *"I believe I have found the person who possesses the book, though I have yet to see it. We'll soon know the exact words of the prophecy."*

Viviana was immensely relieved. On some days it seemed silly, this fixation with the so-called prophecy. But then again, the Jackal, the man who had killed her father, was as intelligent as he was ruthless. His obsession with the prophecy had driven him mad, and in his weakened state, he was overthrown. Was he driven by the fear of a threat to his throne? Would she contend with the same threat?

Upon returning to the Gray City, Viviana had solicited information from her spies in Parliament. She wanted to know what, exactly, the Jackal had learned to drive him to obsession. Viviana discovered that in the years after he'd violently stolen power, the Jackal first heard of the rumors that had begun to circulate among the people of the Gray City—rumors of a prophecy that foretold the emergence of a true king.

The prophecy was perpetuated by a man called the Loon, but he was untraceable. It was said he moved from the city to the mountains frequently with his son, avoiding detection—but the Jackal had managed to capture and question a member of the RATS, a resistance group of Melore loyalists who was associated with the Loon.

The man was tortured, and though Viviana's spies were unclear about the exact wording he used, she was clear on the message he conveyed: that a king would return, leading his army from the mountains. The Jackal had become enraged and killed the prisoner then, but not before he spoke his dying words:

But the tiger! the man had whispered with his last breath. *The white beast!*

Though the man had spoken no more after this, Viviana found it very telling that every white tiger in the kingdom had mysteriously died while the Jackal was in power. The

124

entire species had become extinct. Viviana knew the Jackal was to blame—and judging by the amount of crudely painted white beasts she saw on Gray City alleyways, others in the kingdom felt the same. Although the Jackal had tried to keep the eradication of the tigers a secret, the RATS had spread their suspicion of him throughout Aldermere. The white tiger had become a symbol of the resistance against the Jackal, and it was only a matter of time before that resistance moved against her as well.

Her task now was to find the exact language of the prophecy in order to convince these loyalists, these believers in the white beast, that she was the answer to the rumored prophecy.

There was just one thing that bothered her: *a true king. His* army. She was the daughter of a king, and yet the prophecy insisted on a son. But once she learned exactly what the full prophecy said, she could—more successfully than the Jackal had—make certain that no other ruler could claim the throne. She was one step ahead of the Jackal already: he may have killed the Loon but learned nothing, whereas *she* had found the Loon's book, where the prophecy was sure to be written.

She waved the Clamoribus away and returned to her position in front of the mirror, admiring her new high-collared fur coat, which seemed almost to shimmer in the yellow evening light. Fox fur, beaver, mink, and rabbit—all together in a patchwork of perfectly cut pieces that fit her slender body like armor and framed her face magnificently. She had no idea who the animals had been whose pelts had gone into the coat, and she didn't care.

She smiled at her own powerful reflection in the mirror. It would do nicely for a queen.

Twelve

BAILEY SAT AWAKE IN one of the broad armchairs in the common room long after Hal and the other Tower boys had gone to bed. He mulled over what Phi had told him earlier, about the fear Carin felt out in the woods. Bailey felt certain there must be a mysterious beast out there, responsible for the gruesome death of the bear.

At the bear's funeral days before, Bailey hadn't wanted to mention the animal he had spotted from the rigomotive. It was clear that even Hal hadn't believed him at the time. But the memory of it crept up often, and the more he thought about it the more he couldn't shake the feeling that whatever was out there was dangerous. Perhaps it even had human kin who were equally as dangerous. The animal he'd spotted from the rigomotive had been the largest thing he'd ever seen. If that beast and its kin had followed them to the school, then Fairmount needed to know.

He was sure that if he went to the administration with talk of a mysterious, ghostly beast, he'd be laughed out of the office. He needed proof—and if Phi's words were any indication, that proof might be closer to the school than he thought.

He made a sudden decision. He'd go out and see what he could find now, tonight.

Bailey was extra quiet as he slunk along the wall of the dorms, after a quick and silent trip to his room to grab a jacket and shoes. He held his breath as he shimmied past the resident assistant's door. A floorboard creaked underneath him, and Bailey froze. He couldn't see anything in the dark hallway. He heard a rustle from a neighboring room, and said a silent prayer to Nature that no one would discover him. He waited for a whole minute, frozen. No one came. He kept moving.

Downstairs, he made his way to the cloakroom, where a smaller side door, less likely to creak noisily, took him outside.

He knew he had to hurry across the grounds. Bindley and his night-vision lens could be just about anywhere, and no one had put myrgwood in his tea tonight. He ran due west, around the back of Treetop, toward the bottom of the vast hill where the Scavage fields sat, its stadium seats illuminated by the moon. The patch of trees that backed up to the fields looked ghostly in this darkness. He veered south, to the path that led into the woods, and to where the bear was found. He took a deep breath, and prepared to enter into the shadows.

"Hey, wait!" a voice called. Bailey spun around, half expecting to see a pack of Bindley's hounds charging after him. But it was Tori, hastening down the hill with a cotton robe thrown over a silky button-up pajama top that looked a few sizes too big for her, and boy's pajama bottoms. She had a hand-powered dynamo lamp in her hand, with a crank that made the lightbulb sputter to life.

"*Shh!*" he said.

"What are you doing out here?" Tori asked him as soon as she caught up. She looked excited to see him, as though she'd just been sitting around in her pj's, waiting for an excuse to sneak out of the dorms. Bailey saw the flash of a slim, black snake around her arm.

"What are *you* doing?" Bailey whispered.

"I saw you run past the window," Tori said. "I wasn't tired, so I followed you."

Bailey felt anxious all over again.

"You should go back to bed. You don't want to get in trouble. Two people are easier to catch than one."

"Ants to that!" she exclaimed. "It's so *dull* around here I could scream. I'm dying for a little adventure. Lead on."

"Fine," Bailey said, hoping that she'd get bored and turn back before he found evidence of the white beast or its kin—he wasn't ready to share that theory with anyone yet. Then again, he thought, having a witness if they did come across anything would be useful. "Just try to keep quiet, okay?"

Bailey ignored her as she fiddled with her dynamo lamp, which didn't seem to crank properly. "Ants to this thing!" seemed to be Tori's favorite thing to say. Each time she cursed, he shushed her, and they pressed on in the darkness.

A thick line on Bailey's campus map represented the border of the Fairmount grounds. It was drawn at the westernmost edge of the lower cliffs that led down to the waterwheel, and marked the point of the forest where students were not allowed to cross. Bailey had assumed that the line was only symbolic, and that forest wouldn't change from one side to the other. But as he and Tori walked steadily on past the dirt road, the trees grew closer together. The ground became more uneven, and large rocks jutted up between the roots. When Bailey heard the churning and crashing of water in the distance, he knew that they had crossed that thick line drawn on the map, and were no longer on school grounds. As Tori and Bailey stopped to get their bearings, he heard a low hissing that seemed to come from many creatures at the same time. The sound was all around them.

"Is that . . . ?" he began to ask.

"*Thamnophis cyrtopsis*, maybe even a few *Elaphe obsoleta*," Tori said in an excited whisper. She looked at Bailey, who had no clue what she was talking about. "Snakes."

"Oh," he said. No wonder she thought of Ms. Sucrette as a drip—Tori's Latin was already pretty good.

"Where are we?" asked Tori. The tone of her voice made Bailey wonder if, for all her desire to come, she was actually afraid. As excited as she was to find so many of her kin around, Tori must have inferred from them that something was not as it should be. Her black snake crept out of the neck of her pajama top and settled onto her collarbone.

"It's okay," Bailey said to reassure her, even though he wasn't sure if this was true. "We're out near the low cliffs."

Tori's eyes widened.

"What in Nature are we doing all the way out here?"

Tori began hitting the dynamo light with the flat of her palm, trying to jolt it into working properly. It sputtered, flashed once, and then emitted a beam of dim light. "What are you looking for?"

"I'm not sure yet," he admitted. He wondered whether telling Tori to watch for signs of a giant predator would help the situation at all. Instead, he crouched low and began scanning the tree trunks around them, hoping that whatever marks he found—if any—were old.

"Everyone's being so secretive lately," said Tori. Bailey could tell by the slight waver in her voice that she was nervous, but trying to put on a brave front. "Phi's got her super-secret independent study in the tinkering shop, and here you are looking for 'something, not sure!' in the Dark Woods. I always thought *I* was the mysterious kind . . ."

"What do you mean, about Phi?" Bailey asked. She hadn't mentioned any special classes to him earlier.

Tori shrugged.

"I don't know what it is. But she spends her dinnertime before practice at Tremelo's workshop, and when I asked what they were making, she said she'd show me when the time was right."

A chilly breeze blew through the woods. Tori pulled her sleeves down, and crossed her arms over her buttoned pajama top. Bailey saw a flash of scarred skin on both her wrists. "It's so quiet out here," she whispered. "It's positively creepy."

Bailey had to agree. The hissing had subsided, and the Dark Woods was almost *too* quiet, as if the entire place were holding its breath, waiting for something to happen. He had the strangest feeling, similar to the one he'd felt the night of the rigimotive incident. The feeling of being watched.

"You . . . you don't think there's someone else out here, do you?" Tori whispered, as if she were reading his mind. The skin on Bailey's arms and neck felt shivery.

"I don't," he lied.

Just then, there was a rustle behind them in the bushes.

Before he could even think, Bailey grabbed Tori's hand as the two of them spun around, their hearts pounding in the almost total silence of the woods. A flash, a darting shape, and Bailey held his breath.

It was only a fox, scurrying past them from behind a boulder.

Bailey sighed with relief, and Tori let out a nervous laugh.

"Sorry," Bailey said, letting go of her hand.

Tori straightened her pajama top and smiled.

"It's okay." She exhaled. "I was scared too." Her snake was practically strangling her, and she tried to disentangle it. "What's wrong with you?" she addressed it impatiently. "It was only a—"

But at that second a giant gray wolf, snarling, jumped out at them from the darkness of the trees. Bailey felt the sharp, wrenching pain in his forearm before he even registered what had happened.

He fell backward, holding his arm. Tori screamed as the creature turned to her. She whirled the faulty dynamo lamp, her only weapon, above her head and brought it crashing down on the wolf's nose. What little light the lamp had provided immediately died. In the darkness the wolf backed away a step, growling.

"Bailey!" Tori yelled, holding the remains of the broken dynamo lamp in one hand. "Are you okay?"

Bailey tried to get up to help her fend off the wolf. He'd fallen hard against the trunk of a tree, and his back was throbbing almost as much as his arm. The wolf was still snarling, showing all its teeth, muscles tense. Tori, moving quickly, grabbed a heavy stone from the forest floor, and chucked it, hitting the wolf in the front leg. It growled and sidestepped. Bailey hauled himself to his feet. The wolf dug its front paws into the ground, and Bailey knew it was preparing to leap at them.

"Tor . . ." he whispered, his hands shaking. He grabbed at her to push her out of the way, but his arm felt so weak.

Suddenly, from behind them, a loud, primal scream rang out—it was a man, his voice so loud, angry, and like the roar of a real animal that the wolf paused. An arrow whooshed by them and hit the tree directly behind the wolf with a loud *twang*.

"Get back!" shouted the man, barreling past Tori and Bailey and approaching the wolf head on.

It was Tremelo. His driving jacket billowed out behind him as he jumped in front of them and leveled a heavy bow made of gears and springs at the attacking wolf. Tremelo pulled a clicking trigger and loosed an arrow that whizzed by the wolf's left ear and sunk with a thud into the same tree. The wolf growled and yelped, then slunk away.

As Bailey watched it disappear into the trees, he thought he saw something that made him catch his breath: the silhouettes of two men standing in the trees. He squinted, trying to force his eyes to adjust to the dark, and the men were gone. But he'd seen them; he knew it. He'd been right.

Tremelo threw the bow over his shoulder and stomped toward Bailey.

"What were you thinking?" he asked, furious.

"There were men," Bailey said, and he tried to point before a jolt of pain reminded him that his arm was wounded. "Just over there."

"Come on," said Tremelo quickly, but not before Bailey recognized a surprised look in the professor's eyes. "We need to get your arm looked after."

"But, sir. Their kin attacked us, and with the bear attack, what if—"

"There's no one out here," responded Tremelo curtly. "You're seeing things."

He grabbed Bailey's good arm with one hand and Tori's arm with the other and began dragging them back through the woods. Bailey began to wonder how Tremelo had simply appeared in the woods with a bow and arrows. Had he been following them? Or was he prowling the woods for his own reasons? Did he really believe that no one was out here, or had he been lying? Bailey's head swam with the possibilities, and he began to wonder what, exactly, Tremelo was doing here at Fairmount.

Tremelo's kin, Fennel, trotted ahead of them. Of course, Bailey thought to himself. We saw her just before the wolf attacked. Tremelo knew we were in danger because of her. But why had the fox been following them in the first place?

Then a terrible thought struck Bailey. He'd been caught. Yes, by Tremelo, who broke the rules just as often as anyone, but he'd been caught nonetheless. If Tremelo chose to report him, Bailey would be expelled. No excuses. No second chances.

As they reached the edge of the forest and could see the Fairmount buildings up on the hill, Tremelo let go of them.

"Sir . . ." Bailey tried to say.

"You say one word begging me not to tell Finch, I'll leave you out here with not a single look back," Tremelo growled. "What will be done is my decision now, not yours."

Tori and Bailey looked at each other and stayed silent. Tori looked much paler than usual.

Fennel reached the door of a small stone carriage house that sat tucked among the trees. Tremelo beckoned them over to a low side door and unlocked it. He looked around for lights on in other windows.

Bailey realized that, instead of leading him to the school's infirmary, Tremelo had brought them to his own quarters. He began to feel uneasy.

"What are we doing here?" he asked.

"If you show up in the infirmary with some cock-and-bull story, you'll be out of here faster than you can say *I'm an idiot*," Tremelo spat as they followed him up the stairs.

Bailey and Tori barely had enough room to stand in Tremelo's messy apartment. They stood back to back in the sitting room as Tremelo squeezed past a towering pile of books and disappeared into a side room. They heard rummaging and the clanking of bottles.

"Don't bleed on my floor, boy," Tremelo called. Bailey looked down at his wound. There was a lot of blood, but underneath was only a scratch. It wouldn't need stitches—at least, he hoped it wouldn't. Tori elbowed Bailey in the side.

"Are you *seeing* all these books?" she whispered. Bailey craned his neck around to look at the shelves. They were stacked with all kinds of different books, some of them very old. Some of the newer ones were just cheaply printed pamphlets, with titles like *The False King's Power: The Jackal and Parliament,* and *The Parliament's Crimes Against the People.* Many books seemed to be about the Animas bond's history and power. One book that piqued Bailey's interest was called *The Velyn and their Kin: A Study in Transformation.*

Tremelo re-entered the room. "Ants to this place," he muttered. "I can never find anything I'm looking for. . . ." The corner of a large trunk stuck out from behind a sagging armchair, and Tremelo dragged it out into the few feet of space left in the center of the floor. Bailey and Tori pressed against the closest bookshelf to make room. Tremelo opened the trunk, trying to block Bailey and Tori's view with his shoulders, but not before Bailey saw a jumble of odd-looking glass vials and beakers, and a huge book bound with what looked like real leather, embossed with the image of an animal. He exchanged a worried look with Tori.

"Aha!" said Tremelo, and he held up a small jar of grayish salve. "Very rare, very potent. Hold out your arm." Bailey did as he was told, though he wondered if he wouldn't regret it.

The salve stung like someone had just rubbed bits of sand on a sunburn. His whole arm began to itch.

"Don't touch it; I know you'll want to," Tremelo warned. He released Bailey's arm.

The top of the trunk on the floor was still open. Bailey leaned forward to get a better look, but Fennel leapt onto the top of the trunk, closing it before he could manage so much as a glance. Her golden eyes narrowed.

"Her favorite snack is curious students," Tremelo said with an angry edge to his voice. "Mind she doesn't get ahold of you." He sat down on the edge of the armchair, resting his elbows on his knees and fixing both Bailey and Tori with a stern stare.

"Now, if you two are at all interested in staying at Fairmount— or even staying alive—then listen up."

Thirteen

"I REALIZE THAT I am hardly a paragon of responsibility," said Tremelo. "But I have the power to get both of you booted out of this school, so I suggest you listen to me very carefully all the same."

Bailey glanced at Tori. Her black hair hung messily around her face, and made her look like a small child about to be reprimanded. Her snake had settled inside the collar of her pajama top, and was as still as if it were just a piece of heavy jewelry.

Bailey swallowed.

"Some rules are complete bunk," said Tremelo, pacing. "And we all know it. Curfews, what have you. But going past the school grounds into the Dark Woods at night is pure idiocy. Whatever you have to prove, either of you, you do it within Fairmount grounds."

Tremelo turned his dark eyes on them. He was angry, Bailey could see that plainly. His eyebrows were furrowed, and underneath his mustache, his lips were pursed as though he was trying to stop himself from cursing. But there was something else there too that Bailey could see: the way

Tremelo's fingers, which had shot those arrows so expertly, so calmly, were trembling. The gleam of sweat on Tremelo's forehead. He was worried.

"There are reasons the Dark Woods are forbidden, and they have nothing to do with silly stories or schoolboy dares. Real dangers lurk in those woods. You could have been killed tonight. Do you understand me?"

"Yes," Tori whispered.

Bailey knew that he was already in enough trouble, and that the smartest thing to do would be to answer yes and take his punishment. But he couldn't ignore what he'd seen in the woods. There were *people* out there with dangerous, aggressive kin, and Tremelo didn't seem to care.

"I *don't* understand, sir," Bailey said, forcing himself to meet Tremelo's gaze. "There are people in the woods. I want to know why. Why did they attack us? What do they want with Fairmount?"

Tremelo glared at him.

"You'll recall what I said about being too curious? It would behoove you to stop snooping around when you're only going to get yourself and your friends hurt." Tremelo passed a hand across his eyes. "You are letting yourself get carried away, Bailey, and it's not going to help you do what you've come to this school to do. Your job here at this school is simply to keep yourself out of harm's way and let those who know what they're doing take care of the real threats. Now, I ask you again: do you understand?"

Bailey burned with anger, but he nodded. Tremelo knew more than he was letting on, that much was obvious. Was the professor angrier that Bailey was breaking the rules . . . or that he was asking questions?

Tremelo escorted them back to the dorms. They walked a few paces behind Tremelo as he led them on the path from the teachers' quarters to the main campus.

"How does your arm feel?" asked Tori quietly.

Bailey hadn't even thought about his arm since the tingling from the salve had worn away. He looked down at it now. The blood had dried, and the skin around the wound was healing already.

"It's fine, I think," he said. He ran his hand over the wound. The scabbing was smooth.

"You'll be lucky if you don't have a scar," said Tori, looking up ahead at Tremelo.

Bailey thought of Tori's scars, and the way she was always careful to conceal them with long sleeves. But tonight, in the excitement, she had forgotten; her sleeves were rolled up to the elbow, and in the light from the moon and the few dim lampposts on the main path, Bailey could see the puckered, glossy skin running the length of both forearms. She saw him looking and sighed, rolling down her sleeves again.

"It was a fire," Tori said, sensing the question in his eyes, "in our apartment when I was a kid." She kept her eyes on Tremelo's back as he walked ahead of them. "I was just a couple years old. Some of the Jackal's supporters lit fires in parts of the city when Parliament deposed him." She shuddered. "That's why my parents are so scared of the Dominae. The Gray City always gets caught in the middle."

Up ahead, Tremelo stopped short and swirled around to

face them. They'd reached Treetop.

"We're the only ones who know the extent of your wandering tonight," said Tremelo. "So let's keep it as such, shall we? If Headmaster Finch finds out, this won't be a very happy story for either of you. But in exchange for my silence, you two have to promise me that you will *stay away* from the woods."

Reluctantly, Bailey nodded. Tori said a quiet, clipped "Yes, sir."

"Good," said Tremelo. "Believe me. I'll be watching."

He pointed Tori toward the front door of Treetop. Tori turned her thin shoulders and glanced at Bailey as she slinked away, and her snake flicked its tongue in his direction. Bailey gave a small wave as she disappeared into the dimly lit Treetop entrance.

Tremelo put his hand on Bailey's back and guided him on toward the Towers.

"I'm sorry, sir," Bailey began. He was well aware that this was the second time that Tremelo had caught him out of his dorm late at night, and he didn't know what the professor might be thinking.

Tremelo held up a hand, cutting Bailey off. With his other hand, he reached into the collar of his shirt and fished out a small pendant on a chain.

"This is for you," he said. He lifted the chain over his neck and handed it to Bailey, who was too confused to argue. The pendant was coin-like, a small, round piece of metal with the image of a sleeping fox engraved on one side, and some letters on the other. Both sides were worn, and Bailey could only just make out Tremelo's own name on the talisman.

"I don't understand." Bailey asked. "It's yours. It has your name on it."

Tremelo looked away, as though he was thinking very hard about how to answer.

"It was given to me when I finally Awakened to my Animas," he said. "My father told me that it would offer protection. I don't even know if I believe it at all—he was a superstitious old kook about many things—but I like to think that it's true, in this case."

Tremelo knelt until his eyes were level with Bailey's, and he did not look away.

"You hold on to that for me, and mind what I said about the Dark Woods. Your Absence is a unique problem, I know. And perhaps that's what drives you to un-puzzle things the way you do. But you're not safe—not in the woods. And next time I may not be there to help."

Bailey nodded. He looked once more at the sleeping fox on the pendant, and slipped it into the pocket of his work pants. Tremelo stood and began to walk back toward the teachers' quarters when Bailey suddenly remembered something.

"King's Finger Oak," he called out.

Tremelo turned. He raised an arched eyebrow.

"A tree that bears seeds, but no fruit," Bailey continued. "That's one part of the riddle, isn't it?"

Tremelo didn't move except to stroke his mustache in thought. He seemed about to say something, but then changed his mind.

"Go to bed, Bailey," he said instead and walked away.

Fourteen

TREMELO GLANCED AT THE clock tower as he made his way back to the teachers' quarters. Two thirty, a time when any sane person would be trying to get some sleep. But as usual, Tremelo's mind was too busy to let him rest.

"King's Finger Oak," Tremelo said aloud, and shook his head. Tremelo sighed. He was no better than his father, telling riddles that had no answer. He could see his father now: the bottle-thick monocle and its dangling, fraying string. The frizzed white hair, the patchy velvet waistcoat. The smile. What Tremelo wanted more than anything was the ability to ask the Loon what the night's events meant.

Figure it out yourself, boy! he'd say. *You figure out how things work, you learn the world by heart. Everything is just one gear putting pressure on another.*

Figure it out yourself. Of course, the Loon had never been talking about real gears, but about people.

The Loon was a loving father, but inattentive. He'd worked for Melore as a scholar, but after the king's death, which happened when Tremelo was quite young and now did not remember, the Loon continued his studies obsessively, even dragging Tremelo from the city to the mountains, sometimes with only a moment's notice. He'd been too busy with his theories and stories of the old Seers, the Velyn tribe, and King Melore to take care of a small child in the midst of his conspiring followers, the RATS. The RATS themselves may have introduced Tremelo to myrgwood and rootwort rum when he was a young boy, but they'd also been the ones to help him retrieve his father's books and papers years later, after the Jackal had the Loon killed. Tremelo had been twenty-two then, and after his father's death, the RATS helped him search his father's home and study for the Loon's hidden books before the Jackal's soldiers returned to loot it again.

The past, the past. Recently, the past had been calling to him more and more.

Tremelo reached his carriage house's door and stomped up the narrow stairs. Fennel sat upright on the highest shelf of his desk, waiting. Tremelo lifted open the trunk on the floor and pulled out the heavy, leather-bound book. It was a miracle that the book had survived after the Loon's murder—and a miracle that Tremelo had managed to find it in the Loon's ransacked home without losing his own life. Despite all that, the book had never been of any use to him . . . until now.

Tremelo turned to the first page, and ran his fingers over the familiar handwriting—familiar, and totally unreadable. None of the RATS had been able to decipher it, either. It was, his father had said, the language of the Seers—but after the Loon's death, Tremelo had no desire for another trek through the mountains to find them. The Velyn would have known, and many of them would have helped him, but they were all dead now. The Jackal had made sure of that. After all that bloodshed, Tremelo had done with the book the same thing he'd done with his father's prophecies— dismissed it as an object of a past that no longer meant anything.

But after tonight . . . he was no longer sure.

He had seen the two people Bailey had glimpsed through the trees. Fennel had been hot on their trails, and Tremelo, in a deep meditative state just outside the woods, had seen through her eyes. First, he'd seen flashes of the two nervous kids out where they had no business prowling around, and then two faces and darkly colored handmade clothing. A cloak on one, trimmed with wolf's fur. An earring made from the talon of a crow.

And on the back of a wrinkled hand, a tattoo.

Now Tremelo sat in his armchair in the safe warmth of his familiar apartment, but he felt far from easy. He flipped the pages hastily and then stopped. For a long time he sat staring, unable to move, unable to tear his eyes away from the page.

There, in his father's book, was the same collection of lines and dashes that he'd seen on the hand of the man in the woods.

Fifteen

GWEN WALKED PURPOSEFULLY down a hallway in the high-ceilinged stone Parliament building to fetch an evening snack from the kitchens for the Elder. Even through the fortified walls, she could hear chanting outside.

It had been just over two weeks since the Elder's return to Parliament, and in that time the riots in the city had grown in size and strength. Stirred by the Dominae's promises of power, the poverty-stricken citizens of the Gray City's poorest districts had gathered in the Parliament square to protest. Many storefronts and tenements near the city's center had been looted or, worse, torched. Just the night before, a blaze had started on the streets near the palace. Gwen glanced out a tall window, and through the smoke and flames, she could make out the rioters, holding sticks and clubs, and shouting, *"We will be free! We will be free!"*

As dangerous as it was outside the walls of the palace, however, the real danger was inside. The air in the halls was tense with whispering and worry. Instead of banding together to push back against Viviana, Parliament had only become more fractured, with members disappearing every few days, perhaps afraid of the riots outside.

"Shouldn't the riots prove to Parliament that Viviana is a threat?" Gwen had asked the Elder earlier in his study.

"Violence has a way of distracting us from our goals," he'd replied, watching the melee below. "I'm certain that the Dominae has spies in Parliament who would enjoy nothing more than to see us crumble. Our failure to declare Viviana an official enemy of the people is proof that she has many members of Parliament on her side already."

As she rounded a corner near the kitchens, Gwen saw two Parliament members reflected in a hanging mirror: a large, glowering man followed by a gristly warthog and a spindly woman with a look of permanent irritation. Gwen almost kept going and walked past them, but she drew back when she heard the word *Viviana*.

"Are you ready?" the Animas Warthog said. "I have heard that Viviana will be there in person."

Gwen pressed herself flat against the wall, where she could not be seen. She felt her heart begin to beat faster.

"Just so long as the rabble stays away," the woman replied. "I don't want to be recognized."

From the open window at the end of the hall, the voices of that rabble drifted to where Gwen hid. *"We will be free. We will be free!"*

"Never fear," said the Animas Warthog. "This rally is for the inner circle only."

"As long as the Elder and the other loyalists like him don't find out . . ."

"*Pshh!* The Elder's worn out his welcome, I say. He'll be

the first to go when Viviana takes power. Perhaps sooner . . ."

Gwen stifled a gasp. She could barely believe what she was hearing.

The conspirators were on the move. Their shadows lengthened around the corner as they made their way toward the spot where she stood. Frantically, Gwen scanned the hall for something to hide behind. A door stood ajar only feet away, and just as the twosome turned the corner, Gwen slipped inside a rarely used retiring room. She held her breath, afraid that they'd heard her movement. Instinctively, her fingers flew to her short red hair, which she began twirling anxiously.

As they passed by, Gwen made a decision. She'd follow them. She would go to this rally and find out everything she could; she and the Elder could use that information to expose the spies in Parliament. The Elder had saved her life—she owed him this much. Finding any evidence to align loyal Parliament members behind him could change everything.

Observing them from a distance, she followed the two Dominae sympathizers down a dank hallway in the basement of the Parliament building. The lamps in the corridor were very dim, and the stone smelled like rainwater. She paused as the two conspirators pulled the heavy basement door open and stepped up the stone stairs into the alley. She waited several seconds before she dared approach the door and follow them out into the night. As she emerged into the alleyway, she tried to send out a call—she could feel the presence of the owls that normally roosted in the towers of the palace. She'd need their help to stay on course without being seen by the people she was following. A dark shape flew through the patch of sky that hung over the alley, and Gwen saw an eager young barn owl leading her onward.

She thought about the Elder, alone in his study—he would worry about her if she didn't return soon with a bowl of roasted almonds from downstairs. But she couldn't tell him—he would only forbid her to go, as he'd done so many times before. This was her chance to prove herself to him.

Above her, the owl screeched encouragingly. She hurried on, past a group of men gathered around a waste-can fire and into the dark alleys that led to the Gudgeons. Be brave, she told herself. The Elder needs you.

She was going to meet the Dominae.

Sixteen

AT THE VERY SAME moment that Gwen heard the Animas Warthog threaten the Elder's life, Bailey found himself boarding a rigimotive for the second time. The entire Year One class was embarking on a field trip to the Gray City to hear the famous Equilibrium Orchestra, which was made up of human musicians and their bird kin, who provided the woodwind section. It was supposed to be a beautiful and haunting blend of birdsong and composed music, but Tori, who had already seen the orchestra twice, said it was "nothing you'd flip your lid over."

Bailey had spent the days since his run-in with the wolf distracted and anxious, furious that just when he'd stumbled upon something huge (and potentially dangerous), Tremelo had made it nearly impossible for him to do anything but go about his normal school routine. Fennel had begun popping up in strange places like the dining hall and the path to the Towers, just to remind Bailey that he was being watched.

Other students were anxious too, but for a different reason. Reports had reached the school of unrest in the Gray City—even riots close to the Parliament building.

For that reason, extra chaperones were accompanying the students on the trip, and Headmaster Finch had called a special assembly that morning to assure everyone that any "unsavory activity" was taking place in an entirely different part of the city.

Still, some students had declined to go on the field trip, supposedly because their parents were too worried about any possibility of violence near the opera house. Bailey had written to his own parents to tell them about the field trip, and his mom had written back in length about how she owned two gramophone recordings of the Equilibrium, and how she and Bailey's dad had always wanted to hear them perform live, and did he think that the same gentleman was conducting who'd been with the orchestra when she was a girl? Bailey, relieved, had signed up for the trip with a clear conscience.

Now about fifty Year One students were lined up in the yard next to the rigimotive platform, hooting and waving as the four-story rigi pulled up on the track. Bailey, Hal, Tori, and Phi chose seats on the ground floor near the back of the first car, where a sliding gold-plated door separated them from the last car, occupied by their escorts. Among the half dozen professors who had signed up as chaperones were Mr. Nillow, the History instructor; Ms. Sucrette, who wanted to tie the orchestra into her semester-long study of Latinate bird songs; and Tremelo, who insisted he wasn't going to baby-sit anyone—he was only going, he said, to listen to the music. The teachers were in high spirits, talking loudly and laughing, just as happy to have a day free of regular classes as the students were. Tremelo and Ms. Sucrette sat side by side, trading opinions on which of the latest recordings was the Equilibrium's viola section's most adept.

Phi sat first on one of the wooden benches and, feeling bold, Bailey slid next to her. Tori gave him a sidelong glance and took the bench in front of them. Hal, who couldn't seem to muster up the courage to sit next to her, stretched out his legs on the bench across the aisle. It occurred to Bailey that the ride from Fairmount to the Gray City by rigimotive was over three hours long—and he'd just put himself in the precarious position of having to talk to Phi all that time without sounding like an idiot.

Tori was already in rare form: "When will this ant of a thing get a move on?"

"I've never been to a concert before," Phi said. She tucked a piece of her dark curly hair behind her ear.

Bailey felt like he ought to sound worldly or experienced, but he had to admit, "I haven't, either . . . unless you count a barn dance I went to once."

The rigimotive lurched, and the students in the car all sat up on their seats to wave, even though there was no one in the yard outside to wave to except Mrs. Copse, who hullo-ed back enthusiastically before chopping the ear of an overgrown rabbit-shaped hedge with her shears.

They were off. As the rigimotive sped smoothly along the Fluvian, Hal tried visibly to work up the courage to move closer to Tori. Tori, completely uninterested in making small talk with him, whipped a book out of her beaded satchel and spent the whole ride resolutely ignoring all of them.

Bailey found that the easiest thing to talk about with Phi was the most obvious: their first Scavage game against a rival school, which would take place the next weekend. It was against Roanoake, a trade school from the northernmost region of the Lowlands, which was mostly flat, grassy plains.

By the time the city center was visible in the distance, Bailey had made Phi laugh three times.

She blushed when Bailey complimented her on her tree-climbing skills.

"No, really, I mean it—you're going to win the game for us single-handedly," he said. "I've been through Roanoake, and they barely have shrubs out there! They wouldn't know how to get any height in a game if they were all Animae Eagle."

Phi laughed. Four times. "I like a bird's-eye view!" she joked. "Can I help it if I just happen to see some Sneaks?"

Bailey noticed that Hal was trying desperately not to appear as if he were eavesdropping.

"Hal would probably be really great at recon like that too," he said, raising his voice so that Tori could hear. "His Animas can fly, and plus, Hal can hear anyone coming a mile away."

"I've never heard of a nighttime Scavage game, though," said Tori, who didn't even look up from her book. Bailey expected Hal to stay silent, but he didn't.

"Actually, I think it was three? Four years ago? When Alastair Smith played for the Gray City team, there was an eclipse—the nocturnal Animae players had their best advantage, and ended up clinching the game."

"I didn't know you were such an expert," Phi said. Bailey could have sworn he saw Hal blush. Tori, however, was still unimpressed.

"You couldn't convince me to give a badger's behind about Scavage," she said. "Give me a *real* adventure any day."

As if Tori had just summoned an adventure out of the sky, the rigimotive lurched to a shuddering halt. The force of the stop threw everyone forward in his or her seat, and caused more than a few students to tumble into the aisles. Everywhere was the clatter of paws and claws, the lashing of tails and outraged cawing of various birds.

Hal had been thrown on the floor between the cars, legs splayed inside the students' car, leaning back against the door of the teacher's car. The door was flung suddenly open, causing Hal to fall backward, hitting his head on the delicate blue shoes of Ms. Sucrette.

"Quindley!" she shrieked, as if Hal had purposefully fallen on her foot.

Tremelo stood at Sucrette's side, holding her elbow.

"Everyone all right?" he asked, and was answered by several groans and a bark. "Good," he said cheerily. Sucrette sniffed.

Bailey got up and helped Hal to his feet. At the same time the conductor, a short man with a thin gray mustache, came barreling down the aisle of the rigimotive car toward them. He wore a carefully starched blue uniform with almost comical spangles of gold trim. A tittering monkey sat on his gold-fringed shoulder.

"Out of the way," the conductor snapped. He opened the

metal door of a box set into the wall of the car and pulled out an earpiece. The monkey on his shoulder hopped up and down excitedly as a loudspeaker crackled on.

"Attention, passengers. We have been halted due to a tear in the dirigible. We are approximately half an hour from the center of the Gray City, in an outlying neighborhood. All passengers should please wait here on the rigimotive for us to perform a routine patch. *Don't wander off.*" The conductor then forcefully shut the metal box, and fixed his sharp gaze on the assembled small crowd of students.

"All right, shoo, off with you," the conductor said, pushing Hal and Bailey out of the way.

"This is ri*dic*ulous," huffed Tori. "We'll be stuck here for at least an hour, I'm betting. Some field day!"

The other students wandered back to their seats amid groans and chatter. Hal, Phi, Tori, and Bailey remained standing in the space between the cars with Sucrette and Tremelo. It seemed to Bailey as if they'd stopped in the middle of a wasteland. Though they were inside the limits of the Gray City, they were nowhere near the glittering central square or the opera house. The rigimotive tracks ran along a narrow street that was littered with garbage. The windows of the buildings around them were either broken or shuttered against what light the street offered. Everything was awash in dusty smog. A huddle of children sat on wooden produce boxes and eyed the bright red rigimotive warily.

"Where are we, exactly?" asked Ms. Sucrette.

"Gribber Street," Tremelo answered gruffly, while lighting a pipe. Ms. Sucrette waved the first wisp of smoke away from her face. "I knew a very talented young contortionist in Gribber Street once," Tremelo continued to muse, exhaling. Then he nodded to Sucrette and the two returned to the teachers' car, trailing a plume of myrgwood smoke behind them.

The four students stood facing the steps down from the rigimotive car.

"Well, you asked for an adventure," Hal said bravely to Tori, puffing out his chest. "Seems to me one's just appeared."

Hal stepped down onto the crumbly pavement of Gribber Street and turned, offering his hand to Tori. Phi giggled.

Tori swatted Hal's hand away. "Oh, why not," she said as she stepped down.

"Do you think we ought to stop them?" Bailey asked Phi.

She merely smiled and shrugged, following Hal and Tori into the street. Bailey smiled too, impressed that Hal was leading the charge to break the rules. They quickly crossed Gribber Street and rounded a corner, hoping no teachers would spot them sneaking off. Thankfully, no one followed and they found themselves on another shambling street, which bent and curved around boarding houses and cramped shops.

"Look!" cried Phi. She was pointing not at the dingy street but at the sky. Bailey peered in that direction and saw a strange white bird fluttering down to the ground. It seemed too angular to be a real bird, and its movements were too precise. It landed on top of a swinging iron sign advertising a tax collector's office, emitted a tinny squawk, and then . . . it exploded. Or at least, that's what Bailey thought had happened at first. The bird unfurled with a pop, its many angles unfolding and unfolding until what had been a very small creature was now a large, flat poster, with the face of a beautiful woman—but stern and fierce—and the words *We will be FREE, or we will be NOTHING.*

"What is it?" asked Bailey.

"Dominae stuff," Hal said. "Has to be." He wrinkled his forehead. "Free from what?"

"From Parliament—that's what my mom's letters say, anyway," said Tori. "People say things are no better than when the Jackal ruled."

"And who's this?" Phi asked, pointing to the woman with purple eyes.

"Viviana Melore. She looks like an actress, doesn't she?" Tori said, looking at the woman with narrowed eyes. "My mom says there's something funny about the way she keeps her Animas a secret."

Just then, a small black snake—one of the several that Tori always seemed to have near her—slithered out of her beaded bag and swiftly disappeared into an alley. Bailey heard the frightened squeak of a rodent, and knew that the snake had found something it wanted as a snack.

"Hey!" Tori shouted, dashing after it into the alley. The others followed. As they turned the corner, Bailey saw posters and pamphlets were littered everywhere. On the walls on either side of them were all sorts of painted slogans, written over the layers of old, peeling campaign posters. Some, like the poster that the tiny bird had become, had images of people's faces printed on them, and some were more mysterious, printed only with slogans that sounded like nursery rhymes—The rat's cradle is able and rocks tonight.

"That's all conspiracy stuff," Tori said, holding out her arm for the wandering snake, which had emerged from behind a precarious pile of boxes. It wound itself around Tori's outstretched wrist. "All these old political movements were forced underground when the Jackal took power. You used to see his face everywhere, like he was watching you."

It was a better lesson than anything Bailey had heard in Mr. Nillow's History class. Bailey wondered how far away from this seedy street Tori had actually lived, and if the entire city looked this way.

A painting crudely splattered on a nearby wall caught his attention.

"Hey, Tori, what's this one?" he asked, crossing the alley. He pointed to what looked like a muscular cat. The white paint had faded with age, but it still stood out brightly against the bricks.

"Oh, that. I don't know," Tori admitted. "I used to see it all over the place when I was little."

A filthy, dust-covered rat scuttled out into the alley in front of them. Bailey jumped back in surprise as a man followed the rat out from behind a pile of boxes. He was missing most of his teeth, and he had stringy white hair that had gone so long without a wash that it looked yellow.

"Fairmount kiddies!" he cried with something like glee. "Of the fair mountain!"

Before they could think to run back to the train, the old coot lunged for Hal, and grabbed the strap of his rucksack.

"Hey!" Hal cried out, trying to shake him off.

But Tori's snake was quicker. It slithered up the man's leg and wrapped itself around the old man's wrist. The man screeched, dropped the bag, along with the hissing snake, and backed away quickly into the shadows from which he'd emerged.

Tori was standing, face pale and concentrated, breathing quickly. Then, aware that the other three students were looking at her with amazement, she dropped her arm, adjusted her shirt, and picked up her snake, which had slithered dutifully back to her.

"W-wow. Thanks," Hal said sheepishly.

"That was something else," Phi said.

Bailey could do nothing but stare. The snake had reacted to Tori's instincts as quickly as Tori herself had. He couldn't help but feel jealous.

"C'mon," Tori said, trying to sound nonchalant. "Let's go before that heap of junk leaves without us."

The lobby of the opera house was like nothing Bailey had ever seen. Its grandeur made Fairmount's most beautiful buildings look like tinkerer's workshops. The lobby alone had a ceiling three stories tall, and all painted with famous scenes from Aldermere lore. Tucked inside lamplit archways at different points of the room were glass cases that held ancient books and artifacts. Because of the delay on the rigimotive, the group had arrived forty-five minutes late for the performance, and would have to wait outside the auditorium and enter during intermission. No one seemed to mind too much. The students broke off into small groups and gawked at the painted ceiling. Bailey noticed that their numbers seemed to have shrunk—all of the students were accounted for, but he could swear that a teacher or two had taken advantage of the rigimotive stop to do some exploring. Tremelo, he could see, was tapping his fingers nervously on his thigh, seemingly cross that they'd arrived late.

Bailey leaned his head back to get a better look at the murals on the ceiling.

Directly above him was the goddess Nature, painted in deep teals and reds. She had copper hair tinged with gold leaf. In the folds of her colorful robes stood two small children. The little boy and little girl held hands, and Nature was motioning for them to explore the world together. She had a kind face.

"She deserts them," said Phi, tucking her hair behind her ears as she looked at the mural, and then down at Bailey. She'd walked up and was standing next to him, and Bailey had been too absorbed in the painting to even notice.

"You mean, Nature?" He knew the origin myth as well as anyone. There was even a famous statue of it somewhere west of the mountains, but he'd never seen it. According to the legend, the Twins grow up taking care of each other, and one—the girl—transforms into a fox so that she can catch fish for her brother, and they work together as human and animal.

Phi nodded. "She gives birth to the Twins, but then she isn't mentioned anywhere else in the story, like she just left them on their own. I just always thought that was a funny part of it, you know? The girl Twin feels so empty as a human, like she isn't complete, and Nature's not there to help her. So she has to help herself. She has to change. I think . . ." Phi glanced at Bailey, and then away. "I think if Nature hadn't disappeared from the story, if she'd helped them, the girl could have figured out a way to be whole by herself."

"But then we wouldn't have the Animas bond," Bailey said, though it felt like a funny thing to say. He *didn't* have the Animas bond.

Phi's voice became very quiet.

"I'm not sure the bond was really what she was after. I think maybe she wanted something more."

He stared up at the next painting in the series, of the Twins after the girl's transformation: a boy and a fox, a human and his Animas, holding hand to paw as lightning tinged the painted clouds behind them. He remembered something then—one of the lines from Tremelo's riddle! *Kin rise from ashes, hand over paw.*

These must be the children, he thought. The Twins, brother and sister—but rising from the ashes was a strange image. Maybe Phi was right about Nature abandoning them to a terrible fate. Maybe they'd had to face more than just hunger.

He glanced around the lobby of the opera house for Tremelo. Had he guessed the meaning of the line as well, when he was a boy? He looked toward the ornate archway they'd entered through and saw the professor, now standing alone by the door. He watched as Tremelo looked around him—too quickly to notice Bailey's gaze—and exited silently into the street.

Bailey felt like a cold wind had blown through the opera lobby. He couldn't figure his teacher out. Tremelo insisted that he'd left his training days behind him. But surely a man who had fearlessly fought off the wolf in the woods couldn't merely be a normal tinkerer with nothing odd up his coal-dusted sleeves. And that strange riddle . . . Here, perhaps, was Bailey's chance to find out something more that would explain Tremelo's cryptic words.

Bailey looked around cautiously—none of the chaperones were watching him. Could he sneak away and follow Tremelo? After all, if he was caught, he could simply say he was with his professor—and Tremelo would have to back him, since he was sneaking away as well . . .

"Phi, I . . . I forgot to ask Tremelo something. I'll be right back," he said, feeling guilty for leaving her. She squinted her golden-brown eyes at him and opened her mouth as though to say something.

But before she could, Bailey rushed to the door, and followed Tremelo into the streets of the Gray City.

Seventeen

OUTSIDE THE OPERA HOUSE, groups of wealthy Gray City citizens passed, wearing dresses and suits covered in decorative embroidery. The images of animals were everywhere: not just in the clothing, but in stained glass windows overlooking the square and the stone shapes that menaced from the rooftops. Real animals scuttled across the cobblestones and sat in windowsills, peering at their human kin.

Bailey caught sight of Tremelo on the opposite side of the Opera Square. Quickly, Bailey followed him down a narrow side street. The brightly lit atmosphere of the square dropped away. Here, most of the buildings were shuttered, and Bailey suspected that these businesses were closed because of the riots. Tremelo was leading him closer to the area of the city that was now the most dangerous.

After they'd walked for several blocks, Tremelo disappeared around a corner, and Bailey hurried to catch up. As he turned the same corner, he saw that Tremelo had stopped. Bailey ducked into a darkened doorway. The professor stood in front of a low wooden entrance to a sunken basement storefront. A small plaque was nailed next to the door with a name painted on it: the white tiger. The hairs on Bailey's arms lifted.

Tremelo knocked—six times, in quick but precise succession—and the door swung inward to admit him. Bailey hung back. The basement storefront was nondescript, but Bailey heard loud shouts and even some singing from inside.

The air in the city had turned decidedly colder. Bailey shivered inside his Fairmount blazer. What was he doing? He couldn't just burst in and confront the professor. He decided to wait until Tremelo had gone and then enter the building after him—though he could be waiting on the street for a long time, and he couldn't risk missing the rigimotive back to Fairmount.

Thankfully, he only had to wait about twenty minutes for the door to open and the teacher to reappear. Bailey slunk back into the shadows of the doorway as Tremelo passed him. Once the professor had disappeared at the end of the street, Bailey took off his Fairmount blazer and turned it inside out, so the insignia was hidden against his chest. He spit into both his palms, and mussed up his hay-colored hair. Though he still didn't think he'd pass as a Gray City native, he didn't want to look like a wide-eyed student, fresh off the rigimotive. Unfortunately, the Fairmount blazers were lined with rather loud blue and gold stripes. There was nothing he could do about that.

He approached the door and knocked six times. Almost instantly, it creaked open, and two roughly wrinkled faces peered out at him. One belonged to a very old woman, and the other belonged to the tortoise on her shoulder who was munching very slowly on a withered piece of lettuce. Neither one took their eyes off of Bailey.

"How old are you?" she croaked.

Bailey squared his shoulders and tried to sound tough.

"Old enough," he said.

The old watchwoman shrugged, as if reluctantly admitting that Bailey *had* knocked six times after all, and let Bailey pass before settling back onto her stool and sighing, presumably with the notion to think up a more secret Secret Knock.

At first, Bailey could hardly see a thing. The room was filled with smoke that curled up and over the low rafters. Hunched figures sat in groups around overturned barrels and wobbly wooden tables. A long, tall bar ran the length of one half of the room, and Bailey could barely make out his own reflection through the grime that covered the tilted mirror on the wall behind it. No lamps were lit in this place—the only light wafted in through the bottle-glass windows on either end, which were small and dirty and blocked by whispering patrons.

Had he crossed half the city just to chase Tremelo to a pub?

He approached the bar, where a heavyset man in a long wool cap was watching him with an amused smirk.

"What's your pleasure?" the man asked. His cheeks were the blotted color of a crushed peach.

"I'm looking for someone," Bailey said. "I saw him come in, not too long ago—Mr. Loren?"

"Tremelo, you mean? Just missed him," replied the bartender.

Bailey tried to look disappointed. "Interest you in some rootwort rum? Never too young to get started." The bartender winked.

Bailey looked around for a menu, or even some bottles to indicate what might be on offer in a place like this, but saw nothing except several pairs of suspicious eyes pointed in his direction. He named the first drink he could think of.

"Do you have sap milk?" It was a long shot, a frothy dessert drink that his dad used to bring back from trips to the larger markets in the Lowlands, and which his mom only allowed him to drink a few sips of at a time. The bartender laughed, and fiddled below the bar. He then brought up a full mug, brimming over with the stuff from a low tap.

Bailey took a sip. It was warm and flat, but not too bad. Bailey reached inside his jacket to find a snailback to pay for the drink, and remembered that he still had Tremelo's pendant in his pocket. The metal clanked against the coins.

The bartender held up his hand.

"On the house," he said. He poured himself a mug full of a dark amber liquid and settled his meaty arms on the bar in front of Bailey. A rather fat mole stumbled out from a shadow at the end of the bar and settled at the bartender's right elbow.

"What's a little chap like you doing looking for Tremelo in here?"

"He's an old friend," Bailey said. "Um, of the family's." Several patrons along the bar had stopped their chatting and were craning their necks to take a closer look at him. They were mostly men, dressed in working clothes that had seen too much wear. A couple of toothless older women smiled at him from one table over their pints of dark, cloudy beer. "I have a couple of questions for him, that's all."

"Huh, we all do, that's for sure!" rang a voice from the end of the bar.

Several of the older, grungier-looking patrons of the bar laughed—or grumbled; Bailey found it hard to tell which.

"I, for one, would like to know how to fly!" a very inebriated woman in a plaid jacket cried out, lifting her mug of beer above her head, where it sloshed on the older woman next to her. The bartender laughed.

"He doesn't do work on the Animas bond anymore, Delilah." The bartender shook his head and sighed. "Not since the Loon was—you know."

"The Loon?" Bailey repeated. "What do you mean?"

"Surely you've heard of his father?" a man at the end of the bar asked. His white whiskers were longer on one side of his chin, as though he'd stopped shaving halfway through the job, and had never gone back to finish. He was accompanied by a satisfied-looking sheepdog, who was sitting in the next chair, nodding off. "The Loon was an Animas Rat. And he knew more about the ways of the bond than any man I ever knew."

"Any man who ever lived!" shouted the drunk woman, sloshing her beer again.

"When Melore was alive, the Loon was one of his right-hand men," explained the man with the whiskers. "He and Melore both had powerful bonds, powerful. After Melore died, the Loon was practically an outlaw. He spread this

167

prophecy, see, about a true king returning, even though Melore's kids were both as good as dead. They say the Seers themselves told 'im that it was so. And so he didn't believe in the Jackal's power one bit. He had a whole gang that believed his theories too. The RATS."

"Cheers to the RATS!" shouted the drunk woman.

"Cheers, indeed," said the man, raising his glass. He looked wistfully above Bailey's head. "Followed him blind, we—I mean, *they*—did, spreading bits of the prophecy around to the people, so's they didn't give up hope." Bailey smiled, hearing the man's slip of the tongue. He wasn't sure why, but something about these people and their loyalty to the old king warmed him.

"And your Tremelo, he was raised in the middle of all that," the bartender interjected. "Some think the Loon really did go loony after Melore was assassinated, and that his prophecies about a true king were bunk. But prophecies and conspiracies or not, one thing I know for sure is that that man had the strongest Animas bonds I have ever seen—except for his son."

"*How* strong?" Bailey said, curiously.

"Well," the bartender said, lowering his voice. It was clear that many of the men at this bar were natural storytellers. They all leaned in to hear what the bartender would say. "Delilah over there was joking about flying, but she isn't half wrong—Tremelo grew up learning just about all there was to know of the Animas bond. Its origins. Its tricky nature. How it"—here he made a swooshing, circular movement with his large hands—"flows around everything. Like a . . .

a . . . current! A current, that's what he told me once. Get a little rootwort in him, he'd tell you all kinds of things like that. But when the Jackal's men finally came for the Loon, he gave it all up. Didn't want them coming for him too, I expect. Cut off all ties, 'cept for a myrgwood purchase here 'n' there."

He took a sip out of his mug and continued. "It's a real pity, though. He had a talent. He was taken on at Fairmount when he was twenty years old, and practically a baby himself. He could teach an Animas Sparrow to fly up to the rafters, he could. I seen him make an Animas Cat grow claws instead of nails. Dangerous stuff, powerful stuff. But then old Loony died—ten, eleven years ago—and Tremelo swore it off. Stuck to tinkering. There's some here who think he went mad. 'Course, so many years under the Loon's shadow, I guess anyone might snap. Hard to know these days what side he's on . . ."

Bailey tried to take in everything that was being said. The myrgwood-smoking tinkerer, Tremelo, who was able to make an Animas Sparrow fly, but would only impart a riddle that even *he* didn't quite believe in.

"He told me something once," Bailey said. "A riddle. Maybe you can tell me what it means." He concentrated, trying to remember all the words. *"Trees may bear seeds but no fruit, kin rise from ashes, hand over paw. When locusts turn men from treachery, the sun calls to the loon."* When he'd finished, the bar patrons were staring at him like they'd just seen a dog do a backflip. The bartender was scratching his head, his wool cap balled up in his fist. His hair underneath was a surprising tuft of red.

"Don't sound like much to me, a song I maybe heard once, but I don't know. Though that middle bit—there's something not quite right about it, but it's familiar."

"What do you mean?" asked Bailey, gripping the underside of the bar.

"The bit about locusts and treachery," the bartender said. Several grunts of affirmation echoed down the bar. The bartender went on: "The old king himself said something like that, Nature preserve 'is memory. Was part of Melore's last address, at the Progress Fair, uttered even as the Jackal's men were storming the fairgrounds to kill 'im. I was there, that day, hardly more than a schoolkid. He knew the Jackal's men was coming, and he said that treachery turns men into locusts, but we weren't to forget him . . . Brave until the very last, he were." He brought his rumpled hat to his heart, and many of his listeners mimicked this movement.

An image flitted across Bailey's mind, of the kind-looking man in the top hat and fur-like embroidered coat, holding a pair of scissors: the blurry photograph in Ms. Shonfield's office, his very first day at Fairmount. Bailey nodded.

"They don't teach you much 'bout him in schools these days, oh, no," the scruffy man at the end of the bar blurted out. "The Jackal nearly wrote 'im out of the history books! Just like he did the Velyn, and the—"

"The Velyn?" Bailey interrupted. "Like in the stories?"

"Oh, yes," the man said, scratching his white beard. "They were the Loon's favorite subject, you might say! He studied 'em—even spent a few years living among 'em, when Tremelo were growing up. Most people think the Velyn were some sort of lawless troupe, living only in fairy tales—but they were real folk." The man leaned closer to Bailey. "Tell you something not everyone knows. The Loon's prophecy about a true king? He felt the Velyn would be a big part of that. And the Jackal had them all killed for it, them *and* their kin—only a couple o' years before he went after the Loon too."

The bartender crossed his arms and nodded in solidarity.

"They were amazing people, the Velyn," the man continued. "Lived nose to nose with their kin, and knew all sorts of healing arts. Closest bonds you've ever seen—that's why so many of the stories of 'em are about them being werewolves and shape-shifters. Not far from the truth, they could literally see, clear as day, what their kin was seeing, like they was living in their kins' bodies, and their kin was living in them. The Loon spent years studying their methods—even Melore was interested. Probably why they were an important part of his prophecies, and why the Jackal had 'em all wiped out. 'Cause they was smarter than him. Then he goes and tries to cover his dirt by claiming they were all no-goods. It was a terrible thing. Terrible long years, when the Jackal was in power. Can't even think about what the poor blighter went through who told the prophecy to the Jackal in the first place. Tortured it right out of 'im, the Jackal did."

His sheepdog emitted a low woof of sorrow.

"Go on," Bailey blurted out. He didn't want any of them to stop talking. He wanted to know everything there was to know about the Loon and the man in the hat, King Melore.

"Then of course there's Melore's daughter. Viviana!" added the bartender. At the mention of Viviana's name, a hush fell on the dingy bar.

"Listen to me, boy, and take what you hear back to Fairmount with you—no talk of such things there on your lofty mountain, I'd wager."

Bailey gulped. So they had known the whole time? The stripes probably hadn't helped. But he settled himself on his stool, eager to hear the whole story.

"King Melore had two children—Trent and Viviana. When he was murdered, twenty-seven years ago, the children were locked up in the palace as the Jackal's soldiers attacked."

Down the bar, Delilah muttered, "Terrible, terrible."

"Everyone thought that the little ones were killed. Trent, he was only a little bug. Didn't stand a chance. But Viviana, she was a little older, a little craftier. She made it out of the palace somehow, but she was taken up by some real nasties. No one really knows where she'd been since that awful night. Some say she was a slave all those years she was lost, some say she became the leader of an outlaw gang in the Dust Plains."

"But she's back now," the man with the sheepdog chimed in. "And she wants her father's throne for herself. 'We will be free, or we will be nothing.' Bunch of dreadful tripe." Bailey shuddered at the memory of the fierce-eyed woman on the poster he'd seen only hours before.

"She's the leader of the Dominae? But isn't that what you want?" Bailey asked. "I mean, if Melore was the king, then his daughter is—"

"Everything her father wasn't!" the bartender said loudly, and brought his fist down on the bar. Bailey jumped. "Cruel and self-serving. An embarrassment and blot on the family's name!" The man with the sheepdog nodded emphatically, his eyes closed in sadness. "She blames the Jackal for *this*, the Parliament for *that*—and she talks about restoring progress the likes her father would be proud of, but that's a thin story. Melore was a good king because he believed in the goodness of the Animas bond, but Viviana wants to smash it to bits and call *that* progress instead. She says it's all in the name of good work and invention, but it's about twisting the bond to 'er own means. 'Free' of Parliament, she says, but what she really means is free of the bond—so we can rule over animals instead of learnin' from them. We've seen her factory—we've seen her set animals against each other at the drop of a hat."

"What about the other one?" Bailey asked. "Trent?"

The bartender shook his head.

"Dead." He brought his hat to his heart once more for the dead prince.

Bailey took a deep breath. His mind was spinning.

Behind him, the door to the bar screeched open, and both Bailey and the bartender looked up as a man in a familiar overcoat entered. Herbs and the heads of wild flowers poked out of the tops of bulging pockets, and atop the coat-wearer's shoulders was draped a snoring badger.

It was Roger, Taylor's and Hal's uncle. Bailey turned his face away quickly as Roger passed by to join a group of loud young people in the back of the room.

"Sorry, I . . . uh . . . I have to go," Bailey said, slipping down from the stool and trying to attract as little attention as possible.

Just before he reached the door, he looked back at the bar, where the man in the wool stocking cap stood watching.

"You be careful, boy," he said as Bailey slipped out the door and onto the street, where the sounds of arguing and laughter were immediately swallowed up by the sound of hooves, wings, and working men.

He stood still for a moment on the street, but his mind was running as though a Scavage opponent, a particularly tricky one to catch, was just within marking distance. He realized that in his haste, he'd forgotten to ask about the name of the bar: The White Tiger. But he'd already learned so much.

Tremelo, the son of a man who'd been close to a tragic king. Old words, spoken by King Melore, in Tremelo's riddle. The Velyn, a tribe of people wiped from the mountains and the history books . . . He wasn't sure what all of these things had to do with the Dominae or the shadowy people in the woods, but his curiosity had grown into an undeniable pull: he had to find out what was going on in the Fairmount woods, and he would need Tremelo's help.

Eighteen

GWEN FOLLOWED THE TWO Dominae members down a steep hill toward the Gudgeons, a neighborhood she was all too familiar with—her days as a pickpocket had taken her through these dark streets, and she knew to keep her head low and her steps quick. Her fear beat inside her like a tightly made drum. She pulled the hood of her cloak low over her forehead. She was a spy now, on a mission that the Elder hadn't approved.

The narrow street she'd come down opened to a small, dingy square where groups of men and women waited outside of a run-down theater. The lamps that lit the marquee were dark. Gwen placed her hand on the gritty brick of the building next to her, readying herself to approach. This was the meeting place.

"Excuse me," said an angry-sounding woman.

Gwen's mind seemed to drain of all sensible thought—what would she say? The woman stared at her; she was blond, her hair cut into a bob. Under her trim coat she wore a bright yellow dress.

"Yes?" asked Gwen. Her heart fluttered inside her like

a nervous bird.

"You're in my way," said the woman in a high-pitched voice.

"Oh . . . sorry," said Gwen, as she stepped aside to let the woman descend into the square.

A chirping bluebird flew onto the woman's shoulder and began to sing merrily. The woman sighed, reached up, and smacked the bluebird away. Gwen recoiled.

"Enough with you," Gwen heard the woman say. The bluebird, stunned, hopped away behind a waste bin.

Gwen looked up and saw a very large bird sitting on the corner of the roof above them, watching the woman in yellow as she walked toward the theater. Gwen couldn't tell what it was—but it was no bluebird.

Slowly, Gwen followed the woman into the square. For the first time, Gwen noticed how varied the company really was—these were not just backstreet paupers. Gwen was shocked to see a woman in a fine wool skirt who held the hand of a young boy. Gwen looked around at the crowd—a few other children seemed to have been dragged along with their parents. She was relieved she wouldn't stick out for her age, but she worried too what was in store for minds as young as hers inside that theater.

As the woman in yellow approached, people stepped aside as if she were royalty. The woman smiled kindly and nodded as she passed. The crowd pushed in after her.

Inside, the theater was dilapidated. Many of the original folding seats had been torn away, so most people stood shuffling amid the rows of chairs that had been left behind.

Gwen settled close to the entrance. From there she could see that there had once been a stately balcony overlooking the auditorium, but the floor of it had been removed, leaving a scar in the bricks that circled the space. A portable crank box had been set up next to the stage, powering a set of footlights that shone behind tin sconces. A young boy was stationed by it, charged with the task of cranking the handle if the lights should begin to sputter. The rest of the space was lit by candles that cast a sinister glow on the room. An enormous flag was draped across the back of the stage: red, with a giant image of a hand squeezing a bird claw whose talons reached up like a branch. Gwen felt the violence of the image in her gut—the hand was cruel and controlling, restraining the bird's foot. A looping scroll drawn underneath the image was printed with the words *FREE—or NOTHING!*

A burst of applause announced the arrival onstage of the woman in yellow. On the shoulders of her dress was embroidered a pair of bluebirds that matched her flashing blue eyes. The woman tucked her blond hair behind her ear and gestured for the crowd to quiet down.

"Dominae of the Gray City!" she said in a kind, singsong voice. "Today is a great day—our armies in the Dark Woods are gathering strength, and our movement is growing," she said. "Our leader has gained allies not only in the forests, but in the skies as well. And here, in the Gray City, we are prepared to send our message to Parliament. The citizens are poor, hungry, and *angry*—and they blame Parliament, as they should. They know they deserve better! And our leader, Viviana, will bring about true progress and fullfill the potential that Parliament has squandered. Let me demonstrate how."

The woman lifted something in her right hand—from where Gwen sat, it looked like a switch. As she pressed a button, a cacophony of noise crashed through the hall. Giant black birds had appeared in each of the archways above the main hall. Their beaks were all open, and out of them poured a single human voice: *"My human brethren, we will be free—or we will be nothing!"* Gwen held her hands over her ears, as did many of the other onlookers who'd been taken by surprise. Each of the birds, Gwen could see, represented a different species and were crafted out of fine burnished metal with black enamel. They unfurled their wings, which were as intricate as any living specimen's, and turned to face the stage as their leader entered. The crowd applauded.

Gwen gasped—Viviana was more stunning than her posters had shown. She wore a tailored black suit with a calf-length skirt, which was embroidered from top to bottom in purple, gold, and silver thread. It was impossible to tell from the embroidery what Animas she was, though Gwen knew from the Elder that Viviana was Animas Pig. The embroidered images of two birds of prey wrapped around Viviana's slender waist, their upturned claws imitating the boning of a corset. Her shoulders were decorated with stags, their hooves stomping the birds below. Her dark hair hung down in perfectly crafted waves, and her lips were a deep berry-red.

"Thank you, Joan," she said to the woman in yellow.

Then she turned to address her audience. "You have been promised a demonstration. Progress is one thing—but how we achieve it is quite another. Citizens, let's not dissolve into talk of political woes; instead, see for yourself what we, the Dominae, can accomplish!"

Joan exited behind a curtain along with four men who'd been waiting onstage. They returned with a cage covered with a long canvas tarp, which they wheeled to the front of the stage. The cage was immense—much taller than the petite Joan. A woman in a plain wool suit was ushered onstage. She had broad shoulders and a wide chest, and her large head hung down with a slight hunch.

"Edith," Viviana said, shaking the woman's hand. Behind them, the stagehands pulled the canvas covering off of the cage and let it fall to the floor. Inside paced two young bears. As the audience watched, one bear nuzzled its face into the other's neck.

"Edith, you were raised Animas Bear, correct?" asked Viviana.

"Yes," Edith said.

"And there was a time in your life when you would feel *pain* if your kin was hurt, or in danger?"

Edith nodded. "Just like anyone else," she said.

Viviana placed a reassuring hand on Edith's back and addressed the waiting crowd.

"Yes, just like anyone else—but with Dominance, you can do away with this dependence. Your kin can be hurt or injured, and *you* will not have to feel their suffering."

She snapped her fingers, and a stagehand brought a swift

blow of a whip down on the back of one of the bears. It yowled with pain and tried to burrow itself into the corner of the cage. Gasps of disbelief, followed by a smattering of applause, emerged from the audience. Astoundingly, Edith hadn't moved a muscle. In fact, she seemed to be smiling. In the cage next to her, her kin whimpered.

"Edith has just demonstrated one of the first lessons of Dominance," Viviana announced. "Our bond with common beasts only weakens us! With practice and focus, a human can sever the bond with their kin, and remain strong even when they are in pain."

Gwen shook with rage while the audience around her seemed impressed. The Elder had taught her that the Animas bond made her stronger, not weaker. How could it be considered weakness to care for and receive the help of another creature?

Viviana wasn't finished yet with Edith. She waved a hand to quiet down the crowd, and spoke again.

"Not only has this woman severed her dependence on her kin, but she is learning to use Dominance for her own ends—to control her kin and make them work *for* her."

Viviana stepped to the side and allowed the grave-faced Edith to stand center stage. Behind her, the two bears cuddled together in the corner as Edith shut her eyes and clenched her fists. The bears then sparked to life on all fours, pacing around the cage and growling at each other. They bared their teeth and began to claw at each other. They hadn't been fighting before—it was clear to Gwen that the woman Edith was controlling them and showing the audience how they could be made to hurt each other.

"Through Dominance, Edith can affect her kin's emotions and urges," said Viviana, gesturing to the bears. "She can create discord where none existed, effectively turning her own kin into weapons."

Gwen looked away; it was too horrifying. One man next to her got dizzy and leaned against the wall. Several people covered their eyes. A few groans of pain could be heard from other Animae Bear in the audience. She heard the sound of someone retching.

But to Gwen's surprise, the woman on stage was silent and unmoving. Her eyes, now open, were focused straight ahead. Finally, she breathed out in an exhausted huff, and the bears slowly backed away from each other. Viviana stepped forward clapping, and the audience burst into applause. The mood among the crowd sickened Gwen. The woman may have shown how she could control her own pain and emotions—and that she could force her kin to do her bidding—but at what cost? Her kin were now bloodied, hurt, and confused.

"Thank you, Edith," Viviana said warmly, and then kissed the woman on both cheeks. Edith left the stage, and Gwen could see her hands were shaking. Dominance, it seemed, was not easy work.

"My brothers and sisters, we have many soldiers-in-training like Edith!" Viviana crowed. "The number of true Dominae followers grows every day. And we can be even more powerful, even *more* unstoppable." She turned to her stagehands who carefully opened the door of the bears' cage.

The bears whimpered and backed away from the open door.

"Dominance over one's own kin is easily achievable," she began. The footlights at her feet cast a glow upward, shadowing her face. "But a true Dominae has complete control—not only over his own kin, but over any animal in Nature. Let me show you . . ."

She gestured to the two bears as they stumbled to their feet and walked out of the cage. There was no more fear in their deep black eyes. There was *nothing*. They moved forward until they stood just behind Viviana, and in one movement, they both reared up on their hind legs. Like perfect soldiers, they stood at Viviana's side and stared forward without expression. Whispers of awe spread throughout the room.

"This is the power of the Dominae—power offered to all of you!" Viviana shouted. "In battle, and in our factories, the Dominae will have the upper hand because we can exert our control over *any* kin. Why? Because *we* come before the animals. We are better, smarter, and deserve to control them! If we are not first, we are nothing!"

Cheers erupted from the floor of the theater. Gwen clenched her fists—it was no wonder these people loved Viviana, despite her black heart. Using graciousness and beauty to hide her own evil, this woman played on her audience's desire for power with her "demonstrations" and eloquent speeches. Gwen felt herself shaking with rage. Sweat dripped down her forehead from her concealed red hair.

The applause was interrupted by a piercing, angry screech from above, and everyone craned his or her neck to see what had made the noise.

To Gwen's horror, she saw that it was Grimsen, the Elder's life-bonded owl, in the company of two smaller barn owls. They had entered through a high broken window in the back of the theater. The Elder must have known all along that she'd followed the traitorous Parliament members here. He would have sent Grimsen to make sure she was safe. The two smaller owls circled quickly overhead, beating their wings frantically against the archways and chandeliers. Grimsen flew after them, trying to nip at their feathers and corral them toward the broken window. Then Gwen realized that she had summoned the two smaller ones here. Her anger and fear had pulled them to her like a beacon on a dark sea. They only wanted to help. Grimsen must have flown in after them, to try to turn them away before they caused Gwen to be discovered.

Frantically, Gwen tried to focus. *Turn around, turn around! Go, be safe,* she tried to warn the birds. But she couldn't concentrate. It was her emotional state, and not her desires, that the owls were responding to. She looked toward the door—maybe she could make a run for it, but she'd surely be followed, or worse.

"I know that bird." Viviana's voice was cold, and it hit Gwen's ears like a cascade of icy water. Viviana stood at the edge of the stage and pointed at Grimsen.

"I *know* that *bird*." Her voice rose to a shrill pitch as she screamed. A man behind Viviana on the stage pulled out a bow and arrow, steadied his aim, and shot. The metal arrow cut through the air and flashed in the light of the footlamps. Gwen's breath caught in her throat as the owl tried to take flight—but it was too late.

The arrow pierced Grimsen through the heart.

Grimsen fell quickly, and a heavy flash of feathers and metal landed in the crowd's midst.

All was silent except for a terrified, wounded scream that echoed from the back of the room. A fiery pain ripped through Gwen's heart, and it was only then she realized it was her own voice, her own scream. She was doubled over with nausea and pain, and now everyone's eyes were turned toward her. She stumbled back against a set of stacked wooden crates but slipped, and the crates came crashing down between the door and the Dominae.

"Stop her!" Joan shouted.

The crowd began to move toward Gwen. A snake slithered quickly across the floor to her feet, poised to strike. She was frozen with fear.

Suddenly, a hand was on her arm. She nearly screamed again, until she heard a voice whisper in her ear:

"Go, girl, run. Tell the Elder the rats are here. Come to The White Tiger, tell him!" Gwen reeled backward, barely glancing at the man with dark skin and green eyes. She threw herself over the fallen crates and through the theater door. She ran full tilt across the square. Shouts, barks, and even a roar echoed from the entrance as she scrambled to reach the narrow alley she'd come from. As she turned the corner, she heard another voice echoing off the walls of stone that towered over her.

"Go, then!" Viviana yelled from the center of the square. "Run and tell that demented old man what you've seen—tell him how much hope he has left!"

Viviana's voice seemed to become even louder as Gwen ran, and the echoes even more clear. Only once did Gwen look up, and the sight of three metal birds caused her to scream again. They landed on a roof just above, watching her.

"Go, then; go, then; go, then," they shouted. *"Tell him how much hope he has left, how much hope, how much hope . . ."*

The echoes finally stopped, drowned out in the street noise as Gwen drew closer to the city center. She could barely see where she was going through the tears that fell from her eyes. She kept running, petrified. She had to find the Elder. Any Animas Owl would have experienced an intense pain, as she had, from Grimsen's death—but the Elder would have felt the blow as if the arrow had hit his own chest.

As she turned a corner near the opera house, she collided with a boy and fell to the cobblestone street. He was short, sandy-haired, and wearing an odd jacket with blue and gold stripes. Gwen scrambled to get up, but her cloak had twisted around her. The boy offered her his hand.

"Are you all right?"

She couldn't even find the voice to answer. No, she thought. Nothing is all right. Gwen fought back new tears as she scrambled to her feet and ran. She felt his eyes on her as she ran up the alley, and disappeared into the winding streets of the city.

Nineteen

GWEN'S LUNGS BURNED AS she ran up the narrow staircases to the Elder's tower. Her legs felt as though they would collapse underneath her, but she couldn't stop until she reached him. Through the windows, she saw dozens of owls swooping, mournful and low. Grimsen had been nearly as old as the Elder himself— once life-bonded, both human and animal could live beyond their normal years. To see his life cut down so callously made Gwen's heart break, and the owls outside shared in her sorrow.

Flickering candlelight glowed under the Elder's door. Gwen stopped, and leaned her head on the smooth wood to catch her breath before knocking. She entered in silence.

The Elder sat at his desk, which was piled high with books and maps. His shoulders were hunched underneath his tattered owl-patterned cloak, which had once looked so fine. His interlaced fingers lay heavily in his lap. He did not look up at her.

"I'm sorry," she said. She didn't dare move beyond the door. "I should never have gone. If I hadn't . . ."

The Elder shook his head and reached out a hand to her.

"You did what you thought you had to do. My brave girl. Grimsen's death isn't your fault. "

Gwen rushed forward, kneeling to grasp his hand. He held it tightly, keeping his eyes closed.

"Are *you* all right?" he asked kindly. Gwen shook her head and squeezed her eyes shut, afraid that she would burst into tears.

"You must tell me everything," he said.

Gwen told him about the fearsome mechanical birds, the two conspiring Parliament members, and the terrifying demonstration with the bears. As Gwen described the fight, the Elder's free hand became a fist of anger.

"The Animas bond, when strong, makes us stronger," he said, just as he had so many times over their years together. "Melore unified Aldermere with this strength. His daughter will find only pain down this path. I pity her."

"And I fear her," said Gwen. "She knows who you are. She knows I was there."

For the first time that night, the Elder met Gwen's gaze. His eyes were red and his cheeks glistened where tears had fallen.

"Your fear is not misplaced," he said.

Gwen felt like her heart didn't have enough room in it for the grief she felt. She wished she could set the entire night in reverse and watch it all be undone.

"I'm so sorry," she said.

The Elder shook his head, as though hearing this from her only gave him more pain.

"It's not your place to be sorry," he said. "It was the

greed and fear of others that took Grimsen's life. Not you."

A loud knock sounded at the door. The Elder placed his hand on Gwen's shoulder, as if to protect her if necessary.

"Who is it?"

A kitchen boy's cracking teenaged voice answered with a quick word: "Sap milk."

The Elder's grip on Gwen's shoulder relaxed, and she stood up to let the boy in. In all the terror and excitement, she had almost forgotten that the hour was not so late. The Elder's nightly mug of heated sap milk was being delivered, as though nothing were wrong. As though the world hadn't turned on its edge.

The skinny boy stumbled in and set the hot mug on the Elder's desk. He hurried back out, and didn't look twice at Gwen, who was glad. She was sure that she looked frightful—with tearstained eyes, wild hair, and an unkempt, muddy cloak.

"Gwen, would you care for some . . ." the Elder said, waving his hand in the direction of the mug. "I cannot." He turned away and stared at the owls, who flew back and forth in front of the window. The moonlight made shadows of their wings against the roofs below.

"I'm not thirsty, either." She took the mug and left it in the hallway by the door, where someone would be along to collect it. When she came back into the room, she lifted her cloak off of her shoulders and something fell out of her hood. It clunked onto the floor behind her. She bent down to pick it up and saw that it was a necklace on a gold chain. The pendant was coin-like, with an embossed image of a sleeping fox on one side, and letters on the other. The letters were oddly spaced, but spelled out the name TREMELO. It must have come from the boy she'd collided with. Gwen was sorry to have taken it from him. She tucked it into the pocket of her dress, where it would be safe. She doubted she'd ever see that boy again, but if Nature ever granted it, she'd make sure that his pendant was returned safely to him. For Grimsen's sake.

Her thoughts were interrupted by a strange, gargled howl in the hallway, followed by a thump. The Elder and Gwen looked at each other with confusion. She went to the door, opened it just a crack, and peeked out.

Immediately, her hand flew to her mouth as she stifled a scream. There on the floor was a striped yellow cat, the kin of a Parliamentary clerk who worked late hours at the palace. It lay inert on its side, covered in spilled sap milk. Its face and belly were swollen and distorted. There was no doubt that the poor creature was dead.

"Let me see," said the Elder, who had gotten up and come to Gwen's side. Gwen slid back against the wall and the Elder studied the scene for only a moment before closing the door.

"Poison," he said. His face showed no emotion, only a stern and unshakable comprehension. Gwen felt like she was going to be sick. Someone had tried to kill the Elder—it didn't seem possible.

The Elder looked stricken.

"Parliament is full of locusts," he said. "After tonight, it's clear the Dominae's spies are willing to kill for their cause."

Then Gwen remembered one thing she hadn't told the Elder about that night.

"Who are the rats?" she asked him. "A man helped me on my way out; he said to tell you that the rats were there. What does that mean?"

The Elder's eyes widened, but he shook his head.

"The RATS? They're nothing but rabble-rousers," he said.

"They may be Melore loyalists like us, but they're also daydreamers and idealists—dedicated believers of prophecy and mere rumor. The RATS were against the Jackal, but they don't care for Parliament, either. It's unlikely they'd be any help to us."

He paced between the door and the window, his hands clasped behind his back as if he was unsure where to put them.

"This man did help me," she reassured him, "and he referenced you by name. He knows you're with Parliament but he still said to come to The White Tiger."

"It's too dangerous," he said, shaking his head.

"More dangerous than staying here?" Gwen argued. "It's not safe. You said so yourself."

The Elder was silent. He stared at the wall as if he were listening for advice from someone who was no longer there. Then he moved toward his tall wardrobe, where he retrieved his traveling bag from inside.

The sympathetic birds that had gathered up in the rafters tittered nervously.

"Then we leave at once," he said. "Before the Dominae's spies realize they've failed to poison me."

The Elder began combing through the drawers of his desk and rolling up papers to fit neatly into his pack.

"We?" asked Gwen. "You mean I can go with you this time?" She thought about those terrible days when he'd been away before, how worried she'd been about him, and how lonely.

The Elder stopped and smiled at her, a smile made all the more poignant by the streaks of tears on his tired old face.

"Of course, my child. We're both in danger, and you are now all the family I can claim in this world. Go and pack."

Twenty

BAILEY MANAGED TO RETURN to the opera house and sneak in before the end of the concert. No one said anything to him there, and as he and his classmates boarded the rigimotive to return to Fairmount, he was sure his side trip into the city had gone entirely unnoticed by anyone—anyone except Hal, Tori, and Phi.

"Where did you disappear to?" Tori asked him on the rigi, turning around in her seat to face him. She leaned over the headrest with her slim arms crossed under her chin. Phi sat with her, but she stared straight ahead—all Bailey could see of her was her dark brown curly hair. Hal sat next to Bailey and had his knee propped up on the back of the seat in front of him. He dozed with his mouth open and glasses askew.

"Nowhere," he lied. "I was at the concert. I sat in the back."

"But—" started Phi, but then she seemed to change her mind.

She didn't even turn around to face him. He sat back in his seat, trying to ignore Tori's raised eyebrow. He'd tell them what he'd done at some point—as soon as he had some time to think it over on his own. As it stood, he wanted more information about King Melore's last speech, which had made its way into Tremelo's riddle. He felt closer than ever to solving it—and more convinced than ever that the riddle wasn't the only mystery to be solved.

Between juggling homework and practice every afternoon, and pondering Tremelo's riddle most nights, Bailey had barely any time in the following days to feel nervous about his first Scavage match. But now the day was here: Fairmount versus Roanoake. He felt jittery as he suited up, excited and eager to impress his schoolmates on the field. Even so, he couldn't shake the strangeness of the previous week's events: the panicked girl he'd collided with near the opera house, or his time spent at The White Tiger. He was determined to learn more about Melore and the Velyn as soon as he got the chance—but today, Scavage was king.

The Roanoake team had arrived that morning by rigimotive, and had brought with them a menagerie of kin—deer, rabbit, hedgehogs, and more. Now, as the two teams lined up to take the field, the entire Scavage pitch was crawling with players and animals. The stands were packed with Fairmount students and teachers dressed in blue and gold, as well as a few Roanoake fans who'd traveled there, dressed in green and black stripes. Most of the spectators had binoculars with them so that they could see out over the huge Scavage field. In a special box set atop the highest stands, two Fairmount students were ready to broadcast the game on the school's radio channel. Bailey wondered if his mom and dad, home in the Lowlands, would be tuning the dial on the old kitchen radio at that very moment.

Ms. Shonfield stepped briskly onto an elevated platform in front of the stands, waving for quiet. She lifted a bullhorn up to her mouth.

"Welcome!" she said. "Warmest welcomes indeed to our friends from the Roanoake plains. We're excited you'll be joining us tonight for our Autumnal Soiree celebrating the start of a new Scavage season!" This was met with loud applause from throughout the stadium. Bailey had almost forgotten about the Autumnal Soiree. The team members were required to attend, and act as representatives of their schools. He'd been so distracted with Tremelo's riddle and his trip to The White Tiger that the party had vanished from his mind.

Shonfield finished making her announcements, and then handed the bullhorn to Coach Banter.

"Clean game, everyone!" Coach said. "No biting, scratching, mauling, or use of excrement!" Bailey heard laughter from the stands, and grinned. The players stood in a row at the edge of the field, each team in front of their own "territory." Many of the kin had already scurried onto the field. Bailey envied the fact that everyone else could sense where their kin was, and that those with the strongest bonds could learn something about the field's terrain before the game even started. But he reminded himself that he didn't need the Animas bond to do well in the game. He'd already proven that. His heart hammered as Coach Banter counted down from ten, and he and the other players crouched into a running position. Three Sneaks, three Slammers, and three Squats from each team stood at the ready.

Coach blew the whistle, and they were off. Bailey paid no attention to the other players as he barreled onto the field and into the trees except for Phi. In practice, they'd had lots of success with Phi finding their team's flag first, and leading the Slammers and Squats to it before darting off to find the opposition's. Carin flew high above them, leading them.

When they finally saw it, Bailey's heart took a jump in his chest. Their blue-and-gold striped flag was lodged in a rock face at the far end of the Scavage pitch, close to where the forest terrain gave way to the Dark Woods. They'd have to span out at the base of the rocks and climb if anyone from Roanoake got past them. Bailey left the Squats at the base of the rocks, and then ducked into the trees to find a good vantage point.

He didn't have to wait long for one of the Roanoake Sneaks to cross his path. A nervous deer stepped through the trees, followed by an athletic girl with long legs and blond hair. She didn't see him as she looked up at the flag from behind a boulder. Bailey crept closer to get in better range for the Flick, and saw a flash of blue and gold in his periphery. It was Taylor, making his way through the trees. As a Squat, he was supposed to be guarding their home flag, but he was far off course. Bailey ignored him; he had the perfect shot at the girl and readied his Flick.

Just then, an eagle flying overhead suddenly screeched and the girl turned. She took off into the trees with Taylor in pursuit. Bailey cursed under his breath. Roanoake really did have an Animas Eagle, just like he'd joked to Phi. Now he had to figure out where the Animas Eagle was, and if its kin had already spotted his position.

He decided to switch tactics and take the offensive—moving under the cover of trees and bushes, trying to stay out of sight from above. He saw a blob of green paint against a tree, and knew that someone had had a close call with a Roanoake Slammer. He was in their territory now, far away from his own team's flag.

But he wasn't the only one. Again he saw Taylor. Only a few paces away, Bailey's fellow Slammer seemed to be tracking the Roanoake Sneaks back to their home base, with Taylor in pursuit. Once Bailey was sure that there was no one watching, he caught up to him.

"What are you doing all the way out here?" he asked Taylor. "You're a Squat—you should be guarding our flag."

"What are *you* doing then?" Taylor responded. "Trying to steal the Roanoake flag yourself? That's a Sneak's job. Mind your own business, freak."

Frustrated, and not wanting to cause a fight, Bailey turned away—one of them needed to get back to Fairmount territory and help protect the flag. He dashed back across the terrain, hoping that he wasn't too late.

As he got closer to his team's flag, he saw a flash of green and black stripes at the far side of the rocks. It was the same girl from before—she'd doubled back around after leading Taylor away from his own flag. Bailey's only chance to intercept her was to ascend the steeper rock face and guard the flag from there. He looked around at the base of the rock—where were all the Squats? The other Slammers? It was clear that Roanoake might not have been tree-climbers, but they were awfully good at diversion. His teammates were nowhere to be seen, probably lured away by Roanoake Sneaks just as he and Taylor had been. The Fairmount flag was unprotected.

He tucked the Flick in his waistband and began to climb the rock. He wasn't sure if the Animas Deer had even seen him yet—if not, she'd get a surprise when she looked over the top of the rock. He'd be waiting with the Flick, if only he could get up high enough . . .

Bailey could just see the tops of the stands from his vantage point on the rock, and he heard the cheering echoing across the field. Then something grabbed his foot. He almost lost his grip, but he got ahold of the rock and looked down. A Roanoake Slammer, a broad-shouldered, curly-haired boy had followed him onto the rock, and now held firmly to his ankle.

"Gotcha," he said, grinning. "Now, Ruthie!"

The Animas Deer appeared at the top of the rock and scrambled toward the flag. The Slammer pulled hard on Bailey's ankle, trying to dislodge him from the rock.

"Get off!" Bailey grunted. The Slammer only held on tighter.

"Not a chance!"

Bailey tried to keep his left hand firmly on the rock face so that he could mark the Sneak, Ruthie, with his Flick and disqualify her from being able to capture the Fairmount flag for the win. But he couldn't hold on, even with the uniform gloves helping his grip. His hand slid from the rock, and both he and the Roanoake Slammer hit the ground with a harsh *thud*.

As Bailey and the Roanoake Slammer sat up, groaning, someone darted out from the trees at the base of the cliff. It was Phi.

"Phi, the Roanoake flag is on the far end!" Bailey said as he pointed to the other side of the field.

But Phi was hardly listening to him. Instead, she was looking adamantly into the sky, searching the blue for something Bailey couldn't see. He heard a cheer from the top of the cliff, followed by a loud, high whistle from the stands—the Fairmount flag had been captured. They had lost.

Phi walked closer to him, still scanning the sky.

"Phi, what's going on?" Bailey asked. "The game is over—what are you doing?"

"It's Carin," she said. "She has something."

Atop the cliff, Bailey could hear the Roanoake Sneak's celebratory whoops, and the grumblings of the Fairmount Squats. He stood next to Phi, who pointed up. The falcon was circling closely above them, and she sounded a screech before landing gracefully on the leather gauntlets on Phi's outstretched left arm and plucking a loose feather from her chest.

Something fell from the falcon's talons. Bailey reached out just in time to catch it before it hit the ground. The Roanoake Slammer walked over to them, gaping at Carin.

"What in Nature is that, a knife?" the Slammer said.

What it *was* was a claw—a huge one that spanned the entire length of Bailey's outstretched hand. The blunt base of the claw was rough with dried blood that looked like it had been there for a long time. But Bailey noticed that the tip of the claw ended in a menacing point.

"Wow," Bailey said.

"Ants," said the Slammer.

Phi said nothing, but her eyes widened as big as dinner plates. Bailey handed it to Phi, who held it up in the sunlight.

"It looks ancient," she whispered.

The other players began to descend the cliff and head back to the warm-up areas. The Roanoake Slammer cast one last curious look at the claw before jogging to meet his teammates.

"Should we show Coach?" Phi asked.

"Not yet," Bailey whispered, standing between Phi and the other students. He thought once more about the clean, deep wounds in the dead bear's hide, and the shadowy figures between the trees at the edge of the Dark Woods. If those men had weapons like this, if they'd been the ones to kill the bear so close to the school—as a warning, or a threat?—then the claw was too important to simply hand over to Coach Banter and his blundering bulldogs. No, it was best kept a secret until Bailey could find out more.

Thankfully, Phi nodded in agreement. Without saying another word, she tucked the claw into the waistband of her uniform. The memory of Phi's hurt look when he'd left her alone in the opera house lobby last week flitted through Bailey's mind, and he suddenly felt guilty.

"Um, Phi," Bailey began nervously. He struggled to find the words. There was so much going through his mind—about the men in the woods, the visit to The White Tiger, and now the claw. He wanted to explain why he'd left in such a hurry, yet he didn't know where to start.

"I'm sorry I lost us the game," Phi said, cutting him off. She stared off toward the stands.

"Oh," Bailey said, somewhat relieved she had changed the subject—even if the game seemed trivial now. "That wasn't your fault."

Together they walked across the terrain and out of the woods back into the bright, normal day.

After the game, Bailey, Hal, Tori, and Phi sat in the common room in the Towers with the claw between them on a circular wooden study table. A few other students read or played card games like Rabbit Flash or Rat's Nest nearby, but most of the school was off preparing for the evening party, the Autumnal Soiree. The four friends huddled close so they wouldn't be overheard.

Hal reached out and turned the claw over in his hands.

"It's definitely from something big. Not a bear, though. This looks more like it came from a big cat."

"*Are* there any big cats in this part of the kingdom? Could it be what killed the bear a few weeks ago?" Phi asked.

"Maybe," Hal said, but he sounded unconvinced. Hal moved the claw toward and then away from his eyes, trying to find the right focus through his glasses. It was then that Hal pointed out what Bailey hadn't noticed at first.

"Look at this," Hal said, skimming his finger along the claw's edge. "This has been sharpened recently, with a file or something. What if someone used this as a weapon to take down the bear?"

Bailey took the claw and ran his own finger along the inside of the claw's curve. He nearly sliced into the pad of his thumb. Hal was right; the claw was extremely sharp, and not in the way that Nature had designed.

Hal looked up at Phi. "Where did Carin *find* this thing?"

Phi was quiet for a minute. The falcon was sitting on her shoulder, preening.

"I . . . I'm not sure," she said. She closed her eyes and breathed deeply. Carin, as if mimicking her, stood very still. Phi opened her eyes and sighed with exasperation. "I don't know. I'm not that advanced. But I know she wasn't very far away. She stayed close by the school."

"What does *that* mean?" asked Hal. "A weapon like this, so close to the school?"

Bailey felt a knot tighten in his stomach.

"It means someone's out there," he said. "Someone's watching Fairmount. It could've been a warning."

"Or a threat," Hal added.

"The men you saw—" said Tori. "It's them, isn't it?"

"Maybe," Bailey said. He turned the claw over in his hands. It felt smooth and a little heavy. It was easily seven inches long, with a deadly curve at the end. Its surface was a dark gray, with pale streaks of creamish-white around the base. The men in the woods were big and savage, and when he thought about the damage they might do using

201

this as a weapon, he shuddered.

"But who are they?"

Tori gasped. "The Dominae."

Hal, Bailey, and Phi each turned to stare at her.

"Why would they be hiding out there? Isn't that all just politics?" Phi asked.

"My uncle Roger says the Dominae are out to start a war"—Hal shrugged—"but he can be a little paranoid. Anyway, aren't they more interested in stirring up trouble in the Gray?"

"That's only the half of it," Tori said. "You don't know all the rumors that are going around in the city—people are afraid. My parents told me that there's talk about the Dominae raising a secret army across the kingdom. What if *this* is where their army is gathering?"

Bailey had never seen Tori this animated about anything.

"That seems pretty extreme," he said. "Why would they care about Fairmount?"

"Why *wouldn't* they?" Tori responded. "Fairmount is where some of the greatest work of the Age of Invention took place. If *I* were looking to take over the kingdom, I'd be keeping tabs on what goes on here, for sure."

A tapping on the nearest window caused them to look up. Three bats fluttered against the window, trying to get in through an open pane at the top. The sky outside was dark.

"Ants! We should get back to Treetop." Phi stood up. Carin hopped onto the table and shuffled her wings impatiently. "The soiree's going to start soon."

"Can I keep this?" Bailey asked. He still had the claw

in his hand. It was a frightening object, especially when he thought of it being used by the Dominae. But he couldn't let go of it—not yet. "Just for now," he added.

"If you want," Phi said, looking at him curiously.

"Yikes—good luck getting any sleep with that thing under your pillow," Tori said as she grabbed Phi's elbow and half waved, half swatted them a good-bye.

Bailey and Hal arrived at the grand meeting hall just as the party was getting under way. Despite losing the Scavage game, the mood remained festive. The grand meeting hall inside the library building was decorated with blue-and-gold banners and sheaves of wheat celebrating the harvest season. The school had hired a jig band from one of the neighboring towns, and they began by playing fast and fancy reels that no one really knew how to dance to, but at least it was easy to tap one's feet.

They both immediately looked around for Tori and Phi. Hal looked sophisticated, Bailey had to admit—he was dressed in a lean black suit and vest with light gray patterns of bats' wings on the jacket shoulders and back, and a crisp purple tie. Bailey had nothing nicer to wear than his Fairmount blazer and navy dress pants, but he'd combed his hair, at least, and felt presentable. Hal had offered to lend him a cravat, but he'd politely declined.

They spotted Tori standing by the refreshment table.

"Would you two like to *not* dance with me?" Tori asked. She hadn't changed out of her school clothes—a pair of high-waisted tweed trousers under her Fairmount blazer—and was leaning against the wall of the assembly hall, arms crossed.

"You don't dance?" asked Hal.

"I *can* dance—four years of lessons, thank you—but I don't like to show off. Not in *this* crowd."

"Hmm." Hal nodded. "Yes, it's uh . . . it's good to keep certain skills up your sleeve, I guess."

The tune that was playing came to an end, and Phi wandered over to them from the dance floor, looking a little flushed. Unlike Tori, she'd dressed up in an ill-fitting skirt and blouse, and had swept her curly hair up into a bun.

"Are you still being a sourpuss?" she asked Tori.

"I'm being mys*ter*ious," said Tori. "There's a difference."

Phi looked at Bailey as she smiled, and a terrifying thought occurred to him—he should ask her to dance. The very idea made his throat close up and his palms turn clammy. Even if she said yes, what would he do then?

"Who—who were you dancing with just now?" he asked her.

"No one in particular," she said. "I don't really know how to dance at all. I just move my feet from side to side and see what happens."

Bailey made a sound somewhere between a laugh and a cough. Hal raised an eyebrow at him.

"Yeah, I'm pretty sure I'm terrible at it," Bailey said.

"You told me once you used to go to barn dances," Phi said kindly. "I bet those were fun."

Bailey stumbled to respond. A Lowland barn dance was *not* the same as standing across from Phi at a Fairmount soiree. But Bailey was saved from answering when he caught sight of Mr. Nillow, his History teacher, sampling a glass of punch at the other end of the refreshments table.

"I'll be back," he said to Phi. "Got to ask Nillow something." He could feel the eyes of all three of them on him as he walked away. He truly did have something to ask the professor—several things, in fact, that had been on his mind since his trip to The White Tiger pub—though as he turned his back on Phi, he felt a mixture of embarrassment *and* relief.

"Good evening, Mr. Nillow," he said, sidling up to the table.

"Hello, Mr. Walker. Behaving ourselves?" Nillow said, tugging at a striped waistcoat one size too small. He was a rather rotund man.

"Yes, sir. I was thinking—we haven't covered the Melorian Age of Invention in class yet, but I'd like to focus on that as a topic for my final paper. Do we have any transcripts of his speeches here in the school?"

"My Nature, no," Nillow harrumphed. A dribble of punch escaped down his chin, which he wiped away with the sleeve of his jacket. "A pity. In the seventeen years that the Jackal held this kingdom by the hoof, he decimated public records of Melore's reign. Rotten trick he pulled. The only reliable transcripts, if they exist at all, are in Parliament's archives."

Bailey, though disappointed, felt bold.

"He did the same with the Velyn, didn't he? The Jackal, I mean."

Nillow looked sidelong at him.

"Now you're on about something entirely different. You

ask some people, clearing out the Velyn was the one useful thing the Jackal did during his time in power. Ruffians, the lot of them. Savages." Nillow cleared his throat and downed another gulp of punch. "I wouldn't be much interested in a thesis on them, if that's what you're thinking, my boy. Best stick to history that matters."

Nillow turned away, clearly ruffled by Bailey's question. Bailey wondered what the RATS would have said in response—some history still mattered, to them at least. And it was beginning to matter to him as well.

When he returned to his friends, Phi had disappeared, and Hal and Tori stood side by side by the dance floor.

Tori was actually swaying a little bit—almost like she was having a good time. She smirked at him.

"You fouled that up," she said.

"Fouled what?" he asked, thinking she meant his conversation with Nillow.

"Phi wanted to dance with you," said Hal.

Bailey could feel the blood rushing to his cheeks.

"Really?"

"But you just missed her," Tori said, her smirk softening. "She said she was tired and went back to Treetop." She looked at Hal. "Do you know the Lemur Hop?" she asked him.

Hal straightened his vest and jacket. "Um . . . yes. I do," he mumbled.

"Then let's go," Tori said, grabbing his hand. Hal waved at Bailey as Tori marched him toward the dance floor.

Bailey stood alone for a minute, watching his schoolmates

have a good time. Unsure of what to do with his hands, he fumbled around in his pockets and realized that the pendant Tremelo had given him, which he was used to carrying, was not there. Another disappointment. He'd have to remember to check his room later.

Alone, Bailey left the meeting hall. The sounds of the party echoed in the atrium, and the entrance to the library portion of the building, a grand marble archway, was empty.

Bailey believed Nillow that most records of Melore's words and deeds had been scrubbed in the long years of the Jackal's reign—but he didn't want to give up hope that something, some piece of information, would join together the jagged edges of what he'd learned so far with Tremelo's strange riddle about Awakening. Bailey glanced behind him. The entire school was preoccupied with merriment. He slipped away into the darkened library.

Not entirely certain where to start, he made his way up the stairs to the history section. The autumn moon beamed through the tall glass windowpanes of the stairwell.

Just as he reached the third floor, Bailey heard a clattering sound nearby. Was someone else prowling around the library after hours? He looked down the long, open hallways. No one.

Quick footsteps echoed from below. Bailey leaned over the railing at the top of the stairs, hoping to catch a glimpse of who it was—but only saw the dark shadow of a large, ominous bird perched on the stairwell underneath him. It emitted a loud squawk and Bailey jumped back. Forgetting all about the history section, he slowly retraced his steps down to the second floor to get a closer look at the bird. But when he reached the landing, it was gone, and all was silence.

However, he did notice something else that was odd: a door ajar at the end of the hallway. Had it been closed, the wooden door would've blended seamlessly with the wall. It swung slowly on iron hinges, as though it had only been flung open moments ago. He went in.

Bailey let his eyes adjust, surveying the dark room. His foot knocked against something, and he reached down. It was a dynamo lamp—and it was warm.

Bailey spun the crank and the lamp sputtered to life. He seemed to have stumbled upon a librarian's workshop of sorts. Everything in the room seemed to be covered in a thick layer of dust. Worn books were stacked in neat rows, pots of glue lined a central worktable, and binder's thread and thick needles lay scattered. It was a room for books to be repaired, though by the looks of it, some books were well past the possibility.

On the worktable, a large map lay unfolded. It was the only thing in the room that looked like it had been read in the last twenty years. In fact, there wasn't a speck of dust on it. The dynamo lamp had been on the floor next to an overturned stool. It looked as though whoever had been reading this map had brought it here to read in secret, and had just narrowly escaped.

Bailey leaned over the table and held the lamp above the map. *The Unreachable Road: The Migration of the Velyn Mountain People* was written across the top. In smaller print beneath it said, *By Thelonious Loren*. The title and name sent shivers of recognition down his spine. It wasn't the answer to Tremelo's riddle, but it was something: the Velyn tribes, revealing themselves to him for the second time in less than a week. He wondered who had been in here, reading this map in secret.

The map showed the whole of the Dark Woods that stretched from Fairmount to the southern half of the kingdom, over the Golden Lowlands. The Velyn Peaks had been rendered in white chalk, and lovingly drawn black flowers marked each spot where the Velyn had been known to dwell. A list on the side of the map explained the significance of each marker, and the year that the Velyn had settled there.

The Unreachable Road, he learned, was a pathway that the Velyn used to travel from one location to another. The dense terrain and steep mountainsides of the forest made it nearly impossible to pass—but the Velyn, it seemed, had created the road and were the only ones ever to use it. Except, Bailey assumed, this Thelonious Loren, the man with the same last name as Tremelo. He wondered if Loren might be the same man that the bartender had told him about—the Loon. After all, how many people in the kingdom were this interested in the movements of a lost tribe?

Bailey leaned forward in the chair and followed the chronological key by dragging his finger from place to place. He imagined the mountain people, whole families, trekking up and down the range on their own secret pathway. The stories he'd heard as a child, about the Velyn turning into animals and prowling the mountainsides, all came back to him as vividly as when he'd heard them as a little boy.

As he traced the Unreachable Road with his finger, he noticed one was marked only as the Velyns' "Annual Autumn Dwelling Place," which was at the very end of the path. Bailey noticed the curve of the Dark Woods around the mountains, and a nearby set of cliffs. He saw where the Fluvian was drawn in with a thick blue ink pen, and was certain he was looking at the woods outside of Fairmount Academy.

He came to the final marker at the opposite end of the Unreachable Road. As he traced the map, his finger landed on a perfectly drawn flower . . . near his own hometown in the Lowlands. The forest was thin there, and the Lowlands were separated from the mountains by only a dozen miles of woodland. He noted the number—the last location—and found its description on the adjoining list.

The Lowland Pass, it said on the side, *is the last known settlement of the Velyn tribes. Chosen for its proximity to available goods and trade with the Golden Lowlands, the Pass also made the tribes vulnerable to attack. The Dark Woods grows thin in this area, which, in our recent history, became a noted disadvantage to them. The accessibility of the area gave the Jackal King's soldiers an opportunity to attack. This was the last place where the Velyn tribes were seen alive—and even more surely the place where they were most cruelly murdered.*

Bailey traced his fingers over the words with a shaking hand. Thunder roared outside and the clouds darkened ominously. He moved his finger back to the flower marker, and looking closely, noticed that in neat handwriting, Loren had written *The massacre of the Velyn* and a year. It was one Bailey knew well.

It was the very year he was born.

Twenty-one

THE LIGHTS OF THE Autumnal Soiree shone across the commons as Bailey ran back to the Towers. He saw a flash of lightning over the mountains, and a sprinkling of rain began to fall as he entered the dorm.

He needed to think. It seemed like he'd come across nothing but mysteries and questions since he'd come to Fairmount, but was no closer to answering the one question he'd started out with: that of his Absence.

The year of his birth, written carefully on that map, burned in front of his eyes as though it had been branded there.

He'd grown up never knowing who his real parents were, only that he'd been found near the pass marked on the map, on his own in the Dark Woods. Was it possible that he belonged to the Velyn? They were a cursed people, hated and reviled. Whether they had been shape-shifters, criminals, or just on the wrong end of the history books, their legacy was marked. Being a Velyn would make him more of a freak than he already was.

And what of the marker that lay directly on top of the Fairmount forests? Bailey thought back to the night Tremelo had saved him and Tori from the wolf, and the two men he'd seen. Was it possible that someone was now using the Velyn's Unreachable Road to spy on Fairmount? What if it was this Dominae party that everyone was so afraid of? Could Tremelo know more than he was letting on?

Bailey climbed the steps to his tower bedroom and changed out of his drenched clothing. He laid in bed, anxious over all he'd uncovered.

His dreams that night were of a kind king. He wore an overcoat with pockets full of herbs and a grand top hat. With his hand on Bailey's shoulder, the king led him through the Dark Woods and to the edge of the mountains.

"Look," the king said, pointing. A falcon circled the top of a snow-white mountain with an object clutched in its talons. "What is it bringing us, Bailey?"

But as the falcon grew closer, so too did a terrible roar. From the trees emerged ferocious beasts that bared their teeth. Bailey and the king plunged into darkness, running away as fast as they could.

Behind him, he heard a menacing growl as something huge pursued him.

"Bailey!" the king shouted. His top hat had fallen, and he'd been overtaken by the oncoming beasts.

"Bailey!"

He woke—someone really had said his name.

"Hal!" The same faraway voice called out again, accompanied by a flash of lightning. Bailey sat up in bed. Hal was awake too, polishing his glasses on his pajama top.

"Who is that?" Bailey asked.

"I'm not sure," Hal said, "but it came from outside." He and Bailey opened the window and leaned out. A heavy rain pelted down on them.

Tori stood shivering in her pajamas, rubbing her thin arms. Thunder echoed from across the river, headed their way.

"What are you doing?" Bailey called from their second story window.

"You have to come down, you have to help me!" she said. She was soaked, and wiped the rainwater from her eyes.

Bailey's skin prickled. She sounded truly afraid.

"What's going on?" said Hal.

"It's Phi!" Tori said, trying to keep her voice low over the rain, which was next to impossible. "She's trying to fly!"

"What?!" said Hal.

"We're coming down!" said Bailey. "Just stay there, and stay quiet!" He pushed away the image of Phi on the ground, hurt from a long fall. Trying to fly? What was she thinking?

He and Hal got dressed quickly. Bailey grabbed the claw and careered down the stairs, through the front door. Tori waited just outside, pacing back and forth. The three of them huddled out of the rain under the door frame of the Towers' main entrance.

"She's been gone for hours," Tori said. "I didn't know who else to tell. She's on scholarship—if she gets caught, she'll lose it. But I can't find her by myself. She could be anywhere!"

"Start at the beginning," Bailey said. "What do you mean, she was trying to fly?"

Tori looked down at her hands.

"I thought I knew everything about her—we're together all the time. But lately she's been out of the room, early in the morning and sometimes late at night after Scavage practice. She said she had an independent study with Tremelo. When I asked what it was about, she said"—Tori paused and slowly rubbed her scar where it hid under her sleeve—"she said I wouldn't understand."

Bailey thought back to Phi's words at the opera house— maybe a bond between humans and animals wasn't enough, she'd said. Not for someone who truly wanted to transform *into* an animal.

"Tonight, when she left the soiree, she was acting strange," Tori continued. "I heard her sneak out after we went to bed. I didn't think much about it, we've all snuck out"—she shot a knowing look at Bailey—"but after she left the room, I was really curious and . . . I snooped around." Tori whispered this last part.

"And when I found this, well . . ."

She reached into her pocket and took out a palm-sized notebook, bound in red linen. Hal reached for it and snapped it open.

"So, she wants to fly? That's normal for an avian Animas," he said, flipping through the pages. "I'd be more worried if she didn't want that, frankly. Hmm. Some nice poetry."

Bailey winced. If Phi found out they'd passed her diary around, she'd be horrified.

"Don't read that stuff," he said.

"That's not it, anyway. Keep going," whispered Tori, reaching to turn the page.

Hal held the book closer to his chest and flipped forward a few pages, then stopped short.

"Oh," he said, suddenly sounding very serious.

Tori nodded.

"What? What is it?" asked Bailey. Hal held the notebook open and handed it to Bailey. Next to a page of hastily scribbled notes was a detailed drawing. It was a set of wings, made of thin metal rods and fabric—meant to be attached to a human's back by a buckled harness. Two smaller harnesses were drawn on either side, meant to wrap around the wearer's arms. At the end of these were two handles that resembled a clutch. The setup looked familiar, and all at once Bailey remembered where he'd seen the same machinery before: Tremelo's motorbuggy.

"You think she's actually going to try to make this thing?" said Bailey.

Tori forcefully turned the next page of the notebook and pointed to a checklist written in different handwriting. It was a list of materials, all accompanied by hastily drawn check marks. At the bottom it read, *Do NOT attempt until you've alerted me.*

"She's already made it," Tori said, her voice shaking. "She's already put it all together—and now she's out there, about to break her neck, if she hasn't already."

"Okay," said Bailey. The sounds of the night around them had vanished into some kind of vacuum, and his own voice sounded very far away. "We'll split up. We'll find her."

They made a plan. Hal took off toward the edge of the cliff, where he'd pass the clock tower and the farthermost campus buildings. Tori left to circle the Scavage fields. Both would try their best to learn what they could from their kin who inhabited those areas.

Bailey decided to search the dorms and the stables, and fan out to the teachers' quarters and Tremelo's workshop. He had no doubt whose handwriting had been in Phi's private notebook.

The cold rain fell as Bailey made his way around Garrett dorm and up the hill to the Applied Sciences building. He took extra care to glance up at the windows of Tremelo's office. They were dark, but one window hung open and its shutters beat against the stone exterior wall. Just next to the building, Bailey noticed the gnarled oak tree; its branches reached like a bridge to that same open window. Phi, Bailey thought. What are you thinking?

He turned. Opposite the Applied Sciences building was a knobby hill that sloped downward to the forest proper. Bailey could tell that with a running start and a bit of wind, the hill would be the perfect launching place. He ran toward it, and the landscape opened up as though curtains had just parted on either side of a stage. He saw something large and white in a tree at the bottom of the hill—it was Phi, wearing the wings, which extended at least four full feet from either shoulder. They were caught firmly between two large branches, and Phi was half dangling, half crouching at the top of the tree.

"Phi!" he called, as he ran down the hill to her.

"What are you doing here?" she asked, sounding both relieved and angry.

"Never mind that," Bailey said. "Are you hurt?"

"I'm fine, I think," said Phi. "But I'm stuck and the harness is jammed!" Bailey saw that the right wing had a branch through it. The wires attached to the controllers at each of her wrists were tangled hopelessly with leaves. One raw wire swung down freely and swayed as she struggled. A few bright sparks crackled from the end of the wire.

"Just stay still! I'm coming up there!" called Bailey. As he began to climb the tree, the rain fell harder. The trunk and branches were slick, and he scraped his hands trying to find his grip, but finally he made it to the top. Phi and her contraption were pinned like a specimen under a microscope. It was a creaking mass of wires, rods, and canvas—badly stuck and badly broken. Phi's tears were mixed with the rain pelting her face.

"Don't worry. I can get you out," Bailey yelled over the rain. "But I don't know how we'll get it down."

"What? No, we have to get it down!" protested Phi.

Without responding, he climbed up to the branch above her head and began trying to lift the impaled wing off the sharp wood. Fat raindrops seemed to attack him from every direction.

"Phi! Raise your right shoulder." He saw her back rise as he'd asked, but also shake with a small sob.

"Okay, I got the wing free. Hold on to the branch below you," he warned, grabbing hold of the closest branch to him as well. "I'm going to unbuckle you, and I don't want you to fall."

Phi nodded and did as she was told.

Bailey slipped his hand behind her and tried to undo the back buckle—but it was stuck. Below them the raw wire swung, still snapping sparks at the branches. Bailey thanked Nature for the rain, keeping the tree from catching alight. He took the claw out of his pocket, and began cutting through the heavy strap of Phi's harness. It took only a few seconds, and she was free. With the release of all that weight Phi fell suddenly, as if grabbed by the tree branches below. Bailey lunged and reached for her hands, wet and slick. With some effort he managed to hoist her up to steady footing. He could see her matted hair through flashes of lightning.

Getting down from the tree was difficult. The bark was slippery and it was hard to see. Bailey slid more than once as they made their way to the ground. "I've ruined everything," Phi kept saying. "Tremelo will never forgive me."

"Tremelo will just be glad you're okay," Bailey said.

"But I'm not," she said, shaking her head. "Not if I have to leave it. It's not okay!"

"Phi, everyone's worried about *you*, not that machine. Tremelo will understand."

"Nobody understands!" Phi said, an edge to her voice that Bailey had never heard before. "No one does. All the time, I just wish I could be up there." She looked up at the sky, which bombarded them with raindrops. "If I'm not really flying, then what good am I? I feel like only half a person."

Bailey's heart went out to his friend. He hadn't wanted her to know why he wouldn't tell—in class, in practice, in the dining hall—what his Animas was. But now, it seemed important that she know.

"If anybody understands that, it's me," he said.

Phi went quiet and stared at him.

"I know that feeling," he continued, trying to cover the silence between them. "Like you're only a part of what you should be. I feel like that all the time because . . . because, well, I don't have an Animas."

Phi took his hand.

"I know," she said.

"You do?" Bailey asked, but even as he said this, he knew that she'd recognized his Absence almost as soon as they'd met—and instead of feeling exposed, he felt grateful. "Thank you for not telling anyone," he said.

"I would *never* do that," she said, looking sincerely into his eyes. "I know what it's like to be . . . different. You get good at spotting it in other people too. I could see on that first day at Scavage tryouts that there was something special about you."

"But you don't think it's weird? Or that *I'm* weird?" Bailey asked.

Phi shook her head, and raindrops ran down her face and hair. "At home I'd blend into the background so they wouldn't pick on me. You did the same here. How could *I* think that's weird?"

Before Bailey could respond, the loud baying of dogs sounded over the top of the hill.

"Who's down there?" someone shouted. The light of a swinging lantern broke through the trees. It was Mr. Bindley, the night guard—and tonight, he and his dogs were wide-awake. The light came closer and the silhouettes of the hounds appeared at the top of the hill.

"Phi, run!" Bailey said, pointing away from the hill toward the Scavage field. "Tori and Hal are out there somewhere . . ."

With one last look up at her collapsed pair of wings, Phi darted into the trees and disappeared.

Bailey ran around the side of the hill, in the opposite direction, but the hounds were closing in.

"Stop right there!" Bindley called from behind. The reflection from his lantern flashed off the lens of the night-vision monocle Tremelo had made him.

Bailey veered sharply to the left, and ran into the bushes near the base of the hill. Bindley's hounds were in pursuit; he could hear them stumbling through the overgrowth behind him. At last the trees gave way to a trimmed lawn, and Bailey could see one of the main campus buildings looming before him. As he ran, he realized that he'd dropped the claw in his panic.

The dogs began to bark loudly. Bailey ducked around a corner of the building and saw a row of basement windows peeking out at ground level. Bailey pulled at the first window but its frame was wet and slippery. It wouldn't budge. A flash of lightning reflected in the glass and for a moment, Bailey saw the faces of two snarling hounds. He turned and faced the dogs that blocked his way back to the dorms. Thunder crashed. Bindley's footsteps echoed as they approached, and then Bailey was almost blinded by the light of Bindley's lantern shining into his face.

He'd been caught.

Twenty-two

THE GRASS WAS SLICK with rain and everything smelled of wet dirt; she couldn't track anything over the scent. After a rainfall was no time for hunting.

Above, a large bird took flight, and a spattering of drops fell from the branch it had occupied. She crouched closer to the floor and gazed up—an owl. She stayed still for a moment until it flew out of sight.

Nose to the mud, paws treading softly, she dashed on. Somewhere up ahead was the scent of warm, spilled blood. As she crept along the edge of the trees, the smell of smoke and burning wood became stronger. The presence of humans, none of them her kin.

Her instincts urged her to turn back and hide in darkness. But another urging rose up inside her: her kin's curiosity about these people pressed her forward. For him, she would go on.

She moved alongside the river and saw a passing school of fish, too far below the surface for her to catch. There was a cliff face, where two large rocks rose from the base of the river and met at the top, forming a shelter. Inside was the heat of a flame and humans whispering. There was a woman with long braided hair the color of a gray wolf's in summertime. In her hands she held a ball made of glass and held it to a piece a parchment, studying the light in its orb.

There was movement in the trees; the fur raised on her back and she crouched low once more. An animal to the left let out a low, drawn-out snarl—and a wolf crashed through the trees. There was flesh in its teeth and blood matted on its muzzle, from the nighttime feast still fresh on its lips. She ran away, kicking wet dirt under her paws.

Tremelo opened his eyes, his heart beating hard as Fennel made her escape through the woods. She was fast, and he knew she'd be safe—though it took a moment to fully return to the warmth of his own quarters. His skin tingled with an electric sensation, and he seemed to still taste the wet grass in his nostrils, and the smoke of the campfire in the caves.

He laughed in awe and gratitude. Fennel had found something wonderful.

Twenty-three

THE NEXT MORNING, BAILEY sat in an uncomfortable wooden chair in the center of what was normally used as a music classroom, which had been fashioned into a courtroom of sorts. Headmaster Finch and Dean Shonfield sat at a table on a raised platform used for choir rehearsals. In front of him was a menacing semicircle made up of Sucrette, Nillow, Coach Banter, Bindley, and Tremelo. Bailey felt like a prisoner.

Mr. Finch cleared his throat.

"Bailey, you must know how serious this is," he said, his voice low. "You snuck out of your dormitory and were involved in the destruction of a . . . a pair of . . . well, something very expensive. Is that right, Mr. Loren?" Finch looked at Tremelo, who merely nodded. Bailey felt his face flush.

"We can't have this sneaking around after hours, not from a student with a disadvantage such as yours. You, of all students, should be trying harder to follow the rules," Finch continued. "Our first thought is to expel you from the school. But we want to give you the chance to say something in your own defense. *Have* you anything to say?"

Bailey had spent the whole morning wondering what he would say at this moment. He considered telling Finch and Shonfield about Tremelo's involvement—it was his teacher who'd secretly given Phi the means to fly. But then both Tremelo *and* Phi would be in trouble, and he couldn't bring himself to do it.

He looked up at Finch.

"No, sir," he said.

Finch frowned, and looked almost disappointed that Bailey wouldn't defend himself—but Shonfield stared at him through her horn-rimmed glasses, her dismay was clear on her face. She'd been kind to him on his first day here, even without knowing him. Bailey looked away.

"In that case, Mr. Walker, I'm afraid we have no choice but to ask you to pack your things and—"

"I have another idea."

Tremelo had stood up from his chair. He walked forward, and placed a hand on the back of Bailey's chair as he addressed Finch and Shonfield. The headmaster looked unpleasantly surprised, like he'd just found a frog in his coffee.

"I believe that Bailey's 'disadvantage,' as you put it, is distracting him. He simply needs proper focus. The Animas bond allows many of us to feel grounded, and the boy doesn't have that to help him. I'd like to propose an independent study. I will tutor the boy and we'll see if his behavior doesn't improve."

Finch's brow furrowed. Ms. Shonfield took off her glasses and gave them a quick polish.

"If I may say, Mr. Finch," she said softly, "Bailey has much more to benefit from our guidance. I think Tremelo is right. Turning him away, with an Absence, would be a mistake. Perhaps we set up a trial period. It might allow Tremelo to brush up on some old skills."

Finch looked long and hard at Tremelo. It was clear they didn't like each other much. Finch seemed like the kind of person who could smell troublemaking miles away, and Tremelo didn't seem very interested in rules. But to Bailey's immense relief, Finch said, "A trial period it is, then. Mr. Loren, the boy is yours to mind. And I must say, I'll be *fascinated* to see what you come up with for him."

Bailey wanted to cheer with relief. He wouldn't be kicked out of school—and he'd have a chance to learn from Tremelo, for better or worse.

"But, Mr. Walker, you should know you're now treading on very thin ice. Consider yourself on probation. Any missed classes or Scavage practices—indeed, even showing up late to class—will result in your dismissal. You will be as punctual as a porcupine, or you *will* be expelled."

Bailey nodded vigorously.

"Yes, sir," he said, still grateful.

As everyone replaced their chairs and shuffled to the exit, Bailey approached Tremelo.

"Thank you, sir," he said. He already had so many questions—was Tremelo really planning on training him, or was it just another way to keep him out of trouble?

"Don't thank me yet, boy," Tremelo said as he pulled on a striped jacket over his vest, and patted the pocket to make sure his pipe was still in place. "You're about to work harder than you ever have in your life. We'll have an Awakening from you, if I can help it, by Midwinter Night."

Bailey's Awakening training began the next afternoon, between History and Scavage practice. When he arrived at Tremelo's classroom, the desks had been pushed away from the center of the room to form an open circle—but his teacher wasn't there.

Bailey heard a faint hum emanating from the office at the back of the classroom, and he wondered if Tremelo had lost himself in his myrgwood and forgotten about their meeting. He knocked on the door. No answer.

Pushing it open, he found Tremelo and Fennel sitting opposite each other, each wearing round metal caps connected by buzzing wires. Tremelo stared intently into the fox's black eyes, and Fennel patiently stared back as a current crackled between them. They didn't seem to notice that Bailey had entered. He knocked loudly on the doorframe, causing Tremelo to jump in his seat.

"What is that?" Bailey asked, as Tremelo hurriedly took his cap, and then Fennel's fox-size one, off and set them down on a desk.

"An experiment," Tremelo said. "I have a theory about the strength of the bond. Among many."

"Will I have to wear that?" asked Bailey.

Tremelo looked at him with one eyebrow raised.

"Have to have a willing participant for the other cap, m'boy! But don't worry. Worse comes to worse, we'll just try out a bunch of different beasts and see what causes the thing to spark!" He laughed loudly, though Bailey didn't join him. "I'm only joking," he said. "We won't resort to electro-therapy yet—instead, pure natural instinct is where you should start. Awakening to one's Animas is about honing your instincts. We'll see what you're capable of, what your strengths are, and then perhaps we'll draw out that Awakening. What do you say?"

Tremelo led Bailey to the center of the main classroom, where he had cleared the desks away from the middle of the room. He had a gramophone set up and held up a handkerchief.

"Blindfold yourself," Tremelo said, handing it to Bailey. "And don't cheat."

Bailey did as he was told, though he had reservations about what would happen next. With the handkerchief over his eyes, he couldn't see a thing, not even the faint glow of the overhead lamps through the fabric.

He heard a click and a whir, and a loud, cymbal-crashing march began to play.

"Catch this!" he heard Tremelo yell over the din. Something collided with Bailey's left shoulder.

"Hey!" he yelled, waving his arms in front of himself to block whatever might be coming next.

"All right, take a breath," said Tremelo. "Stand still, and listen." Tremelo walked around him in circles as he spoke; his voice seemed to be coming from everywhere. "We already know that physically, you're in top form for someone of your size. But we need to cultivate the awareness of what's around you."

Something that felt like the heel of a shoe hit Bailey's right arm and he stumbled backward.

"How am I supposed to know something's coming at me with this music playing?" Bailey asked, rubbing his arm.

"I suppose I could say something about how music fine-tunes one's senses, or makes the challenge all the more satisfying once you succeed," Tremelo responded. "But the simple truth is, I like this march. It's stirring. Carry on!"

Bailey felt something coming. He spun out of the way and reached out. The moment seemed to stretch, and the blaring music became fuzzy noise as he concentrated on his own hand and the air around it. The tips of his fingers brushed the flying object, but didn't quite make the catch.

"Good one!" said Tremelo.

The music stopped and Bailey took off the blindfold.

"I didn't catch it, though."

"You came very close, very close indeed," said Tremelo, who was standing by the now-silent gramophone wearing only one shoe. "I'd say it's time we took this lesson outside."

Bailey and Tremelo walked across the campus, away from the classroom buildings to the edge of the wide green expanse. Tremelo carried a canvas basket full of metal odds and ends that Bailey guessed would soon be thrown at him.

A question had been burning in Bailey since the hearing with Finch.

"Why did you decide to train me?" he asked Tremelo. "I thought you'd given it up after your father died—"

"Where did you hear that? My father has nothing to do with this," Tremelo said, cutting him off. "I decided to help

229

you because I see something special in you, but as far as my father goes, you and I will keep a silent truce."

Tremelo smoothed out his mustache, a gesture that made him look as if he was sneering at Bailey.

"Don't think for a second that I'm unaware of your field trip to The White Tiger," he said. "Digby the bartender likes to tell stories that aren't his to tell, and your curiosity may get you in a great deal of trouble. Are you more interested in uncovering the dead, or are you interested in Awakening to your Animas? Because your questions about things that don't concern your Awakening will only complicate your training."

Bailey was quiet. He wanted to Awaken more than anything. He was tired of feeling afraid, worrying that he'd never have an Animas. But he also knew that finding his Animas wouldn't tell him everything about who he was and where he'd come from. It wouldn't tell him who the shadows in the woods had been or where Carin had found the sharpened claw. Bailey didn't want to have to choose. He wanted to know everything. But Bailey had a feeling this was a veiled warning, and that the professor was forbidding him from asking about the Velyn too, and King Melore.

As they reached the edge of the Fairmount forest, Tremelo placed a hand on Bailey's shoulder.

"The truth is, there are things I haven't yet figured out myself. I know how frustrating it can be, but you have to focus on your Awakening. Don't try to solve every mystery that comes along—because in the end, you may not want to know the answer."

As Bailey continued his training with Tremelo, Fairmount saw the steady change from fall to winter. The trees of the Fairmount forest became more and more barren, and snow began to accumulate on the nearby mountains. Students with hibernating kin were becoming sleepier during the day. But despite their sluggishness, all the students in his dorm were excited about the approach of Midwinter Night, and the end-of-semester break. Bailey was looking forward to time away from his busy schedule, made all the more grueling by daily training sessions with Tremelo, either early in the morning before Homeroon, or in the hour after History class, with only enough time to scarf down dinner before Scavage practice. He planned to spend the break at home in the Lowlands, where his parents always provided the bread for the village feast celebrating the Transformation of the Twin. Midwinter Night was nearing, and Bailey wanted to return home with an Animas that would make his mom and dad proud.

In the last several weeks, Tremelo had Bailey perform strange and risky feats to improve his instincts and awareness. Bailey's favorite was running a circle through the woods with a blindfold on, as Tremelo timed him on his speed and graded him on the number of scrapes on his arms. In the early morning hours, he had Bailey climb trees on campus and leap from the branches to the classroom rooftops. Fennel would follow as he scrambled from building to building, the wind rushing in his ears.

Lessons always ended with an intense staring contest,

during which Bailey would have to maintain eye contact with Tremelo, and sometimes Fennel, for whole minutes. At first it seemed crazy, but Bailey had to respect that the professor could not be beaten.

"Eye contact is crucial in the animal kingdom," Tremelo explained. "It can separate the predator from the prey, the dominant from the dead. It creates an equal footing, where both man and beast can begin to understand each other without the need to attack. That's where the bond begins."

Bailey found it most challenging when Tremelo would command him to stay completely still and "feel" the woods around him. The first time Tremelo took him into the forest to try it, Bailey found it frustratingly boring.

"If I'm not actually *doing* anything, then how will this improve my instincts?" he asked Tremelo. They'd come to a wide, flat rock a mile into the Fairmount forest. Bailey's task was to sit, and not say or do anything until he "knew" exactly where to go next.

"Sit," Tremelo answered.

They made themselves comfortable on the rock. Tremelo did not have his pipe with him, Bailey noticed. The air was crisp, and Bailey could smell the smoke of a burning leaf pile wafting to them from the grounds.

"You're too eager," Tremelo said. "You're building strength and agility with all this running around, but you aren't listening to the environment. How do you expect to know your Animas when it comes if you aren't paying attention? How do expect to share in your kins' experiences when you aren't listening to the world they inhabit?"

Reluctantly, Bailey followed Tremelo's instructions and closed his eyes. Cold breezes stirred the dead leaves on the ground.

"What do you hear?" asked Tremelo.

"Um . . . leaves," said Bailey.

"What do you smell?"

Bailey sniffed the air.

"Smoke from the leaf pile on campus; wet ground. Cold."

"Do any of these things make you want to move?" asked Tremelo.

He thought about his answer—he didn't want to be sitting still, so everything made him want to move. But he knew that that wasn't what Tremelo meant. Did anything he sensed seem important enough to go after?

He heard something different then—a snap of a twig and soft haunches pouncing away.

"I heard a rabbit," he said.

"Good!" said Tremelo. Bailey opened his eyes.

"How did you know it was a rabbit?" the professor asked.

"I just . . . guessed," Bailey said.

Tremelo shook his head.

"I bet you smelled something specific that told you it was a rabbit, and not a possum or a housecat. It takes practice to know. You now have your assignment, Bailey! You'll come to this rock every evening before Scavage practice until you can tell me exactly what a rabbit smells like. When you know your environment, you may be that much closer to knowing yourself."

* * *

Whack. Something hit Bailey in the ear.

For a blurry second, he thought he was back in Tremelo's office dodging shoes—but the blow was followed by scattered laughter. Bailey lifted his head and rubbed his eyes. He realized he was sitting in the middle of Latin class and someone had thrown a wad of paper at him. Hal, to his left, grimaced while Tori, one more desk down, stifled a laugh.

Ms. Sucrette stood in front of a chalkboard that listed the various conjugations of the word *surprise*. Her arms were folded in front of her, and she did not look at all amused.

"While Mr. Walker has very accurately demonstrated *surprise*, I am not satisfied he has yet learned the present or past tense of it. Nor have any of you, for that matter. Pay attention!" She clapped.

Bailey nodded absently. Too many naps these days, which always ended with a disgruntled professor at the front of the room. Running from class to training, then to Scavage practice, kept him exhausted. Most nights he stayed awake completing his homework in the Towers common room long after his dormmates had gone to bed—but more and more often, he was simply letting assignments slip by, which he wasn't proud of.

It wasn't just his performance in class that suffered: he felt like he'd barely seen Hal except at night in the dorms, and the only reason he got to talk to Phi was because of Scavage practice. After the incident with the wings, she'd found Tori and Hal, and together they'd managed to sneak back into the dorms without anyone the wiser—except, of course, Tremelo. But the professor had an odd way of choosing his battles, and simply told Phi she was not allowed to work on the wings anymore before dropping it completely.

Tremelo, who actually seemed to be having fun training him, was optimistic and encouraging about Bailey's progress. But after six weeks of training, encouragement wasn't enough to quell Bailey's fears that he might never Awaken. It was already almost winter.

They had just finished their eye-contact exercise. Bailey leaned against Tremelo's office door and sighed deeply. Tremelo had won again, but only after an arduous two minutes without blinking.

"That was a record time for me," Bailey said. "What do you think it means?"

Tremelo was busy returning the bolts he'd thrown at Bailey that day to their proper jars. Fennel the fox was gone, out for a hunt.

"It means you can make eye contact more impressively than you could six weeks ago," he said dryly. "Beyond that, we have to wait and see."

"How long, though?" Bailey asked. "When does all this stuff start to work?"

"You're in a unique situation," said Tremelo, sitting down in his chair. "We can't improve your bond until you've Awakened to your Animas, and you won't Awaken until the time is right."

"I thought coming to Fairmount would make it just . . . happen," Bailey said. "But it's been months, and this training isn't working."

Tremelo shook his head.

"A person's Awakening is something very powerful that can't be controlled by circumstance or effort. We're gathering information about your skills, not trying to trigger something that can't be triggered. And your skills do point to a strong Animas, something with great power, but we can't be certain what it is until you've discovered it for yourself. Take heart, Bailey. You're doing well."

Bailey nodded. Another day without an Awakening. He had over an hour before Scavage practice, and normally he would have gathered his things and gone to eat dinner. But something caught his eye.

On Tremelo's desk was the same book he'd seen the night of the wolf attack. It lay open on the desk, and its pages were covered with scratch-like markings that seemed to be a funny sort of alphabet. Though Bailey couldn't make any sense of the markings, he saw a lovingly drawn flower etched in black ink. They were just like the ones Thelonious Loren had used on the Velyn migration map Bailey had found in the library.

He moved toward the desk to look at the book more closely.

"What is it?" Tremelo asked.

"I've seen those flowers before," Bailey said. "On Loren's map."

Tremelo gave Bailey a stern look.

"What did you just say?" he asked darkly.

Bailey drew away from the book.

"I found something weeks ago—I wanted to ask you about it, but you said . . ."

"What map? What are you talking about?" Tremelo asked.

"I found a map, in a tiny room in the library—the name on it was Thelonious Loren. That's your father, isn't it?"

Tremelo ignored the question—or simply refused to answer it.

"What was this map?"

"It shows Fairmount, as well as the place where I was found. As a baby, I mean. And the map is about the Velyn, about the road they used. I think . . . What if I'm related to them?"

Tremelo stared off into space for a moment. "I already told you—it would serve you well to be less curious about things," he said.

"But what I'm talking about is important!" Bailey said. "What if that's why I have an Absence—because all of the Velyn were killed? Maybe my kin don't even know I'm alive. And if I do awaken, will I be like them? I've heard so many different things, I don't even know what that would mean . . ."

"Nature's ears," Tremelo said. For once, the professor seemed short of words. After a moment of silence, he shook his head. "You can't believe in those stories of mountain boogeymen. They're lies. It's exactly what the Jackal wanted you—wanted everyone—to think. There's a lot you don't know about politics, my boy, and it's a very ugly business."

"Then tell me who they *really* were."

Tremelo paused. He placed his fingers on the leather-bound book, tracing the strange markings. "I knew them—years ago, before . . . My father used to take me into the mountains on his research trips whenever he felt we needed to get out of the city. I would accompany my father as he observed the Velyn and even befriended them. They were kind people, and I knew many of them for years. Then the Jackal . . . What he did was terrible. And after he came for my father too, I wanted to simply leave it all behind and forget them. I had thought the Velyn were all gone. But now . . . Like you, I'm trying to find out more—about the Velyn, about everything. I've been tracking their movement since they arrived at the start of the school year."

Bailey shook his head, trying to make sense of what Tremelo had just said.

"Wait a minute. Tracking *who*?"

Tremelo looked at him oddly.

"The men you saw in the forest, they're not alone out there. There's a whole camp of them. That's who I've been tracking." Tremelo paused. Bailey still didn't understand—the men he'd seen that night with the wolf—he'd thought they were the Dominae, but Tremelo was trying to tell him something different, something impossible.

"They *are* the Velyn, Bailey. They're the only ones left."

Twenty-four

BAILEY SAT DOWN ACROSS from Tremelo and took in a deep breath. The Velyn were not only real, but they were alive—or at least, some of them were. What did it mean if he was also a survivor of the Jackal's war against the Velyn? Would he get a chance to meet the people in the woods, and hear their story? Would their presence in the woods help him find his Animas? The thought made his hairs stand on end. He couldn't shake the stories he'd heard about them, even after learning that those stories were just the Jackal's lies. Despite his fears, he felt a sudden pull toward the woods.

"Sir, Phi and I found something—a claw, but sharpened like a weapon. We thought maybe the Dominae, but could it be . . . ?"

"You mean this?" said Tremelo, opening a drawer in his desk. He took out the claw that Bailey had lost the night of the soiree.

"This is a very traditional weapon for them—for the Velyn. They use pieces of their kin when they die, to honor them. When I went to recover my wings, I found it and

239

figured you had dropped it. Phi had told me her falcon brought it to you."

Bailey took the claw from Tremelo and looked at it again with awe. The Velyn had made this, filed it to its perfect sharpness. He felt a rush of excitement, and fear. The claw had belonged to the kin of the people who could very well be his family.

Tremelo seemed to be very far away, but he was still speaking. The professor turned a page of the strange book and looked at the markings again.

"I spent so many years thinking that my father was a fool. An *important* fool to those who knew him, but a fool nonetheless. I've been proven wrong."

"Sir?" Bailey asked.

"I found something that changed everything," Tremelo said. He pointed to an open page. "Do you see those symbols? They're words. Each and every one of them is a real, honest-to-mice word! You just need a special Glass to see it."

Bailey sat there, confused.

"I'll show you," Tremelo said. He took something out of his coat pocket and lay it flat on the desk. It was a loose piece of leather, embossed with a collection of lines, just like the ones in Tremelo's book.

"I found this outside their camp. It's the name of an animal, I think. But look." Tremelo turned to a page in his book. He pointed at the same symbol inscribed on the page.

Bailey stared at the two symbols. They were exact. But what did they mean?

"This is the Seers' language, which fascinated my father. The Velyn spoke our words, our language, but they would sometimes use this as code. I gave up trying to decipher it long ago, but now perhaps we can finally read it."

"But what is it?" Bailey asked.

"It's an entire book written in the Seers' code. If it contains what I think it does, not only will it help us understand more about the Velyn, but it could change the entire kingdom."

"What do you think is in here?" Bailey asked.

Tremelo sat back in his chair.

"One of my father's particular interests was the Seers who lived west of the mountains, where the Velyn stopped on their yearly migrations. The Seers and Velyn traded both goods and protection. When I was very young, my father was obsessed with the Seers' prophecies. He wanted to know how they made predictions, and he in turn began to make his own. I believe this is a book of *his* prophecies—about the Velyn, the True King, and the fate of Aldermere. This book contains all of it, everything he learned from the Seers, and more."

Bailey felt breathless. It was possible that he'd come from the Velyn, and in front of him was a book written by a man who'd known them better than anyone in the kingdom. Could this book reveal more about who he was, and what his Animas might be? He wanted to grab it from Tremelo and pore over its contents right there. But there was one problem.

"How do we read it?" he asked.

Tremelo's eyes widened and he clasped his hands together.

"It's a beautiful technology! They have a glass device like a prism, cut at many different angles. A crow delivered them a message one day as Fennel was tracking them. A Velyn woman unrolled it and moved the Glass over the symbols. I stayed in my quarters but channeled Fennel's experience. She got close enough so we both could see—when she held the Glass against the symbols, the reflections made sense out of nonsense! The lines reformed and became readable words, in the language that we all speak. If we had that Glass, Bailey . . ." He shook his head and smiled.

Bailey looked at the leather-bound book, amazed that all his questions could be answered in this coded language. The key to reading it was this glass object, in the woods not far away.

"Let's go get it," he said. "If you've seen it, what are we waiting for?"

All the amusement fell from Tremelo's face. "No," he said. "No, we can't do that."

Bailey felt his own face growing hot. "Why not? You just said it could change the whole kingdom! Why wouldn't you want to—"

"It's dangerous! We don't know why the Velyn are near the school, or whom they're loyal to. It's been many years since I interacted with them—even I thought that they were entirely dead—and I don't know if they'll trust us. These are different men than the ones I knew. We have to find out more before we go storming into their camp, demanding something that belongs to them. We have to wait."

Bailey was quiet for a moment. He couldn't wait, not

anymore. If he really was of the Velyn, then the Loon's book might contain information about their immensely strong bonds with their kin. Perhaps there was some secret among the Velyn to unlock an Awakening? Maybe it was possible that they Awaken later—and that he was normal after all?

"Fine," Bailey said. "I'll get it myself."

He tucked the claw in his coat pocket and started to leave. Tremelo jumped out of his chair and grabbed Bailey's shoulder.

"Fine? You're determined to get yourself kicked out of this school before you awaken to your Animas," he shouted. "And that's 'fine'?"

"I don't have to listen to you!" Bailey yelled back. He felt something inside him ready to pounce, and he didn't care if Tremelo got in the way. "You made me think you wanted to help me, but now I might actually find out something about my family and how to find my Animas, but you won't let me. You don't care!"

He remembered the moment he'd read the map in the basement of the library, how immediately those clues had wrapped themselves around his brain like vines. Tremelo's book had the answers he needed, he felt sure of it.

"You don't know what you're talking about," Tremelo said. "You think this book is just about you, and your Animas? There are more important things happening in this kingdom right now!"

"So then tell me!" Bailey shouted. "You don't tell me anything about what's going on—you just talk in riddles and rhymes. You claim to care about Aldermere, but your own friends at The White Tiger bar don't even know which side you're on!"

Tremelo turned away from him and looked back at the book, open on his desk.

"I'm on my own side," he said forcefully. "But I know what's right and what's wrong. Terribly, terribly wrong. I want you to find your Animas, Bailey, but we can't just expose ourselves to the Velyn—it's a very dangerous game. And we won't simply go in and take what's theirs . . ."

"But what about the riddle you told me? Could it have something to do with them, the Velyn?" Bailey asked.

"It's nothing," Tremelo said, his voice low. "It doesn't mean *anything*. When I was your age and frustrated I hadn't yet Awakened, my father used to tell it to me. I never solved it—but in the end, I Awakened anyway, Bailey. I don't know why I told it to you, but just forget it. You don't need it to Awaken—I didn't."

"Forget it?" cried Bailey. "So, you just said it . . . as a joke? What other 'jokes' have you told me? That I would Awaken by Midwinter Night?"

Tremelo opened his mouth to speak, but was silenced by a sharp rap at the classroom door.

"Tremelo?" called a sweet, singsong voice. It was Ms. Sucrette. She opened the door to the classroom and poked her head in.

"We'll finish this discussion later. Get your things and go to practice," Tremelo said softly to Bailey. The professor walked to the office door to meet Ms. Sucrette.

"I was wondering if you had time to show me those papers you'd mentioned," Sucrette asked kindly. She caught sight of Bailey through the office door and waved. "Hello, Mr. Walker! I hope I'm not interrupting."

"Not at all," said Tremelo, as he turned his back to the office, leaving Bailey, if only for a moment, alone at his desk.

The leather-bound book sat on the desk and Bailey slipped it in his backpack without thinking. His heart pounded as he picked up his wool coat and left the office, passing the two teachers, deep in conversation. Tremelo met Bailey's gaze as he walked out the classroom door, and for a moment, Bailey's chest tightened with guilt for what he'd just done. But Tremelo waved dismissively and looked away—and it was all Bailey needed to keep going.

Outside, the clock tower chimed a quarter past four. Bailey still had plenty of time before Scavage practice to find the Velyn and the glass object Tremelo had described. If he could get his hands on it, even for just a few minutes, he could read the book and return it to Tremelo's office—maybe before Tremelo even realized he'd taken it.

He loosened his Fairmount tie and buttoned his coat up as he rushed past classroom buildings and the edge of Mrs. Copse's herb garden. He walked down the hill that led to an opening through the trees.

Tremelo hadn't said where the Velyn camp was, but Bailey's first instinct was to go to where he and Tori had stumbled upon the wolf. There he would sit and listen, just as Tremelo had taught him, and figure out where to go next.

The forest became rockier and he found himself having to climb over roots jutting out from the forest floor. He thought that he'd reached the place where he and Tori had met the wolf. He stopped and heard the rush of the river, but he still couldn't be sure he was going the right way. A lone owl hooted somewhere close by. The noises of animals scurrying in the late afternoon were all around him.

Just as he had every day for weeks, Bailey stood very still. He chose a spot near a spindly birch tree and he closed his eyes. He had learned by now what sounds and smells to expect in the Fairmount forest: the remaining songbirds that hadn't begun their trip south yet, the scratching of mice and moles scuttling along the forest floor. He knew that he would smell the same wet, decaying leaves as he'd smelled for the last several weeks. He tried to concentrate on what was not so usual around him.

After several minutes, he finally heard it. A larger animal—either a possum or a raccoon—stumbled through a prickly bush not too far away, in too much of a hurry to be quiet. He couldn't be sure what had spooked the animal, but he knew that it had come from the south, closer to the cliffs. He walked deeper into the forest, into the more dangerous Dark Woods, and headed toward the river.

As Bailey stumbled over the rocky ground, for the first time he felt frightened. He'd come out here completely unprepared, and Tremelo wouldn't be there to rescue him if anything happened. He reached the edge of the cliffs, where light filtered through the trees and he heard the sound of the river burbling below. He hadn't seen anything else out of the ordinary, and he was beginning to wonder if he'd followed the right trail.

But then he smelled a waft of rotting meat and bones—something had been hunting, something big, and it had left its kill close by. Bailey saw a tree trunk covered in long, fresh scratch marks, clearly made by an animal much larger than a wolf. He pressed his finger into the gash and thought of the enormous claw Carin had found and the wounds on the bear that had died so close to the school. He felt a tingling of recognition: the same animal must have been here.

The Velyn had to be near, but there were no footprints or gaps in the undergrowth—and nothing to suggest there was a camp nearby. Everything felt quiet and completely untouched.

He was almost ready to move on when the skin on the back of his neck prickled. He smelled the slightest hint of burning wood. It seemed to be coming from below, from the river itself—but that was impossible. Bailey walked to the edge of the cliff and looked over.

Huge rocks jutted out from the cliff face, leading down to form a cave entrance at the base of the river. There was a thin, barely used path. Bailey gasped, crawling back out of sight. He scrambled along the edge of the cliff until he was directly over the cave.

He heard voices then, rising out of the rocks. He lowered himself to the ground and crawled toward a thin fissure just a few feet from the cave entrance. From there, he could see three figures around a campfire. Two of them were men, sitting next to each other and talking in low voices. They both wore dark clothing that looked good for hunting—thick fabric reinforced at the knees and arms with real leather. The third form was a massive mountain lion stretched in front of the fire. Just outside of the camp circle sat two wolves. Bailey stayed still and held his breath. A breeze rushed over him, ushering his scent away from the campfire.

"Where's the beast now, then?" asked the dark-haired man. He had a beard and wore a tightly knit scarf around his neck.

"Hunting," said the other, a tall blond with dark circles under his eyes. He wore a hood that seemed to be trimmed with the same color fur as the mountain lion. Both of them had weapons at their sides, and Bailey saw that the blond man wore a claw, just like the one Carin had found, on a strap hanging around his neck. "She's been restless. She's looking for something, same as us, right here at the school."

"How do you know that? You're not her kin!"

The blond man nodded at the mountain lion who lay next to the fire.

"*She* knows it. So I know it."

The same man removed a pouch from around his neck. He reached in and pulled out a glass object, which Bailey knew must be the object Tremelo described.

"She's scared, which means she's dangerous. But we still have our mission . . . We know who we need to give this to. The Seers were very clear on that point. We can't just hand it over to the RATS; it *has* to be to the man who follows the Child of War."

The man with the dark beard nodded gravely.

Bailey's head spun. Seers, RATS, the Child of War—it was overwhelming. He'd be sure to tell Tremelo what he heard here later, if Tremelo was willing to listen.

Just then, an angry hiss echoed through the treetops. Both men looked up, and the blond one shoved the Glass into the pouch before they rushed out of the cave. Bailey scrambled back on the rock to where he could watch without being seen. Outside on the low rocks, the bearded man took up a bow and arrow and aimed it at the sky.

"It's the vultures again," he said.

Bailey shrank back against the cliff face. He couldn't risk being seen and getting an arrow loosed at him.

He heard the bird before he saw it—a dark shadow swooping down from the trees. It barreled toward the Velyn, straight at the pouch in the blond man's hands. The bearded man shot an arrow, barely missing but causing the vulture to careen off to the side. Another bird dropped in from the opposite direction and Bailey felt the urge to cry out and warn the men, but he didn't know them or what they had planned. For all he knew, the vultures might be doing just what Bailey needed.

The mountain lion who had been by the fire jumped up and growled. The second vulture flew at her face, its talons bared. She roared and snapped her teeth. The bird beat against her face with its wings as a third vulture flew at the two men and tore the pouch from the blond man's grip. As it flew away, the bearded man took aim and shot another arrow. He hit the bird in its wing, but the vulture only dipped in the sky before it disappeared into the trees.

"After it!" shouted the bearded man. The mountain lion leapt and grabbed the second vulture with her paws. Bailey looked away as she bit into the bird's neck, though he heard the snap as it broke. The two men and the wolves began climbing the perilous path up the cliff face, straight to where Bailey was hiding.

He scrambled back on the rock and jumped to his feet. He had two choices: hide and follow the Velyn as they tracked the vulture, or run after the bird on his own. The Velyn had yet to appear at the top of the cliff face, which gave Bailey a head start. He dashed away in the direction the vulture had flown ahead of the Velyn.

There was no time to stop and listen for the vulture. As he ran, he tried to exercise the same focus that he'd been honing all those afternoons during training and practice, using all of his senses to know where the vulture was. Above, a high branch was shaking: the bird had brushed against it only a moment ago. He heard the sudden scattering of finches up ahead, as though they were flying out of the predator's way. He caught the smallest scent of carrion—dead meat—on the bird's talons, and he knew he was close. The vulture was due north of him, which meant it was flying toward the school.

His lungs burned as he kept running. If only I were Animas Falcon, like Phi, he thought. A falcon could go after the vulture and hassle it out of the sky. He looked up and saw the shadow of the massive bird, flying low with its wounded wing, the weight of the Glass under it.

He had to stop it before it reached the school. If he couldn't retrieve the Glass, he would have to tell Tremelo—and

250

explain that he'd not only borrowed the book, but snuck into the woods again.

Quickly, Bailey took stock of his surroundings. If the vulture was flying toward the school, it would be flying over rougher terrain, through tall trees that might slow it down. Bailey knew that the hills closer to the Scavage fields were smoother, which made it easier to run and jump, and if he took that route he had a chance to cut the bird off before it left the forest. He had to try.

As he veered left in the direction of the Scavage field, he heard the men not too far behind him. The Velyn were tracking the bird, and though they'd caught up quickly, they weren't as familiar with the woods closer to Fairmount as he now was. As he ran toward the smoother hills, the Velyn crashed onward, following the direct path of the bird. He heard the loosing of another arrow, and a curse from the archer as it missed.

He drew near to the far edge of the Scavage field, where he'd seen the King's Finger Oak, but realized he had no plan for getting the vulture out of the sky. The claw, his only weapon, weighed heavy in his pocket—but he couldn't risk losing it. He imagined himself pouncing on the bird from the branch of a tall tree as it flew past, just as he had jumped off the clock tower—but there was no time to climb high enough. He had to find a way to stop the bird from the ground.

As he neared the place where the trees became less dense, he slowed down. The slightest sound of feathers cutting through wind could be heard above him. He looked and saw the vulture, flying just over him, toward Fairmount. It was struggling to stay aloft, with its wing damaged by the arrow, barely usable. It had the pouch in its mouth, and again Bailey wondered why it had flown in this direction.

Bailey wished he'd changed into his Scavage uniform; the wool coat weighed him down and the Fairmount tie around his neck suddenly felt suffocating. As he tore it off, he had an idea. He folded the tie in half and grabbed at the forest floor for a heavy rock, then placed it in the center of the fabric as he held on to both ends. With three swoops over his head, he unfurled the tie and the rock launched directly at the vulture, the fabric nearly slipping from his hand. The rock hit the bird in the left wing, causing the vulture to falter and drop the pouch. Bailey felt a twinge of guilt for harming someone's kin—but the Glass was too important. He darted forward, but despite its wounds the bird was too agile. It dipped down and caught the pouch holding the Glass again in its talons.

Bailey found another stone, smaller than the first but smoother, with a sharp edge on one side. He cradled it in the fabric and swung again, just as he would with a Flick loaded with paint, and this time the stone hit the vulture in its eye. The vulture bobbed in the air; it fell.

Bailey stood very still, listening. From the place where the vulture landed, he heard ruffling feathers and small croaks as the bird tried to right itself. Though he heard nothing else, he knew the men and their kin couldn't be far behind.

He pushed past a line of trees and found the injured bird. The pouch lay beside it as it thrashed on the ground. It fixed a beady eye on him as he reached down and picked up the pouch. It was heavy—the Glass was still inside. The vulture screeched loudly, and Bailey's heart began to hammer. He backed away, horrified by what he'd done as the vulture continued to squawk and scream, too wounded to defend itself. Still, Bailey knew there was no time to waste. He turned and ran toward campus, hoping the Velyn's need to stay hidden would keep them from following him onto the school grounds. He didn't look back.

Twenty-five

"THIS IS NO WAY for a person or their kin to live," the Elder said, as tensions simmered between a terrier and a raven that had been fighting over a piece of dead mouse. He was becoming more frail these days, and Gwen worried that without Grimsen, he was losing hope.

The night they fled the palace, Gwen had thanked Nature for her pickpocket past. It was only through her intimate knowledge of the Gudgeons that they had been able to find the low-lit bar that housed the RATS. She was excited then to join the fold. After all, the RATS stood for something much larger than any of them: Resistance Against Tyranny and Suppression. They were loyal to King Melore, and feared only the worst would come of Viviana's reign.

But the weeks that followed had been hard on them. Viviana's spies forced them to move operations again and again. The RATS had made their way through a series of safe houses, from attic garrets to abandoned dirigible stations. Sleep didn't come easily; there was an inescapable feeling that they could find themselves in the middle of a war at any moment. Other "RATS Nests" existed all over the city, and as rumors of the Dominae's growing forces reached them, Gwen and the RATS took comfort in knowing that there were many others like them—if only they could all meet at once, without Viviana's terrifying birds watching them.

They had been living in a large underground tunnel for the last several days. It was the remnants of what would have, with time, become the tunnels for the Aldermere's first underground rail-motive: Melore's greatest achievement.

Aboveground, Viviana's mechanical birds were all over the city, alongside the gargoyles on the roofs of buildings and perched on lampposts and stoops. One of their only means of communication was the real rats who scuttled between the safe houses and brought their human kin in the group news from the other nests. To remain undetected, the RATS were only allowed to enter and leave their hiding places one or two at a time—and food was brought in by women from the local markets who made it appear to be a routine stop. But the markets had been affected by Viviana's hordes as well: fewer and fewer farmers were sending their crops to the city, afraid of getting caught up in the Dominae's rioting. Gwen became so used to thinned cabbage soup that she wondered if she'd ever eat anything else. The kin were anxious and tired, and squabbles broke out almost daily between different species.

Gwen took comfort in learning to play the harmonica that the Elder had given her. Enoch the Animas Chameleon—the same young man who had helped her escape the Dominae rally—had taught her the basics one night.

"It's not hard to learn," Enoch told her. "Playing music

should be fun, even if you miss the right notes at first."

The chameleon, Bill, was sprawled across Enoch's shoulder. He turned a pleasant shade of coral pink as Enoch played a fast, toe-tapping melody. With Enoch's guidance, Gwen practiced every chance she got. She couldn't play well, but the music calmed her. In the midst of all the uncertainty, she'd take any small pleasure she could get.

Gwen played absentmindedly on the harmonica to ease her mind, alternating between a lullaby and an energetic jig. She'd noticed in the last few days that as she played, not only did she feel more tranquil, but the various species of kin that shared the dark rail tunnel with her calmed down as well. Just the day before, a scrawny, ruffled little owl had found its way underground and hopped to her as she played. Now there were three of them, listening to her from a crumbled block of concrete, along with a mop-eared sheepdog who yawned peacefully. But in one moment, the peacefulness disappeared.

She heard shouts bouncing off of the arched stone ceiling above them. The Elder woke and sat up in the bedroll next to her. Gwen pulled a blanket around her shoulders and helped the Elder stand. The tunnels were dry, at least, but the approaching winter had begun to creep underground. Gwen could see her breath, and the Elder's, as they entered the main chamber.

Enoch was climbing down an iron ladder that reached up from the unused platform to the street. He'd been on watch, stationed near the palace, as the riots grew stronger and more violent, despite the chill in the air.

"It's finally happened—the Dominae have taken the city; Parliament is poised to fall," said Enoch. "An army of weasels and coyotes from the Dust Plains have swarmed the Parliament's troops—the palace and Parliament are surrounded! The rioters have become one with the Domiane army. It's a mob."

The RATS huddled together in the tunnel.

"What is Parliament doing about it?" someone called out. "Are they just sitting there? Surely they have some sort of plan!"

Enoch shook his head.

"Most of its members fled this morning, and those who stayed have told the Parliament troops to stand down. The traitors . . ."

"Where is Viviana?" someone asked.

"She's taken up headquarters in the old library, in the center of the city."

This was met by shouts and murmurs throughout the echoing chamber.

"We strike now, then! March on the library before they're the wiser!" yelled a dockworker.

"We don't have an army," said Digby, the bartender from The White Tiger. "We can't even organize a meeting between Nests, much less an attack—not with the way her spies watch the city. It's too dangerous to send our rat messengers out. The Dominae would sniff out every last one. I know there are many of us willing to fight, but we don't have the weapons even to defend ourselves here for long."

Enoch leaned against the bottom of the ladder and rubbed

his temples. "It's no use—we can't gather an army the size of Viviana's." His chameleon was currently the color of the brown tweed coat he was perched on. He blinked.

"Don't say that!" said Merrit, an Animas Sheepdog with a lopsided white beard. He took a large swig of bourbon. Gwen guessed it was to calm his nerves.

"Well, then?" shouted Enoch. "What do you suggest?" He pointed to a large man in an overcoat who stood against the tunnel wall. "Roger—you've just come from the Lowlands; what is our hope of finding support there?"

Roger Quindley, an apothecary from the Lowlands, had been bringing news of the rest of the kingdom to the RATS for weeks. He stepped forward, followed by a portly badger.

"The Lowlands is filled with apathy," he said. "What's happening in the city isn't of consequence to them out there. Perhaps if they knew of Viviana's true plans . . . we might have hope of assembling an army."

"We need an army as *powerful* as Viviana's, not just as big," said Digby. "We need fighters who know how to use the bond to their best advantage. We need a *leader*." The bartender sighed. "If only Tremelo were still around. Not just to pick up a spot of myrgwood, but *here* standing with us. His strength could help train an army, turn the tides so us RATS weren't running scared."

Gwen twisted her red hair in between her fingers nervously. There was something nagging at her mind—what was it about that name, Tremelo? It sounded so familiar.

"He's crackers, though," said Merrit, slurring his words. "Holed up in that school of his, only tinkering around with machines and the like. Isn't even interested in his father's work anymore."

Gwen suddenly remembered where she'd seen that name before. She turned her back to the group and fumbled down the dark stone tunnel to where her belongings were stored. She dug in her bag for the gold coin with the image of a sleeping fox and that name. Tremelo. As she made her way back toward the central chamber, she saw a light glimmering off of the stone wall. It was the Elder approaching.

"Is everything all right, Gwendolyn? Where did you rush off to?" he asked.

Gwen said nothing. Instead, she held the necklace out on her palm, where it caught the light from the Elder's dynamo lamp.

He stared at the necklace and lifted a wrinkled hand to his mouth.

"It has the same name," she said.

"Where did you find that?" asked the Elder, a sharp urgency in his voice.

"I found it in the hood of my coat the night Grimsen was killed," she said. "I ran into a boy. We both fell . . . and I think it must have been his. I didn't have it before then."

"What boy? What did he look like?" the Elder asked. He grabbed Gwen's arm and held it tightly.

"I don't know! He was young, maybe a bit younger than me. He wore a jacket with bright blue stripes," she said.

The Elder let go of Gwen's arm and rushed back to the noise of the group. Gwen followed him, confused. She hadn't seen the Elder this upset since the night he'd nearly been poisoned. He marched straight over to Merrit and grabbed his shoulder, shaking him out of his drunken stupor.

"Tremelo, he's the man you wish would lead us? You said he was 'not interested in his father's work.' Who was his father?"

Gwen wasn't sure what to do. The Elder was wide-eyed.

"The Loon, of course. His father, Thelonious Loren." Merrit blinked hard. "What's this all about, Elder?"

The Elder paused.

"The Loon—Thelonious. Of course," he said. "Yes, of course. And you said that this man is a professor of sorts, yes?"

Merritt nodded, still a little dazed. His sheepdog cocked its ear.

"At what school?" the Elder asked.

Digby and Merritt exchanged a nervous look.

"He don't do conspiracy work no more, sir," said Merritt. "And he won't help train an army if that's what you're hoping. We've barely seen him . . . 'cept when he's low on his pipe-stuff."

"He doesn't want to be bothered with the old prophecies," said Digby, sadly. "And after what happened to his father, who can blame him?"

"I wish there was time to explain," said the Elder, "but this has suddenly become a much larger matter than choosing a suitable commander. We *need* to find Tremelo."

Roger approached Gwen and the Elder.

"I'm as much in favor of leaving him alone as anyone—he's not a leader," Roger said. "But if you must find him, I know where you can. He teaches at Fairmount Academy."

"Of course," the Elder said. "Where else but at the gate of the Dark Woods?"

With that, he took off to his sleeping place. Gwen scrambled after him, glancing behind her only once. The confused eyes of the RATS followed them.

"What was that about?" she asked. The Elder had begun pulling together his things. "What does it mean, this necklace?"

The Elder handed his bag to her, and squeezed her shoulder affectionately.

"It means we must travel once more."

Twenty-six

AS BAILEY EMERGED FROM the forest, his first thought was to find Tremelo. Despite his own desire to read the book, it was more important he tell Tremelo what he had seen. The school was in danger, and someone would be coming after the Glass. The clock tower boomed—it was five thirty, time for Scavage practice. He remembered Finch's promise to expel him if he was late, but he didn't care—he had to reach Tremelo.

As he raced up the hill past the Scavage field, Bailey saw Taylor. He had a cruel smirk on his face and a mottled black cat on his shoulder, its green eyes flashing in the evening light.

"Back from another session with your loony professor?" Taylor asked.

"Get out of my way, Taylor," Bailey said. He was breathing heavily, and his body vibrated with energy.

"Why, what's so important?" he asked, motioning to the leather pouch in Bailey's hand. Bailey instinctively clutched it tighter.

"What is it?" Taylor asked. "Some crazy Tremelo contraband?"

"It's none of your business," Bailey said, putting the Glass in his backpack.

"I wasn't making a polite request. Show me what's in the bag, or else."

Bailey stood his ground as Taylor approached, but just then Coach Banter came around the side of the stands.

"Walker!" Coach barked, brushing past Taylor. "Thank Nature you're here. Can't afford to have you late, not with Finch breathing down your neck!"

Bailey felt trapped. He fell in line behind Coach and cast a warning look at Taylor before entering the field. The book and the Glass felt heavy and foreboding in his bag.

"Get yourself into your gear, and let's get started," said Coach.

Bailey rushed into the locker room, Taylor eyeing him from the edge of the field. He changed into his Scavage gear and hid his bag with the Glass and book at the bottom of his locker under his folded clothes. The locker door latched into place and he padlocked it, feeling for the key in his pocket. He ran out onto the field to join the team.

Practice was excruciating, and the air was growing colder. All Bailey wanted to do was leave and find Tremelo. He couldn't wait to see what the Loon's book said about the Velyn, and what it might reveal about his own past. In light of this new information, Tremelo would see Bailey did the right thing . . . at least, he hoped so.

He was too distracted to play well. He got hit with a practice Flick and "accidentally" tripped by Taylor, but he didn't have time to care. As he tried to leave the field after the final practice match of the day, Coach waved him back.

"Where do you think you're going? You were late to practice, Walker—I won't lose you to Finch, but you've still got a lesson to learn! That's three laps around the field!"

Bailey wanted to collapse right there. He needed to talk to Tremelo—now. But instead, it was three laps around the whole Scavage field. The temperature was dropping quickly and his breath billowed out of him. He ran faster than he ever had before.

By the time he finally returned to the changing rooms, he wanted nothing more than to find Tremelo, show him the Glass, and make everything all right.

But his locker door hung open on its hinges, and his clothes had spilled out onto the changing room floor.

His bag, with the book and the Glass inside, was missing.

"No!" he cried. He emptied his pockets and found nothing. Taylor must've swiped the key when he tripped him on the field. He looked around the empty locker room wildly. Whoever had broken into his locker and stolen the items was long gone.

Still in uniform, Bailey ran out the entrance to the Scavage field. He leaned back against the wall to catch his breath. Rage pounded inside him with every heartbeat. He pressed the palms of his hands against his eyes, trying to clear his mind, but he couldn't focus. Any chance of knowing the contents of that book were gone, and he was certain Tremelo would never trust him again. He yelled—a deep, reverberating sound that startled a charm of finches. They flew out of sight into the underbrush—all except one, which still hopped in the dry, winter-ready grass.

It began to skip over to him, holding something in its mouth.

Bailey watched as the finch approached and looked up at him with its beady black eyes. Metal eyes. The finch was an automaton, like a little windup toy. In its copper mouth was a rolled up piece of paper, which it dropped at Bailey's feet. The bird unfolded its clinking wings and flew off toward the forest.

Bailey reached down and picked up the roll of paper. His hands shook as he unrolled it.

It was a map, about the size of his palm, of the forest that surrounded the Fairmount cliff, and of the Dark Woods beyond. A spot in the Dark Woods, just off of the dirt path, had been circled. Bailey saw scribbled handwriting in the margins.

I know of your troubles, the note said. *And I wish to help. Meet here after sunset, and the Seers will help you find the path to your Animas.*

The handwriting was neat and small, and Bailey thought he'd seen it before—but it didn't belong to any of his friends or Tremelo. He wondered if the note could be from the Velyn. But the metal bird seemed to hint at another kind of person, someone with more power.

I know of your troubles . . .

Bailey tried to think of who he knew that was Animas Finch, but he came up with nothing. Could it be from the Velyn?

Tremelo would never speak to him again. His Awakening

training was over. At that moment, he wished he'd never laid eyes on Tremelo's book or heard of the people of the Velyn Peaks. Tremelo had been right—his curiosity had driven him to do something foolish, even deceptive, and he'd lost what could have been the very key to his Awakening.

He looked down at the note. He didn't know who had written it, but he realized that it didn't matter. Tremelo's help was no longer available to him, and Hal, Tori, and Phi couldn't help—not when it came to his Awakening. What other choice did he have? He would go. Overhead, he saw massive snow clouds gathering as the last light sank under the horizon. Bailey reached into his coat pocket and took out the sharpened claw. He hoped he wouldn't need to use it.

Twenty-seven

VIVIANA STOOD INSIDE THE great wooden doors of the Gray City Library. She was too distracted to relish the loud cheers of her followers outside; her mind was racing as she thought of the note from Joan that had arrived only moments ago. She had found the prophecy.

It does speak of a True King who will lead an army—with the Child of War as his standard-bearer, a special child whose Animas has been lost. I have the child in my sights . . . Joan's message had read.

Not only did the prophecy speak of a True King, but a "Child of War" too? She felt dizzy with anger and confusion; it was impossible that another heir to the throne might exist. She knew that the only other child of King Melore was dead. She remembered the flames licking the underside of the locked door, and the small, panicked voice—*Vivi, let me out! Don't leave me!* But the door had been stuck fast; she had been unable to open it. She'd fled in terror, and left the palace with the Elder without saving her brother. No. There could be no true king. Whoever would follow this "Child of War" was an imposter. She had given Joan a new mission now—she would kill the Child of War, and all the omens he represented would die with him.

"My lady looks as though she's seeing ghosts," said Clarke the tinkerer. He emerged from the shadows of the library's foyer.

Irritatingly perceptive man, Viviana thought. But she needed his help tonight. With Clarke's skills, she would give the Dominae a symbol of her power.

"On the contrary," she said, smiling. She'd painted her lips a deep mauve. "The Parliament has fled, and our followers are ready for a new age. I am feeling *very* confident."

Clarke bowed slightly.

"Your grand entrance is ready, then," he said, beckoning to a man and woman who stood back in the shadows. Together they pulled a heavy sheet off of a large rectangular cage. Viviana heard the whir and creak of moving metal. A fierce growl sounded and out of the cage stalked a hulking tiger, its fiery red eyes lit by intricate workings within. Its coat was copper painted with swirling white stripes. It seemed to glow.

Clarke reached for a wide strap secured at the automaton-tiger's neck, and handed the end of it to Viviana.

"The beast is yours to command," he said.

Viviana threw back her shoulders and felt the grain of the strap in her hand—it was real leather of rare quality. Someone's kin had died to make it.

"At the right time, press this button here," Clarke said. He pointed to a small gold button set into the leather strap, which connected to a wire that ran inside a seam.

She nodded, and two attendants opened the massive wooden library doors wide. A deafening cheer washed over her. She'd chosen a long, flowing red opera gown with no embroidery or decoration for the occasion—and it swept around her ankles as she walked slowly down the marble steps.

The square teemed with citizens of the Gray City. Many of them had protested there for days, even weeks—until the pressure became too much for Parliament. Sitting attentively in doorways and on window ledges, watching the crowd, was her army. Weasels, coyotes, badgers, hares, and yes, even jackals, surrounded the shouting crowd, silent and ready, waiting for her next command.

Viviana held tightly to the leash of the automaton-tiger as it roared and pulled at the strap. It was all a show, intricately calculated by Clarke. She pressed the gold button and the tiger turned to face her. It roared, showing off a razor-sharp set of metal teeth. With one exquisite movement, its metal muscles flexed and it bowed low to Viviana. She smiled, and the crowd in the square cheered wildly.

Viviana waved. She had been nervous to greet her followers without Joan by her side . . . but if Joan succeeded tonight, then her power over the prophecy—and the people—was certain.

Twenty-eight

THE BELLS IN THE Fairmount clock tower bellowed, announcing eight o'clock. Tremelo walked swiftly between the dorms, dodging the stream of students coming out of the dining hall. He looked frantically for Bailey as Fennel followed close on his heels.

He saw Hal and Tori walking together. They were talking excitedly, but at his approach their expressions changed into looks of stark concern.

"You," Tremelo said, pointing at Hal and Tori. "Where's Bailey?"

"I don't know," said Hal. The boy squinted behind his glasses.

"I need to find him," he replied. "He has taken something from me, something very important."

Tori scowled at him.

"You think Bailey stole something from you?"

"I think he's done something that he believes will help his Awakening, but he may have put himself in danger."

"What are you talking about?" pressed Tori. One of her snakes had crept out of her bag, and was wrapped around her slender wrist.

Tremelo looked around and stepped closer to Tori and Hal.

"You may recall, Victoria, a certain trunk in my possession, and a certain book in that trunk," said Tremelo. "It can't be read. It's written in an impossible language—but Bailey believes this book has the answers to his questions. This book has a way of attracting the *wrong* kind of attention. We have to find Bailey."

"He might be with Phi," Hal said. "Scavage practice only ended a little while ago."

The group made their way toward the Scavage field, but just over the hill, they heard someone shrieking in terror. Tremelo sprinted up, clearly worried, with Tori and Hal close behind. But it wasn't Bailey—it was Taylor. Phi's falcon, Carin, was flapping her wings around his head and chasing him across the field.

"What did you tell Coach?" Phi was yelling.

"Get her off!" pleaded Taylor. A black cat hissed and tried to pounce at the bird, but he couldn't jump high enough. Fennel bounded into the fray and yipped, trying to herd Taylor's cat away.

"What did you take from Bailey's locker?" Phi demanded. "I *heard* you bragging about it!"

"I didn't take anything! *Ants!* Get this crazy bird away from me!"

Tremelo rushed forward and brushed Carin away with a forceful arm. Taylor's cat was immediately swatted by Fennel.

"What's going on here?" Tremelo asked. "What's this about Bailey's locker?"

271

"I'm *bleeding*," shouted Taylor. "That bird's an anting menace!"

"Believe me, she could do worse!" said Phi. "She was barely trying!"

"Enough!" Tremelo ordered. "Phi, rein in your kin. Taylor, stop your whining and answer my question *now*."

Taylor rubbed a scratch on his neck from Carin's talons, and looked at the ground.

"Is it my fault if he comes running in late, with 'secret' stuff? I just thought Coach ought to know what he's been up to, that's all."

"You were trying to get him kicked off the team!" said Phi. "You can't stand that he's a better Scavage player than you!"

"Calm down!" shouted Tremelo. "What did you take from Bailey's locker, and where is it now?"

Taylor scowled.

"I don't *know* what it was," he groaned. "He came out of the woods acting funny, holding a little pouch. I didn't get to look inside 'cause I got caught opening his locker."

"Caught by whom?" asked Tremelo.

"By Sucrette," said Taylor. "She confiscated the bag and gave me detention. Then she took it away with her while Bailey ran laps."

"What was she doing in the Scavage locker room?" asked Hal.

"Ms. Sucrette . . ." Tremelo raised his hand to his mustache. At his feet, Fennel now sat very still, looking up at him.

"Can I go now?" asked Taylor.

Tremelo ignored him, turning to leave.

"Follow me," he said to Hal, Tori, and Phi.

They formed a silent parade to the Linguistics and Interspecies Communications building, with Carin flying low overhead before settling onto the leather gear on Phi's arm. Outside Sucrette's classroom, Tremelo knocked once before opening the door.

The orderly classroom was deserted. The posters with verb conjugations hung in their tidy rows, and the desks had been expertly straightened.

"Ms. Sucrette?" Tremelo called. The door to the teacher's office at the back of the room was ajar. "Joan?"

Tremelo began to feel his skin prickle. Something was wrong.

He marched to the office door and pushed it open. Inside, the scene was chaotic: desk drawers flung open and emptied, loose papers and pens littered the floors, and the chair behind the desk lay overturned on the floor. A thin scratching caught Tremelo's attention—a rat huddled in a corner, nibbling on bits from Sucrette's overturned candy dish.

"I don't understand," said Hal. "Where's Ms. Sucrette?"

Tremelo shook his head.

"Perhaps the more important question," he said, as his hands trembled, "is 'Who is Ms. Sucrette?'"

Twenty-nine

BAILEY WALKED QUICKLY OVER the rocks and mossy crags, out again into the woods. His breath stung in his lungs and he felt a sharp chill as the light faded. He hadn't bothered to bring a lamp with him, but he felt reassured by the mysterious claw he clutched deep in his pocket. The snow clouds he'd seen over campus had released their hold, and flakes of white danced in the air around him.

Somewhere overhead a bird cried and Bailey was reminded of the vulture, its wing damaged and bloody. He began to run, both scared and exhilarated as he vaulted himself off of the tops of the rocks. He had no inclination to stick to the dirt road that the teachers used to get into the woods—his urgency drove him into the trees. He was farther from the school than he'd ever been, and he felt stronger now—or more reckless—after his outing in the woods just a few hours prior.

He knew this was dangerous, but he had no other choice now that he'd lost the Glass and the book. Getting answers about his Animas seemed worth the risk.

As Bailey hurried on, the rocks grew larger and slick with

wet leaves. Finally, he found an open grove just past the curve of the stream. This was the spot on the map in the mysterious note. He charged down the slope and stopped at the edge of the trees. The grove was empty, and his heart beat so quickly it felt like a creature all its own. He could feel the cold in his fingertips.

But something else besides the cold made Bailey pause. A slender woman in a tailored coat stepped into the grove. A lumbering herd of bears and wolves followed her into the clearing, then stood at attention. The woman pulled back the hood of her coat, and Bailey saw the shiny blond bob of Ms. Sucrette.

A harsh wind sounded above, and an entire kettle of vultures careened into the clearing. They settled onto the branches and gazed down, cold and knowing. A young vulture with piercing black eyes flew down and onto Ms. Sucrette's slim shoulder. Bailey realized her customary bluebirds were nowhere to be seen.

"Ms. Sucrette?" he said. "Why are *you* here?"

Ms. Sucrette reached into the pocket of her overcoat and drew out a gleaming knife.

"So, Mr. Walker," she said, her voice light and airy even then. "You received my note."

Thirty

IF ANYONE WITH A keen eye had happened to glance out the window of the now-empty Latin classroom, they might have seen four suspicious-looking figures darting through the falling snow. This person might have thought nothing of the gaunt professor and three worried students hurrying out toward the teachers' quarters. But in Tremelo's mind, the windows of the classroom buildings were full of closely watching eyes. The destruction of Sucrette's office had lodged a stone of worry in him that would not be shaken loose. He couldn't piece it all together yet, but he knew two things: first, that he had to find Bailey before any harm came to him, and second, that it was very likely to be a deadly night.

He rushed up the narrow staircase to his quarters. Hal, Tori, and Phi followed behind him, nearly breathless. The floor of his apartment in the carriage house was covered in angrily strewn papers, and the books he'd overturned lay opened with bent pages. He left the students in his sitting room and threw open the door to a cramped closet. He grabbed his spring-loaded bow and the quiver of arrows he'd stashed there the night Tori and Bailey had been attacked by a wolf, as well as a handful of other objects. The two girls waited together next to the armchair, watching his every move. Hal stood, stiff and alert, by the door.

"I have my own ideas about where our friend might be," Tremelo said, looking carefully at each of the students' faces. "But if any of you know of a particular place *besides* the woods, then do speak up."

As he'd expected, no one said anything to the contrary.

He placed the bow and quiver down and handed Hal a bag of objects that looked very similar to stony, chipped marbles.

"You'll be able to make good use of these with your hearing," he said. "They're stunners. If anything approaches you in the dark, launch one of these. Once they collide with something, they'll explode, and a flashing light will stun your opponent. Just don't let them get set off within five feet of yourself, or you'll be blind for a good ten seconds—blinder than you already are, that is. Got it?"

Hal weighed the bag in his hand. "Got it," he said.

Tremelo turned to the girls. "We'll have to find something for you two as well," he said. But just then, he felt a tug of awareness— Fennel had caught Bailey's scent in the woods.

It was difficult to channel Fennel's experiences when he was this anxious, though this was when his concentration mattered the most. Tremelo took a deep breath and closed his eyes. He saw a green light begin to glow, like a photograph being slowly developed. He felt the wet grass beneath Fennel's paws and tracked Bailey's scent, in a way that no human nose ever could. But where was Fennel running?

A sharp knock on the door yanked Tremelo out of his concentration. Phi and Hal looked wide-eyed toward the entrance; Tremelo noticed that Tori didn't look scared, but determined.

"Did you see anything?" she asked him in a whisper.

Before he could answer, Headmaster Finch walked in. His brow was tightly knit as he cast a glance over the room. Tremelo realized he was still holding an assortment of weapons, and that his bow and arrows were leaning on the wall behind him. Hal slowly pulled the bag of stunners behind his back.

"I require an immediate explanation from you, Tremelo," Finch said as he pushed up his wire-frame glasses. "Just what is going on here?"

"An explanation . . . of course," said Tremelo. His hands shook. Somewhere, Bailey was in grave danger. "Perhaps over a pint of Dust Plains moonshine? I believe we have mutual acquaintances in the Gray who could procure such a thing."

"I don't partake in prohibited behavior, and I'm sure I have no idea what you're referring to—" He would've likely continued, but a girl poked her head in from the hallway. She was about thirteen, Tremelo guessed—with bright red, cropped hair.

"I'm so sorry to interrupt," she said. She squeezed her way into the crowded room and looked around, pausing on Tremelo. "Is this the professor?" she asked Finch.

"It is," Finch replied. "Tremelo, you have visitors who demanded to see you at once. She and the gentleman have

278

just arrived on a rigi from Parliament." Finch gestured to an old man who appeared at the doorway, just behind the girl. He looked frail, but he stood tall and walked on his own.

"I'm Elder Finn," said the old man, "and this is my apprentice, Gwen."

"I have other things to attend to and will leave you to your guests," Finch said. "But we *will* discuss why these students are here with so many dangerous objects at their disposal." He muttered to himself as he exited down the stairs, and left the strangers at the entrance of Tremelo's sitting room.

Before the old man could speak, Tremelo grabbed the bow from where he'd put it down. Tori and Phi moved toward the door.

"I'm sorry to delay the satisfaction of my *immense* curiosity," Tremelo said, flexing the bow to check its tension, "but these students and I have a very urgent appointment, so if you don't mind—"

"I am a friend of your father's," the old man interrupted. "And what I have to say is most important. And sensitive . . ." He paused, casting a sidelong glance at the students in the room.

"Say it quickly, then. And don't worry about these three. They know how to keep a secret."

"This belongs to you?" the Elder gestured to the girl, Gwen. She reached into her coat pocket and brought out the gold charm that Tremelo had given Bailey so many weeks before. It was the familiar letters of his name and the shape of the sleeping fox.

"How do you have that?" he asked.

"It was a mistake," said the girl.

The Elder stepped forward. "Your confusion is understandable, but forgive me—the more pressing question is how *you* came to have it. This is where you got your name, yes?"

"It *is* my name, always has been," said Tremelo. "Just as I've always had that."

The Elder smiled. He leaned on Gwen's arm, and for a moment Tremelo thought the old man would faint.

"Are you all right?" Tremelo asked.

"I'm more than all right." The old man cleared his throat; Tremelo saw his eyes were bright with tears. "I knew the man you call your father, Thelonious Loren, long before he became known as the Loon. He was childless. He had no son."

"Then you knew him before I was born."

The Elder shook his head and placed a hand on Tremelo's arm. "You have no memory of the first five years of your life, do you?" he asked.

Tremelo's stomach tightened reflexively. "Many people don't."

"And perhaps it's best that you never did. It would've been difficult to know at such a young age . . ." The Elder lifted the pendant from Gwen's hand. "He must have rescued you from the palace, just as I rescued your sister before she was taken from me. He knew your true identity and kept it a secret. But he left you clues, so that you would find your destiny when the time was right. His prophecies—they were true all along, because he knew that he was protecting the true king."

The Elder lay the pendant flat in his own hand, and pointed a bony finger to the widely spaced letters on it: TRE MELO.

"I know this pendant. I remember fetching it from the jeweler on the night you were born. Your father somehow knew that you'd be Animas Fox, like him. But some of the letters have worn off—very likely in the fire that caused us all to flee the palace that terrible night. Look."

The Elder ran his fingers along the letters again, pausing between the existing ones.

"Trent Melore." The Elder raised his eyes to meet Tremelo's. "The sleeping fox, awake at last."

Tremelo backed away from the Elder. What the man was saying was madness. But before he could speak, the Elder sank down to one knee.

"What are you doing?" Tremelo felt that the air in the room had grown thin.

"My dear, lost boy," the Elder said. "I was taught to always bow before a king."

Thirty-one

AN ASSORTMENT OF BEARS, wolves, coyotes, and badgers stood in a semicircle behind Sucrette. Bailey's head spun with fear and confusion. How was she doing this? It was clear now that the bluebirds had never been her real kin—but how had she controlled them, or any of these animals? Behind him, Bailey heard low growls from the direction he'd just come from.

"Wh-why are they acting like this?" Bailey stuttered, eyeing the tree line for an escape.

"They obey me because I am better than they are," Sucrette said matter-of-factly. "Silly Bailey. You were much easier to catch than I'd even imagined! Your hunger for an Animas makes you weak."

"What do you want?" Bailey asked. His throat felt dry. The surrounding animals horrified him. They stared at him with empty eyes, cut off from their own will. This couldn't be the Animas bond as Tremelo described it. He knew in his bones that this was something different, something evil.

"I have what I want," Sucrette said. She revealed Tremelo's book from beneath her coat, and pulled the

Glass out of her pocket.

"No," Bailey said, despite himself. "What do you want them for?"

The vulture on Sucrette's shoulder opened its beak and hissed. Bailey was almost sure that it too was laughing at him.

"It's not *I* who wanted them, but Viviana, the rightful heir to the throne. Do you think I like teaching Latin? I've spent months here, following around your dear Tremelo, trying to find a way to steal this book, and finally you do it *for* me! My queen will have everything she wants."

"You . . . you're with the Dominae," he said, breathless. He remembered the fearful whispers in The White Tiger pub. "And I helped you."

He looked around at the array of animals, ready to strike at Sucrette's command. The bartender's words about Viviana echoed in his mind. *Twisting the Animas bond to her own means.* So this was what they'd meant. Dominance. The beasts stood like machines instead of flesh-and-blood animals. His knees wobbled, and he felt dizzy. In their midst, Sucrette stood still and powerful, holding her blade steady.

"It's funny, really!" Sucrette chirruped. "Because the book and the Glass led me to a much bigger prize . . . *you.*"

Bailey backed away instinctively. He stopped when he heard a twig snap, and another growl only a few paces behind him.

"What do you mean?"

She stepped forward and fixed her eyes on his face, as though she was looking for something.

"The boy with the lost Animas—you're what the Seers called the Child of War, the boy who would lead an army and herald the new king. It's my job to stop that. There can be no new king—the son of Melore died in the ashes of the palace, and his daughter survived. *She* will become *queen*."

He didn't understand. He was to herald a new king, just like the RATS had hoped . . . but he felt no hope now, as the mocking look in Sucrette's eyes froze him through with fear. And what did she mean by a "lost Animas"? Not that he could ask; Sucrette looked in no mood to answer his question as she inched closer with the handle of the blade clutched in her hand.

"I've never killed a child before," she murmured. "I suppose it's no different than tucking you into bed, except your sleep will be eternal. Though I regret, little Bailey, I have no talent for singing lullabies"—one of the vultures flying above let out a piercing, broken screech, and Sucrette laughed—"as you can see."

And in a flash, Bailey remembered. The lullaby that his mother had sung to him, the one he'd tried to remember when Tremelo had first told him the riddle—he could almost hear her singing it now:

A father fox lulls his kit to sleep
With talk of the coming morn:
"Sleep, little fox, and when you wake
The rooster sounds his horn,
The cicadas play their merry tune,

The loon calls to the sun.
But now the crickets hail the moon
For another day is done."

It seemed to Bailey that the many parts of the riddle were
dancing together in his mind: a lullaby about a sleeping fox,
a brother and sister rising from the ashes, the Loon, the line
about locusts from Melore's speech, the "King's Children"
growing on the gnarled tree . . . Snowflakes swirled in the
air around him and settled silently onto his coat and hair.

All at once, the riddle's clues formed together and became
clear: The riddle had led him to "King's Children"—but
they weren't Nature's children, as he'd thought in the opera
house. They were the Melorian brother and sister. They'd
both survived the palace fire, and the sun wasn't calling to
the loon. It was backward—and *sun* meant *son*! The Loon
was calling to the Son, Melore's son, who was alive, who
had *not* died in the ashes!

Bailey ducked, as one of Sucrette's vultures swooped at
him. It snapped its beak at his hair, and he instinctively
swung his arm up to knock it away. The vulture circled
above him as Sucrette laughed, relishing his fear.

But it wasn't only fear that he felt—his mind was humming
with information, strands of prophecy and song weaving
themselves together. *Locusts turn Men from Treachery . . .*

He focused on the words Locusts, Men, Treachery—
Treachery, Locusts, Men . . .

Treachery turns Men into Locusts. Bailey repeated it in
his mind, and something else began to form.

Tre. Me. Lo. The Loon calls to the son who rose from the palace's ashes—Tremelo.

The riddle wasn't about Awakening—it was about the lost king, the sleeping fox who would wake again. The sleeping fox. Just like on Tremelo's necklace.

"Tremelo is the sleeping fox," Bailey whispered. No wonder the Loon had repeated the riddle to Tremelo as a child. *He's Melore's son.*

"What was that?" snapped Sucrette. Bailey tried to stay calm despite his sudden realization. Was he the only one who knew?

"Why kill me?" he asked, stalling. "I don't care about the Dominae movement. I'm . . . I'm just a kid."

"Don't play dumb, Bailey. I know Tremelo was grooming you to be another one of his spies."

"What do you mean?"

Sucrette paused. Her usually neat blond hair was tousled, her blue eyes narrowed and menacing.

"Your oddball tutor was using you, Bailey. I watched him closely."

"That's not true," said Bailey.

"Oh, it is," Sucrette said. "He's a political radical—and you were merely his pawn. You ran around spying for him and found my map, which I *don't* appreciate. But now I've read this—the Loon's prophecies about the return of the True King." She gestured to the book. "And I plan to finish what the Jackal began."

She lunged and he sidestepped her, but Sucrette snapped her fingers and a roar tore through the air. On her command, he was thrown hard onto the ground by a huge wolf with snarled fur. It leapt away, but paced before him, ready to attack again.

"But why me?" asked Bailey. "What does it say about the Child of War? About my Animas?" His body ached and he could barely pull himself up to sit. The woods around him spun. Warm blood began to pool at the back of his head, and every exposed part of his skin burned from the cold.

Sucrette advanced slowly this time, her knife at the ready. Bailey crept his hand into his coat pocket and closed a tight fist around the sharpened claw.

"The book says you have an Animas after all, Bailey Walker," Sucrette cooed. "Take comfort in that before you die."

She lunged. At the same time, he drew the claw from his pocket and slashed at Sucrette, barely skimming her cheek. She deflected him with the blade of her knife. Pain ripped through his arm and Bailey cried out, dropping the claw. The wolf bared its teeth and snapped its jaws an inch from his face.

"Congratulations, Bailey. I didn't think you had it in you." She staggered back a few feet, clutching her bleeding cheek with one hand, grinning. She kneeled and picked up the claw. "Oh, how *perfect*. The irony! An A-plus for imagination, Bailey."

Still clutching her cheek, she kneeled over him. A drop of her blood spattered onto his face. When he tried to turn away, the wolf pinned him with a heavy paw.

"A fitting end," she said, as she raised the claw high in the chill winter air, "for the Child of War."

Bailey closed his eyes as she brought the claw whistling down toward his chest. But the blow didn't fall. Instead, he heard Sucrette let out a mangled scream.

He opened his eyes just in time to see an animal pounce from the rocks behind him—its massive snow-white body at full extension as it flew through the air.

Thirty-two

TEETH BARED, THE BEAST leapt straight at Sucrette. It swiped its giant paw at her shoulder and sharp claws ripped at her flesh. She screamed, stumbling backward. Bailey couldn't breathe. He felt like he was falling from a great height, the same way he'd felt after leaping from the clock tower. The giant animal he'd seen from the rigimotive *was* real. Its hide was a brilliant white, with light gray stripes. It was no ghost, but a beautiful white tiger.

The tiger crouched low, poised to strike Sucrette again, but the gray wolf hurled onto its back and the two animals became a snarling mass of blood and fur. The tiger reared up on its hind legs and whipped its head back, biting into the wolf and heaving it off. It landed a few feet away in the snow, yelping.

The tiger then turned to Bailey. It growled, but softly—a deadly rumbling that echoed in Bailey's bones. He slowly pushed himself up into a sitting position. His head and arm throbbed.

"Stop them!" Sucrette yelled to the beasts behind her, though Bailey barely registered her screams as the tiger paced before him, its tail lashing.

A pair of black bears ran across the clearing and lunged at the tiger. Bailey scrambled backward as the three animals crashed onto the ground. The other animals moved into the clearing and closed in on the tiger. Their warm breath rose up as bits of vapor in the cold air.

"Finish it!" shouted Sucrette. But the tiger landed a crushing blow to one bear, then the other, and each of them fell in furry heaps in the snow. They were replaced by a handful of wolves, who leapt into the fray, baying. The tiger snorted and growled as it fought them off—as it fought them *away* from Bailey.

Bailey crouched on the ground, trying to understand. His heart was beating, and he tasted something metallic in his mouth, like blood. Each blow the tiger suffered made him feel panicked and sick. He looked for a break in the rocks behind him, but there was no escape.

Sucrette was at the opposite end of the clearing, and between them, the fight raged on. Teeth and claws and blood. The white tiger rose on its haunches and seemed to spin in the air, knocking the wind out of several wolves with a swipe of one massive paw. It landed close to Bailey, and for the first time, the two of them were eye to eye.

Bailey could swear that in that moment, time stopped. All was quiet and still, and even the snarling pack of beasts seemed to fade from his awareness. He could see nothing but the tiger's face. The breaths of both boy and tiger appeared in the air between them, rising and dissipating in the dark.

Bailey kept his gaze focused on the tiger's eyes—irises

laced with shades of blue and gray.

He did not blink or look away. Neither did the tiger.

And then, as if through a trick of magic, Bailey saw the forest in reverse. The same trees, the same grove—but the figure in front of him was not the hulking white tiger.

It was himself.

His new wool coat was torn in one shoulder and he held his right arm, which lay limp and useless against his chest. He smelled strongly of the lentil soup he'd had for lunch, and of healthy, pumping blood. He watched his own eyes widen and fill with understanding. He was seeing himself, from the tiger's perspective.

He knew—of course he knew. It felt so undeniably true that he laughed, as if he had just realized the sky was above him.

He was Animas White Tiger. He had Awakened, and here was his only kin in the world.

His vision seemed to jump, like frames in a picture show, between the tiger's perspective and his own. The tiger's eyes softened, and its whiskers flickered. Bailey knew the tiger—a female whose name, Bailey simply knew, was Taleth—was experiencing the same sudden realization, after years of feeling incomplete. She had felt a pull here, to the woods just outside Fairmount, never knowing it was the need to be near her kin. Until now.

Bailey felt nothing but awe and joy. Their two perspectives switched back and forth as they stared at each other.

But a hoarse, angry cry cut through the quiet, "Kill them both, you filthy beasts!"

Thirty-three

AT SUCRETTE'S COMMAND, A massive bear threw itself on Taleth's hide from behind. The tiger roared, her pain shattering Bailey's trance.

The tiger shook the bear off, and Bailey ran to her. The claw marks in her side were deep, but she kept fighting. Bailey grabbed a hold of her flank with his good arm and heaved himself up onto her back. Though his arm throbbed with the effort, he grasped the tiger's hide with both hands. His head was spinning.

Sucrette stood on a tall rock outside the clearing, close to the spot where Bailey had first entered. She was clutching her side, and blood was flowing freely from her cheek. But she was alive. The Dominated animals continued to approach them, ready to fight.

The tiger reared up on her hind legs and shook her striped head, teeth bared and glistening. Bailey gripped her neck tightly, trying to clear his head of dizziness.

Taleth leapt forward, crashing through the melee toward the rock face. A wolf bit into her back leg, but Bailey kicked at its nose until it let go, growling. With one shuddering movement, the tiger hauled herself up onto the rock, with Bailey holding on to her back for dear life. Taleth towered before Sucrette, who did not back down.

"How brave," she spat as the tiger crouched in front of her. "And how kind of you both to deliver yourself to me so conveniently. Two parts of one prophecy, killed in one stroke."

The hum of an engine and a strange rattling noise cut through the air. Bailey heard too the flapping of hundreds of wings, and he took his eyes off Sucrette and looked up. The gray evening sky above the clearing was full of birds—falcons and owls—flying in circles through the falling snow.

A bright light bounced between the trees, and Bailey shaded his eyes as the mechanical hum and rattling grew deafening, and something crashed and sputtered onto the large, flat surface of the rock. The tiger reared, and Sucrette fell backward in surprise. As Bailey's eyes adjusted, he saw that it was Tremelo's motorbuggy. Tremelo himself was standing with his feet balanced on the back fender, aiming his crossbow straight at Sucrette's heart. An old man sat in the sidecar, looking determined, but very uncomfortable in Tremelo's spare goggles. Tori sat in the driver's seat with an expression on her face that was both fearful and also very, very smug.

With one look, Tremelo surveyed the scene in the clearing below and cocked his crossbow.

"Where is the Glass?" he shouted.

Bailey was about to yell back that Sucrette had it in her pocket, but as he looked at her, he saw that her bag had spilled when she'd fallen back. The Glass was lying several feet away in the snow, out of reach. At the same moment, Sucrette saw it too.

"There! It's there!" Bailey yelled, and pointed over the tiger's back with his damaged arm.

Two of Sucrette's vulture kin swooped toward the Glass.

"Phi!" Tremelo shouted, and as Bailey watched, a huge bird shot through between the vultures and the Glass, distracting them from their glittering prize. The bird slowed down, and with amazement, Bailey realized that it was no bird at all. It was Phi. The enormous repaired wings allowed her to weave in and out of the formations of the vultures that Sucrette was now sending toward the buggy. As Phi flew closer, Bailey saw that she wore metal spikes on her feet, affixed to her boots, in the shape of curved birds' talons. She kicked and dove, distracting the animals enough to give Bailey a chance to get his bearings. Several wolves pounced after her, and Bailey's heart jumped at the thought that she could be pulled from the sky. The tiger, feeling Bailey's rage at seeing his friends attacked, rushed toward Sucrette. But before Bailey and Taleth could reach her, a gray wolf jumped at them from behind. As the tiger whirled around to fight it, Bailey saw that some of the animals from the clearing had begun climbing the rocks and were lumbering toward them.

Suddenly, Bailey heard a snapping noise, and a bright light burst just a few feet away from him, stunning the wolf as well as several vultures that were circling close overhead. As his eyes adjusted to the light, Bailey saw Hal running out of the woods, past the rumbling motorbuggy. Tori had leapt from it and shielded her eyes from the light enough to reach the Glass before Sucrette had a chance. She lodged the Glass in her beaded bag and then, as Bailey cheered, drew an enormous sword out of a metal scabbard at her side, and swiped at the vultures who had regained their sight. Tremelo had left the buggy behind, flipped his crossbow onto his back, and was fighting off a bear with a short ax.

"Bailey! You hurt?" Hal asked as he ran past. Hal's eyes grew wide as he registered that Bailey was sitting on top of a wild, fighting tiger. Bailey didn't even have time to respond as he reached out with his good arm and punched away a badger who had tried to climb up onto Taleth's shoulder. The forest beasts were becoming too much for them. No matter how injured the wolves, bears, and badgers became, they didn't stop coming. Dominance had made them unstoppable, oblivious to their own pain. For the first time, Bailey understood the true horror of it.

Bailey knew that they had to get through the animals to Sucrette, or they'd never leave the woods. Exhausted, Bailey clung to Taleth's back, until suddenly a vulture flew toward him, its talons extended and aimed for his eyes. As it flew in Bailey's face, he lost his balance and thudded backward.

At first, Bailey thought he'd been struck blind as he hit the ground, because all he could see above him was a black cloud. But as he came to, he realized that the cloud was real. Bats, hundreds of them, swarmed into the clearing and surrounded Sucrette, creating a tower of flapping wings around her.

Sucrette dove forward, breaking through the cloud of

wings, the knife in her uplifted hand. Bailey ducked out of the way of her swinging arm, and the tiger inserted herself between them.

A sharp plunk, and the sound of air being split came from behind Bailey, and suddenly Sucrette screeched and cradled her arm. A metal arrow had pierced the tree behind Sucrette, but not before grazing her arm on its way.

"Joan!" Bailey heard Tremelo call. "Stop this madness, or I aim for your heart next!"

Tremelo stood at the trees' edge, his spring-loaded bow aimed directly at Joan Sucrette.

Sucrette held her bleeding arm and merely smiled.

"Parliament has fallen and the kingdom belongs to the Dominae. Stop this madness? The madness is everywhere." Sucrette closed her eyes. The forest beasts began to plod obediently toward Bailey and the others. Sucrette was weakened, but her power was far from gone.

"Now, Gwen!" Tremelo called out.

Just then, a strange humming sound emerged from the trees. Bailey watched as a familiar-looking girl with red hair stepped onto the rock beside Tremelo, with an instrument—a harmonica—at her lips. She played a low, mournful tune, while Tremelo kept his aim steady.

"What is this?" Sucrette mocked.

Gwen walked forward, shielding Tremelo from Sucrette. While still playing, she held her other hand out as though she could stop Tremelo from walking into harm's way. Tremelo's pendant dangled from his neck, exposed to the light. Sucrette looked from Gwen to Tremelo, then to Bailey and back to

Tremelo again. She laughed in disbelief.

"It's *you*! Of course!" Her voice sounded almost excited, as if she'd just found the last piece of an impossible puzzle. But then her face fell, and her eyes widened. "I'm too late," she said. "Too late to kill the boy . . . I'll just have to kill you all." She drew herself up tall, and breathed deeply. Bailey knew that she was preparing to command the dead-eyed animals in the clearing, and her gaze was fixed directly on Tremelo.

"Look out!" he said weakly.

Gwen's playing became faster and louder. The mournful tune became a fast-paced, heady jig, and as the music rose, the air filled with the sound of flapping wings. A vast parliament of owls flew into the clearing and settled one by one into the treetops. As she played, Bailey watched the advancing horde of angry beasts slow and hesitate.

"What are you doing?" screeched Sucrette. "After them!"

But the animals looked confused and frightened. Some of them slunk away into the trees. Others inched backward, whimpering. The music, Bailey realized, was *freeing* them—it was healing the bond, and turning it back to good, freeing them from Sucrette's control.

Sucrette turned on Gwen.

"What is that? What have you done?" She took two steps as though to stop Gwen from playing, but she was too weak. She collapsed to her knees. The snow was spotted with her blood.

Gwen kept playing.

Bailey watched as the wolves that had attacked him earlier

began prowling around the clearing, this time with their sights set on Sucrette.

"I ask you again, Joan," said Tremelo, "stop this. Come with us back to the school, where we'll decide what to do with you."

Bailey looked at her, Joan Sucrette. Whereas this morning in class, she had been chipper and dressed in bright colors, repeating verb conjugations, here she was now: broken, madness in her eyes as easy to see as the blood on her face and dress. Her blond hair was streaked with blood and dirt. Bailey felt a stir of pity.

Sucrette turned her gaze to him. Shivers ran down Bailey's spine. She raised her one good arm, and prepared to throw the knife straight at Bailey.

A roar, a flash of fur and teeth, and a scream—Joan Sucrette lay in the snow, and the wolves that had once been her captives were on top of her. By the time Tremelo managed to clear the beasts with a volley of arrows, they were too late.

Sucrette had large gashes on her chest and neck, but she was still breathing. In fact, she was still smiling.

She gasped, and looked at Bailey.

"There is no stopping the Dominae," she wheezed. "The old ways are done, and humans will be the masters of this world. Soon all of you will meet my lady. She will find you." She laughed—a small, gurgling sound that rose from her wrecked throat and echoed in the snow-filled air of the clearing. "Soon you will all belong to Viviana."

She gasped once more, and then was still.

The vultures who had remained unharmed during the battle stood scattered on branches. One of them voiced a long, keening squawk before, one by one, they each slowly took to the sky. They wound their ways up into the clouds and disappeared. The clearing was suddenly silent, the only movement the still-falling first snow of the year.

Thirty-four

THE FIRST PERSON TO move was Gwen. She turned around to look back through the trees behind the rock where she and Tremelo had entered the fight. Her gaze fell upon something farther back in the woods, and she cried out and bolted ahead. Tori, Hal, Phi, and Bailey ran after her.

Behind the rock, underneath the shade of the trees, the old man who'd arrived with Tremelo lay crumpled in the sidecar, bleeding heavily from wounds on his head and his chest. Gwen kneeled next to him. As Bailey approached, he looked at Hal and Tori, who stood closely together.

"He's called the Elder," Tori whispered. "He came today, to tell us—" She stopped, and shook her head. "There's just too much to tell."

The Elder coughed and shuddered as Gwen took his hand. Bailey saw that the wound on his chest, just below his heart, was not large—but it was deep.

He turned quickly to Tremelo.

"We're not far from the Velyn camp," Bailey whispered. "They were healers—I mean, they *are*. Maybe they can help?"

Tremelo looked uncertain, but he nodded.

"We have to try. But the motorbuggy won't make it any farther over these rocks."

Bailey felt something heavy and soft brush against his good shoulder. The white tiger had crept behind him and was nuzzling him gently. Bailey placed his hand on the rough fur of her neck. Without a word or even a gesture, Bailey felt Taleth offer her help.

"Thank you," Bailey whispered, even though he knew he didn't have to say anything for her to know how he felt.

Together he, Tremelo, Hal, and Gwen lifted the Elder carefully onto Taleth's back. Phi flew ahead to warn the Velyn that they were on their way.

"Give them this," he said, placing the Seers' Glass carefully in Phi's open palms. "It belongs to them."

Hal and Tori walked on either side of the tiger's flanks as they set off over the rocks with Bailey in the lead. The Elder groaned softly. Gwen walked at his side as Taleth crept through the Dark Woods. Just once, Bailey glanced back at Tremelo. The professor's jaw was firm and his eyes were red. He looked like he carried the weight of the Elder on his own shoulders.

It was a slow and silent walk through the snow and the darkness. At last, the group reached the Velyns' camp. A fire crackled at the mouth of their cliffside cave, illuminating the giant white wings that Phi still wore strapped to her back. She stood waiting for them with the tall, light-haired man that Bailey had seen when he'd stolen the Glass. He felt a heavy guilt settle over him as the man's eyes met his own. A few others, including the man with the dark beard, stood on the other side of the grove, watching them approach. Already many of the animals that Sucrette had controlled with her Dominance had found their way back here, and the clearing was full of the groans and muttered curses as other Velyn tended to their wounded kin.

Tremelo walked forward and held out his hand to the light-haired man.

"I am . . ." He hesitated. "I am Trent Melore."

The man clasped Tremelo's hand in his own, and bowed his head.

"Where is the man who needs our help?" he asked.

The tiger crept forward into the grove. With the assistance of Gwen and Tremelo, two of the Velyn men lifted the Elder off of Taleth's back and lay him down carefully by the fire. Bailey stayed close to the tiger. Her white fur was matted with blood—both the Elder's and her own.

The light-haired man and a Velyn woman with long reddish-brown hair and freckles knelt over the Elder, examining his wounds. Another woman brought over a bowl that contained a sticky substance just like the salve that Tremelo had used to heal Bailey's arm. He recognized the sweet, plant-like smell of it.

"What is that stuff?" Bailey asked someone next to him— the Velyn man with the dark beard he'd seen guarding the Glass against the vultures.

The bearded man regarded him cautiously.

"It's a paste made of the flowers of the King's Fingers," he said gruffly. "The seeds bloom in winter into a little black flower that, when crushed, is very potent."

Bailey nodded, thinking of the black flowers drawn on Loren's map.

The Elder cried out as the Velyn applied the salve to his head and chest. After a short time, the light-haired man stood up, and the two women backed away.

The man shook his head.

"He has suffered too great a wound," he said. "The flesh could heal, but without his life-kin, he is too weak to overcome it."

The girl Gwen uttered a sharp, soft cry, and lifted her hands to her eyes.

The Elder reached up his hand and pointed at Tremelo. The professor crouched at the Elder's side. The Elder touched Tremelo's face gingerly, then lay his hand back down on his chest.

"I see him in you," he said. "I never thought I'd see that face again. There are so few photographs . . ."

Tremelo took hold of the old man's hand and held it tightly.

"I tried to save you," the Elder said. "I thought I had lost you the night the palace burned. I saved your sister, only to lose her to the hordes in the streets. I had intended to save you both, and I failed. She told me"—the old man closed his eyes, reliving the memory—"she told me that you were surely dead, and I believed her. I took her to safety, and have lived every day since then with the guilt that I could not save you too. But now you're here. You're found, at last."

Gwen let out a sob as the Elder's head sank back onto the stone. His eyes darted in her direction.

"Please don't go," Gwen whispered. "What will I do?"

"Child," the Elder said, so softly that Bailey only saw his lips move, "don't cry. I am proud of you. So strong, and so good. The kingdom . . . It needs you. Your place is with your king." He gestured weakly at Tremelo. "His faith is not enough, not yet. It is your task to help it grow. He cannot be a king without it . . ." His voice broke, and his cloudy gray eyes took in the students standing over him. "The kingdom . . ." The old man gasped and gazed upward at the sky.

"Grimsen," he whispered, smiling. Then all was silence.

Thirty-five

GWEN WEPT, INCONSOLABLE, AS the group left the forest and made their way in secret to Tremelo's quarters. Her grief and exhaustion were overpowering, but she couldn't sleep. She didn't know if she would ever sleep again.

She was alone. Completely and totally alone.

Now, in the early hours of the morning, before the first hazy light rose over Fairmount's cliffs and forests, the students, Tremelo, and Gwen sat huddled in Tremelo's small apartment in the teacher's quarters. They drank from steaming mugs of sap milk.

"No one here at the school will know you were involved in Sucrette's death," Tremelo assured all of them. "As far as anyone knows, you students—and you, Gwen—weren't anywhere near that grove. If anyone were to find out, the Dominae would come looking for all of you."

The students nodded, and Gwen stared into the swirling cream of the sap milk. She wanted to believe that she was safe—but now that the Elder was gone, she didn't know where she belonged, and safety seemed like something she'd merely dreamed of.

"They'll come here anyway," she said. "One of their own

is dead. They'll want to know why."

She met the eyes of the students as they turned to her.

"The Elder said that dangerous times were coming," she continued. "I believed him—but I didn't know just how dangerous. You're all lucky you have each other."

It was Bailey, the sandy-haired boy with the wounded arm—the Child of War—who spoke first.

"We have you too, don't we, Gwen?"

Phi, whose wide-eyed falcon was perched on her shoulder and nestled in her wild hair, placed a hand on Gwen's knee.

"Yes, you'll stay, right? With us?"

Gwen looked at Tremelo, the professor—and the king. She recalled the Elder's words: *Your place is with your king. His faith is not enough . . . Help it grow.* She could see that the Elder had been right. Tremelo—Trent Melore—looked worried. His shoulders hunched as though he could already feel the eyes of the kingdom on him, and wanted to shy away.

"Of course you must stay here with us," he said to her. "Far too dangerous to let you back to the city on your own, and you have information that we need about what's happening in the Gray. We'll need you."

His words made her think of the RATS, and how they so desperately needed a leader. Their leader was sitting in front of her, and with the Elder gone, she was the only person they would trust who knew his true identity. The Elder had left her one final mission: to bring Trent Melore and his people together.

Gwen managed a small smile. She nodded to Tremelo. Yes, she thought. I think you will need me after all.

Thirty-six

THE NEXT EVENING, A somber group stood atop the highest hill on the Fairmount grounds, overlooking the snow-covered campus and the Fluvian River beyond.

Tremelo, Bailey, Gwen, Hal, Tori, and Phi were accompanied by a few other professors who'd offered to help send the Elder back to Nature. Earlier in the day, Mrs. Copse and her helpers had built a pyre for the Elder. Now they all stood alongside her as she set the pyre alight. With the setting sun as the funeral's backdrop, it seemed to Bailey as though the entire sky were in flames. Freshly cut cedarwood had been brought in from the deep forest, and the air smelled of spices and woodland. Bailey's arm was set in a sling. Gwen stood next to him. She played a low, melancholy lullaby on the harmonica.

"I'm sorry we couldn't take him home to the Gray City," Bailey said.

She shook her head and stopped playing. "He's closer to the mountains here," she said. "I think he'd have liked that."

No one spoke. Headmaster Finch had muttered, on his way up the hill, that a Parliament member's funeral was a

307

first for Fairmount, and no one seemed to know the right thing to say. But Parliament, Bailey reminded himself, had fallen. The Dominae had taken the city, and Viviana had an army that would guard against any uprisings from loyalists in the kingdom. What would be proper, or official, for the funeral of a Parliament member didn't seem as important now. Instead, those who gathered listened to the strains of Gwen's harmonica as the Elder's body turned to ash under its canvas shroud. Bailey and Hal stood with Tori, Phi, and Gwen. Tremelo was clear-eyed, standing at the front of the group.

As the mourners began to turn away, a flock of owls flew overhead. They hooted their good-byes to the group below, and then circled back to the woods.

Bailey and Tremelo walked down the hill and toward campus in silence. The others lingered at the top with Gwen, who wanted to wait until the fire died completely. When Bailey reached the path that led back to the dorms, he stopped. A shiver of warmth ran down his spine. He turned, knowing he would see his kin just beyond the hill. The tiger had been wounded in the fight, and Bailey felt the ache in his own muscles, as though he were feeling both of their injuries. But his wonderment was greater than his pain.

Taleth stood proud on the embankment of rocks beyond the hill. They looked at each other, and Bailey felt a surge of confidence, tempered with longing. The tiger had seen her kind almost completely wiped from the mountains, and the loneliness she felt echoed within Bailey—a sadness so deep he could hardly bear the feeling, or the beauty of sharing something so intimate with another soul.

Tremelo had invited the Velyn to attend the funeral, but they had declined. It wasn't yet the time to reveal themselves. But Bailey was thankful even that *he* knew. After all, they were his people. After the battle, the tall man with light hair like his own had taken a knee before him.

"You know what it means, don't you—that the tiger is your kin? It means we're your kin too." It wasn't customary for humans to refer to other humans as their kin, but he liked how it felt. "We can't replace your parents," the man had continued. "They're gone, just like so many of our kind. But you're one of us, Bailey Walker."

The man put a strong hand on Bailey's shoulder and squeezed.

"Taleth will be safe here in the woods with us," the man said. "It's too much of a risk to allow her to come to the school with you—she's the last of her kind."

Bailey felt an intense longing then, even stronger than the yearning he'd felt to find his Animas—he wanted to go with the Velyn and learn from them, learn about his real family. He wanted to stay wherever Taleth was, so they could protect each other. But he saw Tremelo, standing and talking with Gwen and his friends, and he knew where was most needed.

"I know," he said. "Thanks."

The Velyn warrior stood to go. Bailey couldn't bear to see him walk away.

"Wait," he had called. All of his questions burned in him like a flickering campfire, but he could hardly voice them.

He settled on one. "What's your name?"

"Eneas Fourclaw of the Velyn. If you ever need me, I'm here for you."

With that, the Velyn had receded into the forest to care for their wounded, bloodied kin.

Now, as Bailey walked back to campus with Tremelo and Fennel after the Elder's funeral, he felt pulled back toward the woods. He'd made a decision to stay with Tremelo and help him become a king—but he knew he'd always feel that longing. It would be a part of him, as surely as he was Animas White Tiger.

"I wanted to ask you something before," Bailey said. "When Ms. Sucrette tried—" He gulped. It still seemed too strange that someone had tried to kill him. "In the woods, she said something about finishing what the Jackal started. It had something to do with the white tiger, and my Awakening." Bailey pointed to Taleth.

Tremelo nodded. For once, Bailey noticed, his professor didn't smell of herbs. "You knew, already, that the Velyn people had disappeared and that the white tiger was rumored to be extinct. But the Loon knew the white tiger did not die of natural causes—they were hunted. Massacred, along with their kin, the Velyn. They were no more outlaws than you or I."

"They're warriors," Bailey said.

"Just like you," said Tremelo.

"I still don't understand, though," said Bailey. "What do I have to do with the True King? With you?"

Tremelo stared straight ahead. Behind his eyes, a hundred

questions seemed to float by, unanswered. Bailey understood the feeling. They'd both been taken by surprise, and both faced a kingdom filled with uncertainty. Tremelo reached into his pocket, and took out the Seers' Glass.

"Eneas gave me this after the battle. He claims it belongs to the king." He fixed Bailey with a look that was part excitement, part awe. "We have some reading to catch up on."

The shadowed figures of Tori, Hal, and Phi descended the hill. Gwen followed closely behind. As they approached, Hal smiled at Bailey, and Phi placed her hand gently on his hurt arm.

"I thought it was an Absence this whole time," said Tori. "But you're Animas White Tiger. I'm . . . impressed,"

Bailey smiled. "You? Impressed by something? I'm honored."

"You should be," she said firmly.

"Are you the only one?" asked Phi.

"I don't know," Bailey said, looking from Phi to Tremelo. "I think so."

"But even so, you're not alone," said Gwen. "You and the tiger have each other now."

"That's true," Bailey said, and his heart felt so full at the thought.

The sun dipped below the horizon, bathing the cliffs of Fairmount in an orange light. Bailey shivered, but not from the cold. For the first time, he knew where he had come from, and also where he belonged. Tremelo, the True King, stood beside him—and they would soon prepare to lead an army. Though he was small, and young, Bailey felt powerful enough to fight. Tremelo touched Bailey's arm, and pointed at the rocks where the tiger had sat only a moment before.

"Where did she go?" Tremelo asked.

Bailey shook his head. The tiger was out of sight, but her strength remained, coursing through his blood.

"She's close by," Bailey said. But those words fell short of describing the kinship he finally felt—with Taleth and with his friends. His senses told him his kin was just beyond the trees. More than that, his senses told him that what Gwen had said was true: he wasn't alone, and that even in the worst times, he never had been.

He smiled at his good friends and his king, and they continued on the snowy path toward home.

Acknowledgments

I WOULD LIKE TO THANK the editorial team at Paper Lantern Lit: Lauren Oliver, Lexa Hillyer, Beth Scorzato, and especially Rhoda Belleza. Their encouragement, advice, and hands-on help built the world of Animas and all its inhabitants in ways I could never do alone. Thanks are due to Stephen Barbara at Foundry Literary + Media, as well as Rotem Moscovich and Julie Moody at Disney • Hyperion for their dedication and support. Writers Aine Ni Cheallaigh, Nora Olsen, and Kelly Kingman have my gratitude for giving such wise counsel, in addition to Michele McNally and Jen Whitton, and of course my family for always lending their ears to my wonderings. And I'd also like to thank the Genealogy and Local History room at the Adriance Memorial Library in Poughkeepsie, NY, for being somehow both cozy and grand all at once—the perfect place to write a book.

C. R. Grey

C. R. Grey was born in a house on a pier in Maine – literally on the ocean. She then grew up in Memphis, Tennessee. She received her BA in Theatre from SUNY New Paltz and her MFA in Fiction from Ohio State University. Grey lives in a sunny apartment in Poughkeepsie, New York, with one black cat, one white cat, and a Boston Terrier named Trudy. She can often be found weeding through ephemera in antique shops and walking over the bridges that span the Hudson River. LEGACY OF THE CLAW is her first novel.